FOREVER DEAD

FOREVER DEAD

A Cordi O'Callaghan Mystery

Suzanne F. Kingsmill

A Castle Street Mystery

THE DUNDURN GROUP
TORONTO

Editor: Barry Jowett
Copy-editor: Andrea Waters
Design: Jennifer Scott
Printer: Webcom

National Library of Canada Cataloguing in Publication

Kingsmill, Suzanne
    Forever dead : a Cordi O'Callaghan mystery / Suzanne F. Kingsmill.

ISBN 978-1-55002-705-1

    I. Title.

PS8621.I57F67 2007   C813'.6   C2007-900087-8

1   2   3   4   5   11   10   09   08   07

We acknowledge the support of the **Canada Council for the Arts** and the
Ontario Arts Council for our publishing program. We also acknowledge the
financial support of the **Government of Canada** through the **Book Publishing
Industry Development Program** and The Association for the Export of Canadian
Books, and the **Government of Ontario** through the **Ontario Book Publishers
Tax Credit** program and the **Ontario Media Development Corporation.**

Care has been taken to trace the ownership of copyright material used in this book.
The author and the publisher welcome any information enabling them to rectify
any references or credits in subsequent editions.

                                        J. Kirk Howard, President

Printed and bound in Canada   www.dundurn.com

    Dundurn Press   Gazelle Book Services Limited   Dundurn Press
3 Church Street, Suite 500   White Cross Mills   2250 Military Road
Toronto, Ontario, Canada   High Town, Lancaster, England   Tonawanda, NY
      M5E 1M2   LA1 4XS   U.S.A. 14150

For:

John, Tim, and Jesse
&
Bill, Allison, and Dorion

Prologue

Jake Diamond eyed the angle of the sun and knew he'd never get out of the bush by nightfall. That he would never get out at all didn't cross his mind as he gripped the axe in his left hand and sliced the finely sharpened edge viciously downward, slashing a long, narrow strip of bark from the cedar. There were a hundred more such blazes snaking their way back behind him through the endless stand of trees.

Diamond surveyed the slashes with a mixture of satisfaction and frustration. He hadn't expected it to take so long, but then he hadn't counted on unwanted company either. Another dozen or so to go. He continued on through the heavy undergrowth toward the next tree. His deeply tanned arms glistened with sweat in the sticky summer sun, and his thick curly black hair lay matted at the line where it met his broad forehead. He had the chiselled features of a statue not yet finished, the lines sharp and blocked out, the nose straight, the chin square, the eyebrows with a startled look, as if slashed on at the last moment by the sculptor. It was a face that would have aged well, given the chance.

"Come on, Paulie!" he called, searching the woods for his cat, knowing she was there, never far away — not since the day he'd been bullied by his four-year-old nephew into caring for the little three-legged cripple, and she had latched onto him.

She darted out of the tangled woods to his left and rubbed her long, lean, velvet black body against his leg, purring loudly as she looked up at Diamond with her startling yellow eyes framed by the black obelisk of her face.

"Easy now, Paulie. Easy, you'll rub all your fur away!" he laughed as he shifted the axe to his right hand and reached down to scratch the cat's ears. "Just a few more and we're done."

The little cat raced off ahead of him as Diamond moved quickly, taking a compass reading after each blaze. He broke out of the woods onto the smooth, pale granite that formed the top of a cliff overlooking a lake. The shimmering blue of the water stretched beyond his sight to the north, and he could just make out the tell-tale white froth of the rapids to the south, their dull roar sounding like wind racing through the trees. Across the lake, beyond the first undulating mountain of ever-greens, he could see a pale wisp of smoke coming from the new logging camp carved into this wilderness. For one nasty moment he thought he heard the distant buzz of a chainsaw, and the anger surged in him — sweetened only by the revenge that now lay within his grasp. But the buzz was only a dragonfly caught in a spider's web, wildly flapping its wings.

The clifftop where Diamond found himself was cleft in two from some great wrenching upheaval of the earth's inner guts; a thin jagged tear ripped down the cliff face almost to the water's edge, along an area of weaker rust red rock. He carefully scanned the lake, looking for any sign of movement. Finding none, he turned back to face the woods, and, with one foot on either side of the narrow crevice, he took a quick compass bearing from the last blazed tree. Just a precaution in case something happened to him — he'd never forget how to get there. After all he'd been through, how the hell could he?

"Let's go, Paulie, or we'll never beat the sun back to camp. One more night, girl, just one more night."

By the time they reached the campsite the sun was sinking into the water, its red eye bleeding into the clouds above, leaving behind a tangled whirl of angry purple and crimson swirls. Several large cedars stood shadowing his campsite, but all other brush and trees had long since been cut down or burned by other campers. Diamond threw his ratty green canvas backpack to the ground, sat down, and dug out his cup from one of the many pockets on his pack. He filled it from the water bag he had left hanging in the shade of one of the trees. The water was tepid and bitter from the chemical taste of the iodine tablets he'd used to purify it. He checked the impulse to spit it out and instead let it sluice down his parched throat and made a mental note to switch brands of tablet. This stuff was about the worst he'd ever tasted. Paulie jumped onto his lap trying to whisker away the water.

"All right, all right. There's a whole lake down there for you. Why do you want this horrible stuff, eh?"

But he let her lap briefly at his cup as he looked out at the setting sun. Normally he loved the solitude and beauty of the north woods, but tonight, for some reason, the quiet was almost oppressive — noisy in its silence. Jake suddenly found himself straining to listen to it, to catch it off guard and hear it by its very absence, but he was puzzled to find that tonight instead of comforting him, it felt oddly menacing.

Paulie stopped drinking and with a sudden movement turned to look behind her, her body tense, ears quivering. Diamond followed her stare, wondering what it was that she was hearing, when he became aware of the trees moving in the newborn wind.

"Is that what's bothering you, girl?"

It was shuffling to life in the trees overhead, easing through their branches like a gentle, foreboding hiss. It felt obsequious, fawning, as it caressed Diamond's body, whistling a strange keening that made Diamond shiver. He was momentarily unnerved by the flood of feelings it released: a fathomless, inexplicable sadness and an unexpected, gnawing fear of something he couldn't identify. He shook himself like a dog, trying to dislodge the melancholy mood, and struck off into the woods to haul down his small food pack from where he'd left it hanging from the limb of a tree.

Diamond's last evening melted into a clear and warm night with the stars crowding the sky in a pointillistic masterpiece. He lay sprawled on his sleeping bag, belly full of beans, outstretched in front of the dying embers of the fire with Paulie nestled in the crook of his arm. His head was propped up on an old canvas pack, and he breathed in the smell of ten days of grime and soot, sweat, bug dope, cedar, woodsmoke, triumph, and the river's sweat on his clothes and in his mind.

A rustle in the woods made him roll his head lazily to one side and glance into the darkness beyond the golden circle of his campfire. Something was moving quietly through the underbrush. Paulie stirred beside him in her sleep.

"Just a coon, Paulie. You afraid of coons, girl?" The cat stretched out and burrowed up into his armpit, but didn't wake up. Diamond laughed uneasily and scanned the woods again.

"All right, girl, maybe it's something bigger than a coon." He scratched the cat behind her ears and gently extricated himself, watching her as she whimpered in her dreams. He'd never known her to be so tired that his touch failed to wake her up. He reached over for his backpack and brought it back into the warm circle of firelight, aware that he was strangely groggy and that sleep was stalking him in the way it does after a hard day of physical labour. He unbuckled an outer pocket and withdrew the flare gun he used to fend off the occasional curious bear.

"This ought to make you feel better." He caressed the fine black fur, but still the little cat didn't stir. It made Diamond unsettled to see her so far away, and he suddenly felt very alone. He hefted the metal gun in his hand before cocking it and propping it inside his running shoe. He placed it ready, near his right hand. Its presence stilled a growing uneasiness that puzzled him more for its persistence than for anything else.

It was the distant thunder that woke Diamond, or perhaps it was the wind, now wailing through the trees overhead. Perhaps it was neither. The fire was dead, the bleak, black embers as cold as they had been warm. The wind had whipped the ashes around the clearing and there was a fine dusting on his clothes. His head was heavy and his limbs felt like lead pipes. He must have slept deeply to feel so groggy, like the heavy-headed feeling after an unearned afternoon nap, he thought. Diamond lay listening to the thunder, collecting his thoughts, sticky as molasses. The quiet between the distant thunderclaps and gusts of wind felt strangely ominous, as if the quiet was trying to tell him something. How long had he been asleep?

He saw that the crescent moon had moved through the sky and there were thunderclouds scudding past it, chasing themselves across its blinkered eye. As they darted across the moon, snuffing it out, it became eerily dark in the woods. He sat up slowly. He could hear the rapids in the distance, and he could smell the dampness of the water mixing with the pungent odour of the cedars and the cloying smell of fish, and something else. What? He shivered, held his breath, and listened to that endless, wild silence. The feeling of unease grew in him like a dull, gnawing pain, slowly coalescing into the first stirrings of fear.

"Goddammit, Diamond," he said. "Pull yourself together. You're acting like Paulie. Afraid of your own shadow."

He reached out his hand for the comfort of the little cat and stiffened. There was no warm, friendly little body curled up next to him.

"Paulie?"

His voice hit the quiet of the woods like a hammer on granite, hardly denting or scratching the silence all around him. It sounded dead, flat, alone.

"Paulie?" he called again.

There was no familiar scrambling of little feet, no warm, wet snout nuzzling his hand, no purring, nothing. Diamond felt around with his hands, sure Paulie must have rolled away from him in her sleep. No Paulie.

Slowly, carefully, he reached for his flare gun, silently groping in the darkness for his running shoe. His hand gripped the familiar outline and followed the sole along to the tongue. The shoe was empty. He groped all around, like a blind man, tapping his fingers amongst the carpet of cedar twigs, but there was nothing.

"What the hell?" he whispered, jerking his head up to scan the woods around him.

A twig snapped nearby, then there was a slight rustling in the trees. Diamond turned to face the sound.

"Paulie?"

For an instant the moon came out from behind a cloud, and in the woods beyond him it reflected off something shiny before skidding back behind another cloud. He stared after it, willing his eyes to see, and slowly he picked out something on the very edge of his vision, a darker smudge staining the blackness of the night, standing in the shadows of the trees, barely perceptible, upright. Too small for a bear. Human? He felt the goosebumps rise all over his body, a cold prickle of fear rapidly building into a crescendo, overwhelming in the suddenness of its vicious grasp, rearing out of his grogginess like some nightmare. He struggled to his feet, his heart racing like the rapids, and cried out in frustration as his sleeping bag entangled his legs. When he looked again there was nothing. He waited, head cocked, listening.

"Who's there?" His voice was caught by a gust of wind and flung into the silence, as if to the wolves. He could taste the fear now, like some unwanted sickness, clammy, unhealthy, rising like bile. He stood there scanning the trees and called out again and again, in an odd, strangled mixture of fear and anger. Nothing. Only the shadows playing tricks on him.

Too late, he sensed movement behind him and whirled. In the split second it took for the horror of what he saw to surface, he raised his hands to shield his head. The impact of the blow across his chest knocked the wind out of him and sent him sprawling onto a rock outcrop, his head glancing against the rock and stunning him as he lashed out with his arms. He felt his mind spinning out of control, weaving in and out of consciousness.

A grisly, high-pitched scream careened through the forest. He felt a sudden overwhelming weight on his chest, pushing out the air he tried to breathe in, and he knew, in a spiralling crescendo of fear and terrifying clarity, that the scream had been his.

The dull roar of the rapids merged into a roaring in his head. His mind fell into slow motion, tumbling over memories and daydreams, and the pain, the violent jabbing pain, was followed miraculously by a delicious feeling of overwhelming calm that enveloped him. Its fingers gently probed the recesses of his mind, easing the pain until, quietly, gently, like wind whispering through trees, Jake Diamond was gone.

chapter one

"**I** wanted to kill him," I said, as I scrambled out onto the rocky shore and steadied the canoe. I waited for my brother to respond, but he just grimaced at me as he slowly unwound his six-foot frame and stepped out of the canoe. The water lapped gently against the gleaming silver hull, safe now in the eddy, as it nudged the rocks where I squatted impatiently. Out beyond the eddy I could see the smooth, luminous sheen of the water, stretched like cellophane almost at the ripping point, as it gathered speed and funnelled between the two tree-lined rocky shores. Somewhere around the corner and out of sight it would rip apart and splinter into thousands of ragged shards of white boiling water — just as my life sometimes threatened to do, I thought.

The canoe suddenly jerked toward me as Ryan hauled out the first of our packs and, grunting, dumped it unceremoniously on the rocks beside me.

"Leave it alone can't you, Cordi?" he groaned. "You're like a dog with an old bone, slobbering and chewing on it even though there's nothing left." When I didn't answer he sighed and said, "We've gone over it a thousand times. So he's a jerk. It's past. Over. Done with. Finito. For God's sake, let it die."

As if to underline his words he stooped and flicked the bow painter at me, then went to secure the canoe with the stern line. He was right, of course, but I couldn't get it out of my mind because I knew I should have said something to the suave bastard. I'd been checking the glass tanks that housed my frogs in the zoology building where I worked as an assistant professor when Jim Hilson quietly materialized behind me and curled his hands around my hips and squeezed. "Cordi, my dear, have you heard the news?" I elbowed him in the gut, and he let me go as I turned to face him. He held up his hands in self-defence and with an ingratiating smile said, "I just thought you should be the first to know."

"Know what?" I asked, marvelling that such a handsome face, with its burnt umber eyes, thick straight shaggy brown hair, full lips, and a button nose, could be so irritating. We'd worked together as partners on and off on some research projects, and he always, without fail, seemed to come out on top, with his name front stage centre and mine trailing behind. Why I kept co-authoring papers with him I could not fathom. He was so irritating.

"I think you might be out of a job," he said, pulling a long face, but the cheery tone of his voice revealed his real feelings. He didn't say anything more, forcing me to ask why, which irritated me even more.

"You didn't make tenure." I didn't say anything at all, fighting back my anger and disappointment as he stood there peering at me solicitously. I had been so sure I'd be considered for tenure.

"How do you know that?" I asked in anger.

He smiled knowingly and said, "Poor little Cordi. You have to know the right people to get the information you want." Which translated into he did, and I didn't. "That's why you have such a hard time getting ahead." I bit my tongue hard and tried to think of all the devastating retorts I could say, but all I could think of was "Go to hell," which wasn't exactly imaginative.

"I could help you, Cordi. You and me — we make a great team," he said, sidling closer to me. After two years of this I was getting sick of Jim's game. I backed away and ignored him.

"Don't you want to know?" he asked, moving closer.

"Know what?" I asked, and backed away again.

"If I got tenure?' He waited for my response, but I just stared at him.

"You'll be sorry to know that I didn't," he said. But of course I was glad, which made me feel a bit guilty, but only for a moment.

"It's just you and me now, Cordi. And one of us won't be here this time next year."

I looked at him and said, "Would you please get to the point."

"I also heard that an assistant professor is on the chopping block, come spring," he said, "and I think it's going to be you."

He smiled again and shrugged, holding out his overly muscled arms to me, inviting a hug. I moved away, saying nothing, too afraid my voice might crack, furious at myself for not being able to come up with some witty remark.

"You know why it won't be me, other than the fact that I've published more papers?" he crowed.

When I didn't answer, his face suddenly twitched in annoyance and he abruptly answered his own question. "Because for your last year here they're saddling you with the perennially unpopular entomology taxonomy course, now that Jefferson's heart problem has sidelined him." He sighed. "I'm really sorry, Cordi, but it sure won't be easy to impress the tenure committee with an insect taxonomy course, not that that's a prerequisite or anything."

He shook his head in commiseration, grinned suggestively, blew me a kiss, and turned to leave, but then couldn't resist a final jab. Did he know the damage his words were doing, or was he biologically incapable of comprehending?

"I've had two papers accepted, you know, and I drew Jefferson's animal behaviour course this year — hard to make a course like that bomb out, eh? But who knows? Maybe you can do something with the insect taxonomy course that will blow us all out of the water." He disappeared down the hall, leaving me shaking with frustration at myself for letting him see my shock and the stinging tears in my eyes. At times like this I felt like a real loser even though I knew the jerk was exaggerating. I was good at what I did. I just had to convince myself of it somehow.

I tried to shift my focus away from my depressing thoughts and glanced at Ryan, who was securing the canoe. He had a million new freckles on his arms, legs, and face from the endless days of sun, and the rusty red baseball cap that hid his unruly red-blond hair seemed to have done little to prevent the sun from bleaching most of the red out. I smiled and remembered trying to count all those freckles once when we were kids on the farm: it had been like counting the grains of sand on a beach. We were so different, he and I.

I sighed and got up to tie my line around a large

boulder at the base of a cliff that soared above us. The jumble of rocks at its base had once formed part of its face, now battered, craggy, and forlorn from years of losing pieces of itself.

The entrance to the portage trail was framed by the huge trunks of two large pine trees on a height of land. Ryan turned on his heel and disappeared into the woods to scout the rapids. I followed him down the soft earthen trail and saw him veer off the path in the direction of the rapids. We broke out of the bushes onto some sun-warmed, rust-streaked granite rocks overlooking the full force of the rapids.

"Would you take a look at that!" yelled Ryan from his position atop a huge boulder.

The words were whipped away by the wind and the thundering roar of the rapids. I clambered up beside him and looked at the roiling mass of suicidal waves at our feet. I glanced apprehensively at Ryan out of the corner of my eye. He was eyeballing the rapids with the look of someone possessed, and when he caught my glance I rolled my eyes in exasperation.

"No way, Ryan."

"Aw, c'mon, Cor." He gripped my arm and pointed. All either of us could see was the ominous white cauldron of water, torn here and there by jagged rocks and a fallen tree hanging out over the water. Further down I could just make out the telltale line where the river suddenly dropped from view as it plummeted over a series of unseen cliffs.

"We could canoe this far side," said Ryan eagerly. "See? Over here. We take the route between those two boulders, veer sharply left to miss all the mess close to shore there, and then angle back to miss the shelf. We hug the shore and find a backwater just before the tree and the falls. Easy!"

"That's what you said about the last one," I yelled, "and we nearly skewered the canoe on that godawful rock just past the mini ledge!"

"Whose fault was that? You were in the bow!" shouted Ryan.

"Don't remind me," I said. I hated being in the bow, being the first one down into a boiling cauldron of water, madly trying to take the correct route to get us through. The person in the bow never got the respect they were due. All the stern had to do was follow the bow's lead, but the bow? The bow had to choose the right route, usually with split-second precision and twenty-twenty vision, neither of which I was particularly blessed with.

"It didn't look like a ledge when we scouted it!" Ryan protested as he looked back at the river, a look of disappointment on his face.

"You'd canoe Niagara Falls if you could," I said, knowing there was a spark of truth to it. Ryan seemed to have no strong sense of his own mortality, but fortunately it wasn't contagious. I suffered from no such illusions of immortality, especially when it came to a wet death.

I looked at the river again, shivering suddenly, as if the water already had me in its grip. "This'd kill us," I said, and I shivered again as the spray misted my face and left me feeling strangely apprehensive.

Ryan suddenly caught me by the wrists, shaking me out of my thoughts, and pulled me close, whispering in my ear, "Lighten up Cordi, I'm only joking."

He jumped off the boulder then and headed back into the coolness of the woods. Of course he was only joking. I knew that, so why had I let it bother me so much?

"Come on, lazy, let's get the packs," he shouted.

"Lazy? You call me lazy?" I yelled at Ryan's disappearing back. "The only reason you wanted to run these rapids was so you wouldn't have to portage the canoe."

I could just hear Ryan's answering chortle as I ran to catch up.

The sun was at its hottest, directly overhead, and the water looked deliciously cool as it gently cradled the canoe, but there was nowhere safe to swim, hot as we were. We'd just have to scout around for a good spot at the other end of the portage. Ryan's pack was now light enough for him to hoist it onto his back without my help. Most of the food from our two-week trip was gone, but my pack — with the tent, sleeping bag, clothes, and my small collecting pack — remained the same. Ryan, no doubt feeling guilty, helped me on with my pack, which practically dwarfed my 5'6", 120-pound frame. After two weeks I'd adjusted pretty well to the heft of it, and the growing strength in my arms and legs felt good. I adjusted the wide shoulder straps and pulled the leather tumpline over my forehead to take some of the weight off my shoulders and then took off ahead of Ryan.

I padded softly down the narrow trail, the needles of the pine trees on either side jiggling in the sunlight, dancing and leaping in the wind and sending shadows skittering across the path in front of me.

I slithered down a damp, rocky incline and felt the pack try to take me in one direction. I lurched the other way to compensate, just as a green beetle gyrated past my nose and landed ten feet in front of me, right on top of a large piece of some dead animal, its smell ripe and pungent. I came to a sudden halt, struggling to keep the pack's momentum from taking me with it.

"For God's sake, Cor. Give me some warning, will you?" said Ryan as he endeavoured to stop himself from slamming into me. But I ignored his flailing and kept my eye on the bug. I didn't want to lose it.

"This one's a beaut!" I said.

Ryan struggled up beside me.

"What's a beaut?" He stopped dead, as the stench reached him. "Oh, Jesus! What's the stink? Who died?"

"Probably part of a raccoon or porcupine, or maybe a deer. But there's no hair so it's impossible to tell."

"You *would* call a dead raccoon a 'beaut.'"

"Not the animal, Ryan. Take at look at what's on it."

"Oh, gross. This is revolting, Cordi. How can you stand the stink?" Ryan pulled his shirt up over his nose. "It's crawling with bugs!" he said in disgust and looked away.

"They're not bugs —"

"I know, I know." Ryan cut me short, pitched his voice higher, and I heard my own words coming back at me. "'All bugs are insects but not all insects are bugs.' You biologists are all alike. But to me a bug is an insect is a bug. It's such a good guttural sound. Why waste it? You can really wind your disgust around that one little word: *bug*." He dropped his voice so low that "bug" came out sounding like a twin of "ugh."

Ignoring Ryan's diatribe, I pointed at the big green beetle balanced on a piece of the dead animal, its little antennae quivering in the wind, but Ryan kept his back studiously away from the beetle and moved upwind.

"Oh, come on, Ryan. This'd look terrific on the cover of one of your magazines. Maybe *Insect News* would buy it? Lime green. The art department will go nuts, and besides, I don't recognize it. Maybe it will be a brand new species and I'll become famous." I heard the wistfulness creep into my voice and smothered it with a nervous laugh.

"Yeah, right," said Ryan, who to my relief hadn't seemed to notice. He was too preoccupied with the stink of the dead animal. "I can see the headline now: 'Beautiful bug on putrid porker.' Besides, you know

Insect News pays diddly-squat." Ryan sold his photos to the big-name magazines for good money, but bugs were seldom in great demand by the big guys, and so he usually tried to avoid taking their pictures at all.

I simply ignored him, having heard it all before. I eased off my backpack and pulled out another, smaller knapsack. Inside was a fisherman's tackle box where I kept all the vials and live jars for my day's specimens until I could transfer them at night to other large containers strapped to the undersides of our canoe seats. Insects weren't really my main line of research, but I'd taken enough courses and done enough research to know quite a lot about them, and that had landed me Jefferson's notoriously boring entomology course. That, and the fact that I was low woman on the totem pole. I rustled through the plant specimens, scats, and other animal paraphernalia I'd already collected and pulled out some jars with mesh lids.

"Cor, do we really need this? It's crawling with bugs." Ryan's voice was muffled through his shirt. "Can't we just pretend we didn't see it? God, when I agreed to help you on this trip you never said anything about collecting bugs from dead animals. I'm fine with the mice and shrews and frogs, even the butterflies and spiders and the little nets and stuff, but frankly, this is revolting."

"Look, I'm not sure I'm any happier about this than you are." I sighed. "But I don't have any choice. I've got to come up with something for this taxonomy course that's not boring. Maybe if I offer some live labs along with all the dry dead stuff I can generate some interest."

Interest my ass, I thought. How many undergrads were going to flock to the taxonomy course this year? And if they didn't, what would the tenure committee think? Jim Hilson's smirk floated in front of me like an irritating mote in my eye. He'd make himself too valuable to lose, and it was either him or me. I had less than two months to pore over the old course and come up with a new, madly exciting course before the fall term started. To boot, I had a paper that was close to being accepted for publication, but the reviewers wanted some extra analysis of my data. I wanted to concentrate on that, not on the entomology course.

Ryan dumped his pack rather noisily on the ground next to the dead beast, but the insect miraculously stayed put.

"You move the insect away from that 'thing' and I'll snap its picture. Then you can collect your grubs for your live labs," said Ryan in a voice that held itself away from the gruesome scene like a pair of verbal tweezers. He didn't mind taking the photos for me as long as he didn't have to get cozy with the bugs themselves.

"Really, Ryan. If I try to do that he'll fly. Just plug your nose."

Ryan resignedly squatted down beside me. He unclipped his camera gear from his pack and extracted one of his close-up lenses and a tiny tripod and set to work. Once the photos were done I cornered the little bug with a miniature bug net and put it in one of my jars. I then collected a number of the grubs, some of which were stuck to a cedar twig that went into a jar as well. While I was waiting for Ryan to store his equipment away I slung my collection bag over my shoulder and padded back down the trail. The pines lining the portage acted like a sieve for the early afternoon sun, which squeezed through the cracks, weaving a tapestry of light patterns that swarmed over the forest floor. The thumping roar of the rapids, the moist smell of rich humus, and the sticky heat of the sun were like an elixir — it just was not possible to stay depressed out in the wilderness.

I walked further along the path a short way to see

what lay ahead of us and suddenly stopped, cocking an ear in the gentle breeze. I could hear something crackling in the woods off to my left, but it quieted when I stopped and all I could hear was the loud buzzing of a bee as it flew past me, the hot sun dripping on me like heated honey. The crackle began again and slowly approached me. I could see the bushes jerking and could clearly hear the soft sound of an animal swishing toward me. I waited, watching the branches moving, judging the animal to be small: maybe a coon, maybe a weasel. It couldn't be anything much bigger. I hoped Ryan wouldn't come gallivanting down the path and scare whatever it was. I stood statue-still on the path, holding my breath as the animal came closer until I caught a glimpse of a small, slim black form. Not a coon. Maybe a marten. Too big for a weasel. And then it was there on the path in front of me, its golden eyes glowing in its black face, one small black ear dangling at a strange angle. The cat stopped and stared back at me. Slowly I stooped and held out my hand.

"Hey ya, kitty." The bedraggled cat held its ground, the leaves swished gently overhead, and then slowly, carefully, the cat moved, stiff legged, toward me; I noticed that it had only three legs as it brushed its body against my own.

"What happened to you, eh, puss?" I asked as I glanced uneasily at the cat's ear, matted with blood, its tip hanging on by a thread. There was a huge gash down the cat's left flank, caked with dried blood, as though some animal had raked it with its claws. But the loss of its leg was an old injury — there was no blood there. I reached out my hand and tried to scratch the cat, but it backed off and stood staring at me, not moving. Suddenly it meowed loudly and moved off down the portage trail. It looked back once and then stopped as if inviting me to follow, all the while emitting a low, haunting whine that made me shiver. Why was the cat alone? Where was its owner? I called out to Ryan, and when he came loping down the path toward me he stopped dead when he caught sight of the cat.

"Is that a cat?" he asked incredulously.

I didn't answer. Instead I moved forward slowly, but the cat loped away into the woods ahead of me, its agility surprising after the loss of a leg. When I reached the spot it had run to I could see the cat sitting under some bushes looking back at me, waiting. I looked up and saw something glinting high up in the trees about a hundred yards into the bush. As I watched, it seemed to swing slowly back and forth, like a pendulum sparkling in the sun. The cat sat patiently waiting, tilting its head, silently, unnervingly watching me. I glanced down into its golden yellow eyes and suddenly felt an inexplicable coldness steal through my sweaty body like a thief. I couldn't fathom what it was trying to steal, but I didn't like the feeling one bit. Instinctively I backed away and then felt foolish as the cat broke the spell by running back toward me and rubbing itself against my leg.

"Someone must have left something behind, besides the cat," I said as Ryan came up behind me. I pointed toward the woods.

"Twenty feet up a tree?" quipped Ryan.

I repositioned my collecting pack from my shoulder onto my back. "I'm going to take a look," I said. "Just in case the cat's owner is hurt."

"And I'm going to stay right here and have a snooze! No way I'm bushwhacking my way down that poor excuse for a trail. It's probably only a piece of tinfoil."

"But what about the cat?" I asked.

Ryan shrugged, sat down, leaned against a tree, and pulled his cap over his eyes. "Let me know what you find."

chapter two

I peered unenthusiastically at the tangled undergrowth converging on the old trail. It was going to be a lovely bushwhack. Did I really want to do it? I glanced at the cat. Something in the way it stared at me sent a shiver of fear down my spine. I looked back at Ryan, who had slouched further down against the tree in a spectacularly contorted position that looked impossibly uncomfortable, and yet he was already softly snoring. A wisp of his red-blond hair, like a coiled golden snake, had escaped from the confines of his cap and now sproinged across his right eyebrow, which suddenly twitched in annoyance. I took a deep breath and waded into the woods after the cat, shoving aside the branches and twigs of the dead layers of jack pine that grabbed at my legs and arms. I stumbled over a tangle of hidden roots and watched in envy as the cat nimbly moved through the underbrush, patiently waiting for me each time I got tangled in the bracken.

Eventually the undergrowth thinned and we broke out of the bush into a glade, a legacy of the sudden violent death of a pine whose great gnarled and naked roots stood upended in a mocking reversal of life. After being torn from the earth, the great tree had toppled and taken out a handful of other younger trees. Directly in front of the downed tree and dangling from a rope thrown high over the limb of another tree was a medium-sized olive green canvas pack.

The glint I had seen from afar came from the sharpened edge of the blade of a bush axe. As I approached the pack I could see that it was held in place by the other end of the rope tied around the girth of the same tree. The result was that the pack swung below the limb by about five feet and above the ground by about fifteen feet. It was a professional job: whoever had hauled the food pack off the ground to keep the bears and other wildlife at bay was no newcomer to the bush. I suddenly felt like an intruder and did not particularly want to be caught drooling over someone else's food, but then again curiosity is sometimes a strong incentive to ignore common sense. I looked around. There had to be a campsite nearby.

I picked my way over to the tree. I could see that the rope had been wound around the trunk several times and then knotted, but the knot had been gnawed through by animals and the rope had broken, slithering around the trunk as the pack slipped until the rope had caught and wedged itself in a crotch of the tree. Not far enough for the animal, whatever it was, to get at the pack. There was a scrunched-up ball of blue paper litter caught in the rope. I pocketed it with the rest of the litter I'd picked up that day, which I'd burn on the fire that night, a reflex habit I'd gotten into years before. I couldn't resist pulling on the rope to feel the weight of the pack. I watched as it jerked at the end of the line, the axe head glinting in the sun. The movement disturbed a cloud of flies that swarmed off the pack and circled it. I watched, puzzled, as they regained their quarry. I grabbed the taut line and shook it once more and watched the flies in growing alarm.

I struggled to free the rope from where it was wedged and then carefully paid out the rope and watched as the pack slowly descended to the ground. Even at a distance of a few feet the stench of rotten potatoes was overpowering. Who in their right mind would haul up a food pack and then let the perishables rot? It didn't make any sense, unless the owner was hurt, a decidedly unwelcome thought. I backed away and looked around in alarm, but no one came limping out of the woods or screamed at me to get away. Quickly I hauled the pack back up out of reach and secured the rope to the tree. How long did it take for potatoes to rot in the summer sun? I looked around for another way out of the glade and saw a trail leading back toward the portage trail from the direction in which I'd come. Too bad I hadn't seen it from the other end. I could have saved myself a slew of cuts and scratches. I'd go back that way. I scanned the grove looking for another route, the route taken by whoever owned this pack, and saw the cat sitting at the entrance to a trail, mutely watching me.

The narrow path wound through the jack pines and rock boulders and made its way toward the water. The cat darted off ahead of me and disappeared.

After a hundred yards or so the earthen path led me out into a well-used clearing with flat spaces for five or six tents. Beyond it I could see the blue waters of a small bay in the lake we had just paddled across.

Immediately in front of me I could see the backside of a big white canvas tent, and as I approached it a red squirrel chattered noisily and scooted away to the safety of a tree where it continued its shrill rant. A clothesline had been hung between two trees to one side of the tent and there were some socks and a large pale blue flannel bush shirt and some running shoes, with most of the toes missing, hanging from it. Next to the clothesline there was a large ten-gallon tank, and as I shoved it with my toe there was a slosh of water. Whoever had set up camp here had spent many weeks in comparative luxury.

"Anybody here? Hello?"

The words reverberated through the woods like a physical assault and made the following silence seem unreal, as the flies buzzed and a woodpecker pecked and the breeze shook the leaves in the trees overhead. But no answer.

I turned back to the tent. The front was open to the elements, the bug netting and door tied back to the tent proper. It was big enough for a man to stand erect in. Cautiously I peered inside. There was an old makeshift wooden table, the kind found in thousands of fishing camps all over the country, and a couple of logs as chairs. Tin cans of food were stacked on shelves made from rocks and old, swollen plywood. Dirty plates and cutlery were laid out on the table as if someone had been interrupted in the middle of a meal, and a bottle of iodine tablets had rolled under the table. Opened tins of sardines lay scattered about the needle-carpeted floor of the tent, all now licked clean by chipmunks or coons.

I came out of the tent and cupped my hands around my mouth and yelled again, but there was no answer, just the red squirrel chittering away like a dentist's drill.

It was then that I noticed the second tent. It was the colour of the clump of jack pines that surrounded it on three sides. It stood on a small rock outcrop twenty yards from the mess tent and close to the water. It was a faded old green canvas tent with an awning over the front door, which was tightly zipped shut. One of the poles that held the awning up had fallen over, and the wing was flapping in the breeze. I noticed then that the cat had taken up a position in front of the tent, as if guarding it.

I turned away from the cat and the tent, firmly convincing myself that I didn't need to look inside it. Instead I walked through the camp, calling out as I went, more to reassure myself of some semblance of normalcy than expecting an answer. At one point I thought I heard an animal creeping through the forest, but when I stopped and listened there was nothing and when I glanced back at the cat it seemed unperturbed. Probably just a coon. Lots of coon sign about.

I called out again and walked down to the shore, the cat silently watching me from its position near the tent. The land jutted out into a peninsula forming one end of the bay, and although I couldn't see our canoe I knew it was there, just around the corner. I turned back then and looked along the shore and almost missed it, so well did it blend in with the driftwood on the beach. The warm wooden sides of a cedar strip canoe lay hidden among some bushes as if it had been thrown there, its stern line still dragging in the water, the bowline pulled taut from the base of the tree where it was tied, as if it had been yanked or blown by the wind. On the bow there was a white silhouette of a really badly drawn eagle in full flight looking as though it were trying to flee the confines of the canoe.

Where was the guy? If his canoe was still here but the food in his pack had gone rotten and the awning of his tent was flapping enough to drive someone nuts, where was the person who owned all this? As long as there had been no canoe I had almost managed to convince myself that whoever had been here had left in a big hurry in their canoe. In which case it hadn't been my concern. No more.

The forlorn feel of the place, the juxtaposition of the obvious care and pride put into the site with the equally obvious neglect, was disquieting. I glanced uneasily at the cat and the green tent, its tarp still flapping ominously in the gentle breeze, and I knew I had no choice. I approached the tent the way I used to approach my dentist's office: with great reluctance.

The cat rubbed against my leg as I squatted in front of the tent looking for the zipper to unzip the door. Maybe the guy was a heavy sleeper and had just not heard me yelling out. A *really* heavy sleeper.

"Hello?"

My voice sounded tiny, hesitant, and almost made me jump as it garrotted the silence. But there was no response. I fumbled with the zipper on the tent door, and when I got it opened halfway the cat pushed its head in ahead of me and went inside. I carefully pulled the tent flap back, peered inside, and then reeled back in sudden panic as something moved on the far side of the dimly lit tent. I backed away, my eyes glued to the door. There was a squeal and a nasty wet gurgle and the cat suddenly slipped out, a dying chipmunk in its jaws, and disappeared around the side of the tent. My heart slowed to a sprint and I approached the tent again, angry at myself for being frightened by a chipmunk.

The inside of the tent was musty and damp with the stale air of disuse. As my eyes adjusted to the light I saw the bunched-up shape of a large down sleeping bag and two substantial foam pads that served as a very comfortable mattress. This guy sure knew how to camp in luxury.

I scanned the area where I had seen the chipmunk move and saw the remains of a Mars chocolate bar tucked into a pocket on the side of the tent. Right below it was the telltale hole in the tent where the chipmunk had chewed its way in to death. A small palm-sized black book with an orange slash on the cover and a man's name printed across it lay close by as if dropped there by accident. An expensive-looking camera lay on top of the sleeping bag, partly out of its case, and an empty black plastic film canister lay beside it, as if someone had just loaded the camera and been interrupted. Nothing here to say what had become of the owner.

I backed out of the tent and let the flap drop behind me as I breathed in fresh air. I saw the cat sitting near the mess tent, its tail flicking lazily from side to side as it licked its paws. Its cool aloofness was beginning to give me the creeps.

I shivered. A warm snug campsite was warm and snug only when filled with a human body. Like an empty house it loses its warmth and humanity the minute its people leave it behind. It loses its soul. There was no soul here now, only the tantalizing potential of soul. Where was the owner?

I surveyed the campsite one last time, then followed the trail back to the glade and the dangling food pack. I resisted the sudden urge to look behind me as I skirted the glade and found the trail I'd seen earlier that would lead me back to the portage trail. I hadn't walked very far when I rounded a bend in the trail just where it merged with the portage trail and the stench hit me like a physical blow. I stopped and then I saw it, a large formless shape lying to one side of the trail, silent, mute, and threatening in its inevitability. And I saw what I didn't want to see. Sticking out of the heap, white, flaccid, and bloated in the strong summer sun, was a single human finger curled into a miniature fist of death.

I stumbled away from the body, the nausea coming in waves that touched and sickened not only my stomach but also my mind. A million whirling thoughts crowded into my brain, pulling and twisting it like a

Chinese puzzle. The sun shone down through the trees and the birds still called sweetly, but for one human being life was now over and there was nothing to mark the passing of whoever it had been; someone who had once had hopes and dreams, now gone. The smell of the hot sun on warm earth enveloped me and I breathed in the freshness of air not touched by death. I sank to my knees and threw up.

chapter three

"Ryan! Ryan!" My voice came out sounding like the croaking rasp of a cricket. Why is it that when you really need your voice it so often betrays you?

Ryan was lying slumped against the tree where I'd left him sound asleep, months ago it seemed.

"Ryan!" This time I put more force behind my voice but it still croaked, so I leaned over and grabbed his shoulder, the nausea rising again inside me so that I let go quickly and straightened up.

Ryan grunted and slowly propped himself up on one arm and looked at me, his eyes taking a long time to focus. Suddenly he sat up and rubbed them as if to clear away an unpleasant vision, and then he looked at me again.

"What's up, Cordi? Jesus, you look awful," he said. "What's wrong? What's the matter?"

I couldn't seem to find any words that would work. My tongue felt thick and fuzzy and trying to make it perform balletic manoeuvres with words seemed impossible.

"What's wrong?" Ryan asked in growing alarm. He stood up, gripped me by the shoulders. Nothing like a concerned brother to loosen my tongue.

"There's a dead guy just off the portage trail, or what's left of him," I squawked. "Near where you took the photo."

"'Dead guy,' as in *human* dead guy?"

I nodded. Ryan didn't say anything at all, just reached out instinctively and hugged me.

"Or dead woman," I added. "The animals have got at the body. There's not much left to recognize," I said into his armpit. "I don't even know if it's male or female it's all so bloated and covered in grubs and twigs."

When Ryan didn't respond I pulled away and looked at him. He just stood there looking dumbly back at me, his jaw hanging loose, his eyebrows raised in an I-hear-you-but-I-don't-want-to expression that ordinarily would have made me laugh.

"Who is it? What was he doing around here?" said Ryan.

"I found a food pack hauled up between two trees. It was crawling with flies." I waited for some reaction, concentrating on my words to keep the images from crowding out my tenuous self-control.

"Flies on the food pack?" he finally asked.

"Yeah. Strange, isn't it?"

"Who'd let food rot?"

"That's what I thought," I said, glad to find my voice returning to normal. "There's a campsite over there. Two tents, one's a mess tent and the other is for sleeping. Only there was no sign that anybody had been around for at least a few days. There's a canoe hauled up and battered by the wind and it looks abandoned.

But it's all mostly so neat and tidy, so I looked inside the tent."

I brushed a pine needle off my arm and watched it fall to the ground as I tried to obliterate the vision of the body before I continued.

"But there was nobody in there. No sign of the owner. So I came back and the smell hit me."

"You think it's the guy from the campsite?" When I didn't answer he said, "Where is it? We'll have to report this."

"It's down the path near where we picked up our grubs. It's in at least two pieces along the trail and ..." I suppressed a gag and pointed back the way I had come.

Ryan rallied at this. "Oh gross, Cordi, don't tell me we took grubs off a dead body, a dead *human* body ..."

When I didn't answer Ryan stared at me and raised his hairy eyebrows.

"Better lead the way."

"You sure you want to see this?" I said.

"You did."

"Yeah, but I had no choice. I practically tripped over it. It's not a pretty sight."

He shrugged. "Maybe there's a photo op here for the local paper. I owe them a favour."

It was my turn to roll my eyes.

"And you call me gross. No paper in their right mind would print a photo of this unless they wanted to scare their readers away."

"For God's sake, Cordi, I didn't mean taking pictures of the body. I was thinking of some pictures of the campsite, lonely, deserted. Imagine the pathos you could build up. And I could get a good writer to write the text: an article about camp safety and the dangers of camping alone. It could be very powerful as long as the writer doesn't go all gushy and sentimental, and if we can find out how he died."

I had to admit that the campsite did look sad and lonely and it would make a powerful picture, especially knowing what lay in the bushes this side of it.

We picked up our gear and I led the way. We walked back along the portage trail to where we had collected the grubs. Ryan grimaced at what we'd thought was part of a coon as I located the partly overgrown trail that led to where part of the torso lay half concealed in pine needles.

"Jesus," whispered Ryan. "What the hell happened to the guy? He looks as though he's been ripped to shreds."

"He has. By scavengers."

"Oh gross, Cor." Ryan shivered. I heard the tremble in his voice and watched his face turn a paler shade of white as he struggled to keep his breakfast down. He took two deep breaths and turned away from the body. I felt somehow relieved that he was handling it as badly as I had and then felt ashamed of my thoughts.

"How'd the guy die?"

"Maybe he had a heart attack or hurt himself and couldn't get to help," I said, not wanting to say what was in both our minds. Of course, Ryan had no such qualms.

"You think it was a bear?" he asked, as he struggled with his pack.

Ryan's voice quavered on the word *bear*. Ryan wasn't afraid of much, but he did have a pathological fear of bears. He'd once blasted a poor little mouse with the flare gun outside our tent when we were kids, thinking it was a bear. After all the screaming and yelling in the dark had died down he promised our parents he'd never use a flare gun again. He now uses pepper spray, and I watched as he struggled to get it out of his pack.

"I'm getting the hell out of here," said Ryan as he moved away from the body, shook the can of pepper spray, and checked the nozzle. Not for the first time I wondered what would happen if the wind changed direction just after he used it, or the spray bounced off the bear and back at us. Three blinded creatures lashing out in panic. Charming thought. Perhaps a flare gun would be better after all. What a team we made. I was afraid of rapids and we were both afraid of bears. So why wasn't I afraid now?

We figured our best bet to get help and still get out of the bush by nightfall was to portage our stuff and then go report the discovery of the body. The topographical map showed a lumber road near the end of the portage. We hoped we could flag down a lumber truck or something. The portage got progressively worse, with large sections of mud and swamp in the lower stretches of the trail. The rain in the last few nights had made everything a boggy, mucky mess. There were no recent signs that anyone had passed this way before us, and I wondered if the last person to travel this trail now lay dead by its side. At the end of the portage we dumped our gear and I emptied the specimens from my collection pack to lighten the load. It was pure habit. I never went anywhere without a collecting pack. You never knew what you might find.

"Cordi, why not just leave it this time? We don't have time to collect with a wild bear out there."

I swung the pack over one shoulder and, with Ryan twitching and jerking like a marionette on the lookout for bears, we retraced our steps back over the portage to get the canoe.

It still lay peacefully in the water, safely tied bow and stern to some small boulders where the cliff that soared above had given up some of its weight.

"You take the bow. I'll get the stern," I said above the din of the rapids. I untangled and untied my line and, holding tight to keep the canoe near the ledge, bent down and grabbed the gunnel.

Ryan was still struggling with the bowline. The canoe still had some water in it. We hadn't done a good job of bailing after the last set of rapids. When we pulled it out of the water it would all come my way first.

"Hang on," I said, as Ryan prepared to hoist it out. "No way I'm going to get soaked."

I grabbed hold of the rock ledge with one hand and stepped into the canoe, letting the water sluice by my feet to the stern. The bailer was behind the stern seat where my bug collection was strapped and I reached back with my free hand, retrieved the bailer, and began to bail.

Ryan squatted down and held on to the gunnel amidships to steady her.

Suddenly I heard a sharp intake of breath and looked up to see Ryan reaching his free hand into a crevice among the rocks. "Would you take a look at this?"

When he pulled his hand out he was clutching a roll of film. It must have fallen out when we'd taken the packs out of the canoe. I thought of the hours of patience represented by that roll of film. He must have spent twenty to thirty hours stalking things or waiting patiently in a blind. I mentally went through all the pictures he'd taken, wondering how many of the really good ones he had almost lost. Good pictures were worth a lot of money. He had one he had sold over a hundred times, grossing twenty thousand bucks.

How the hell could he be so careless? As I went back to bailing, an osprey called out a short sharp squawk of alarm, and I looked up to see it veering away from the cliff that soared straight up above the rocky ledge where we'd moored the canoe. There was a blur of something purple on the clifftop, and as I looked I saw the cliff move; I watched as if in a trance as a boulder the size of a basketball tumbled down toward us against the cold blue sky and the unforgiving granite of the cliff face.

"Above you! Look out!" I yelled at Ryan, shaking myself out of the confusion of what I thought I had seen.

He looked up in alarm, twisting his body at the last moment, his face grimacing as the boulder glanced off his right shoulder. He slipped on the rocky ledge and fell sideways into the canoe.

The weight of his body jerked the canoe against the rock in an ugly scraping of fibreglass. My body was flung toward the rock as the canoe began to tip in toward it. I flung out my hands to grab the rock and prevent the gunnel from going under, but there was nothing to grip, and the canoe suddenly tilted dizzily in the other direction as Ryan tried to sit up.

I fought to keep myself from being flung out of the canoe and grabbed a paddle just as the current slammed against the canoe, catching the stern and swinging it around to face the rapids below.

"We're going down backwards." I yelled at Ryan. "Turn around!" He scrambled on all fours to the bow, now suddenly the stern, and grabbed his paddle. I just had time to glimpse an angry open cut on his shoulder and the blood streaming down his forearm before the river had us. I grabbed the gunnels, clutching my paddle firmly in my right hand, and swung my legs around in my seat so that I faced downstream.

"Jesus, Ryan, we'll never make it!" I yelled, but my words were lost in the roaring of the raw power of the river. I looked ahead and stifled the panic building inside me.

The whole river ahead of me was torn up, shreds of water spewing everywhere, boiling, seething, and we were barrelling down toward that cauldron at a break-neck pace. Huge standing waves were breaking up in front of us, and two boulders were causing angry waves to jerk and thrash.

I gripped my paddle, eyeballed the river, and made a quick judgment, trying to remember what I had seen from the head of the rapids when we had joked about running them and I had thought about immortality. We would have to go right between the two boulders. Going left meant huge standing waves, and I could see water leaping up, the telltale signs of shallow water just beyond them. We'd never get by that. The boulders it would have to be, but we were too far right. We had to get the canoe over.

I thrust my paddle into the water, leaning way over the side of the canoe, and pulled the blade back toward the canoe to draw the bow to the left, waiting for Ryan to rudder the stern around to line us up so that we were pointed right between the boulders.

I could see the air bubbles churning over one of the rocks as the canoe swept down upon it, and just when I figured we were going to broadside Ryan pried the stern out and the canoe swept by the right boulder, missing it by inches.

I tried to remember what came after the boulders. What had Ryan pointed out? Hug the shore, take the ledge on the right, and eddy out before the waterfalls — or was it take the ledge on the left? I couldn't remember what path to take. Everything looked so different now we were in the rapids.

Just ahead and to our right a jagged rock suddenly reared out of the water. I hoped I was right: we needed to go to the right of it, to give us a good chance of avoid-ing the ledge. I started paddling to draw the bow to the right, but the current was too fast and I frantically switched sides and pulled the bow left to avoid broadsiding the rock. Ryan took my lead and we flew by on the wrong side.

We were in the centre of the rapids now, heading for the shelf, which I still couldn't see. The foam and the spray washed over me as I strained to pick out our route.

And then, suddenly, I saw it: the long, low uninterrupted line of the shelf. We were too far to the right. We were on a collision course.

"Left!" I screamed into the wind, frantically leaning way out and pulling my paddle in toward the canoe to pull the bow over. The clamour of the rapids killed all other sound and my words were whipped away on the wind, but I knew, as long as Ryan was watching, that the meaning in my wildly pumping arms made it very clear just exactly what was expected of him.

Ryan held the canoe angled, with the bow pointing to shore, and it looked to me like we would broadside. I jabbed my paddle again and again into the churning white mess, blade parallel to the canoe and as far out as I dared reach, then hauled back on it to draw the bow forward and to the left. My arms screamed for rest and my jaw ached from being clamped tight while my adrenaline raced the river for how fast it could drown me. The bow was clear, but it was touch and go if I was really clear enough for Ryan to start bringing the stern around. If he did a strong pry too soon, the canoe would swing around and we would hit the shelf. He held off till the last possible minute and then, with a mighty pry, the stern swung around and the canoe shot past the shelf, so close that I could see the flecks of quartz on the rocks that would have claimed us.

I could see the churning cauldron to my left and the easy, smooth, fast-running water to my right, but to get to it we had to go to the right of a big boulder fast approaching. We had shipped some water, and the canoe was sluggish and not responding as quickly to steering. We hit side on.

The canoe tilted crazily. I reached out and slapped the water hard with the flat side of the paddle blade. The canoe came upright, shipping water as it entered a rolling field of haystacks, huge standing waves sculpted by the hidden boulders beneath. We back paddled to keep the canoe riding the waves.

The eddy we had seen from the shore had to be somewhere ahead, somewhere we could take out — had to take out before the falls. And suddenly there it was, the big boulder and beyond and to its side the small square of dead water and safety. But to my horror, straddling the rock and pushing out over the water to block our route was a "sweeper," a great bloody pine tree, partly submerged.

If we hit it broadside the canoe would tip and fill. We'd be swept under and held by the sweeper. But there was no time to go around it. If we hit the sweeper bow-on I could leap onto it, if it held, but Ryan would swing around or, worse, dump as I leapt.

Broadside it would have to be. We would have to leap in unison, just before it hit. I made the decision, drawing frantically to pull the bow around as Ryan pried, hoping to God we could time it right, that Ryan was reading my signals properly. I braced myself as the canoe hit broadside, flinging my weight downriver to counteract the canoe's crazy tilt upstream into the current. I could see Ryan, closer to shore, flinging his body onto the tree, even as I felt my hands close around a limb. I felt the branches beneath me ripping through my shirt as I grabbed the ones on the surface and then felt the weight of my body dragging them into the water, its power slamming into me like a freight train. I could feel my grip slipping as the water grabbed my legs, pulling them down, dragging me with them. I felt the canoe broach, felt my hands slip. I grabbed wildly for another branch and struggled as my legs were pulled along by the water. I hung on desperately, but the branch was pliable, soft, and my weight pulled it under; I felt my body being pulled under the branches, still with their needles untarnished by death, and then my momentum stopped suddenly as I was jerked back by the straps of my pack.

I was face up and felt like a pinned insect amongst the submerged branches of the tree, barely able to breathe as the water sluiced over my face. I was afraid to move, for fear the backpack would suddenly let go, my left hand in a rigid grip on a small branch, my right hand and arm pressed up against another branch. I stayed as still as I could and waited. Where was Ryan?

I could feel my energy dwindling away as the force of the water pounded me mercilessly. And then he was there above me on the main tree trunk, reaching down, touching my face. I could see his lips moving but heard nothing, just felt the water pressing hard against my ears like a vice; I couldn't move my head in any direction, as it was braced by the water on both sides and was being pushed down against the ominously flimsy branches beneath. Ryan said something again but it was useless — I couldn't hear him and suddenly he was gone.

I timed my breathing to coincide with the least amount of water sluicing over me, terrified that I would start to choke. I felt the panic in me begin to rise and forced myself to think of something else.

And then Ryan was back and I watched as he pulled out his knife and cut the end off a plastic Coke bottle. He reached over and indicated that he wanted me to breathe through it. I started to lose it. I was sure I was going to drown, the bottle would be wrenched from my mouth by the power of the water and I'd be gone. Ryan grabbed my free hand and pressed it, and then pointed to the sturdy branch right above my head. He placed the bottle upriver of it and fed it into my mouth so that the branch braced the bottle. I clamped down with my teeth on the rim of the bottle and took a tentative breath through the tube, fearing water, getting air.

Ryan disappeared for what seemed like hours. The water was sluicing constantly now over my face, and my teeth ached from their iron grip around the bottle. Suddenly I felt Ryan's nails digging into my hands.

"Cordi, can you hold on?" he yelled over the raging of the river. He was gone and then was back with a coil of rope, one end of which he tied with a bowline to one of the tree's branches that soared out of the water. Struggling, he lay over the partially submerged trunk and reached down into the lunging strength of the current. After what seemed like an interminable amount of fumbling he finally got the other end of the rope under my arms and tied another bowline.

"I'll pull the rope tight first," he yelled as I struggled to hear him. "Then I'll have to cut through your pack before I can pull you up." He looked at me, and I saw the fear etched in his face.

Jesus, what was I doing here? This couldn't be happening to me. I felt as though I was being pulled apart and I was getting tired. All I wanted to do was sleep. The sun was overhead now, lunchtime. It seemed that years rolled by and I lived in a dream, and the dream got lighter and lighter, and then I felt the pressure of the rope and saw it tighten over the horizontal trunk of the tree above me. I felt some branches in the water tighten over my chest and the pull of the back-pack on my shoulders. I lay suspended between two forces and waited. Suddenly Ryan was back, his hunting knife in his hand.

He yelled something at me and motioned to the straps on my shoulder. I felt his hands then as he groped for the straps and suddenly I swung forward with the current as the backpack released me. The branch slid through my hand as I struggled to hold on. And then the rope jerked me to a halt.

Ryan was hauling on the loose end trying to winch me out of the water, but my mind was floating up there with the sun as I clutched the underwater branch in my hand, as if it were the lifeline and not the rope.

"Let go, Cordi!" bellowed Ryan "Let go. For God's sake, Cordi, let go!"

I could feel the sun and wind on my face and the roaring, rasping power of the water. I didn't want to let go of my branch. It was my lifeline, wasn't it?

"Let go!" The terror in Ryan's voice seared into my brain; like an automaton, I reacted instinctively to the insistent fear in that voice, and I let go. Suddenly I was free of the river, winched back to safety, coughing and retching in the blessed sunshine, my mind numb. Ryan hauled me out of the water onto the tree trunk and hugged me in a grip almost as fierce as the river had hugged me moments before. I was awed by the tiny distance between life and death.

My legs felt like cement blocks as we struggled together along the fallen tree toward shore. We collapsed in a heap in each other's arms on the sunlit rocks, inches from the water. We lay there side by side, holding each other, shivering, and neither one of us spoke. The sun still shone, warming us. The wind still blew as though nothing had happened, and yet we had nearly died.

I watched the slight breeze shifting the leaves overhead, smelled the soil and the leaf litter, felt the soft, rich earth beneath my clammy, clothes-covered body, felt the scratches on my face, the ache in my limbs, the warmth of the sun as the roaring surge of the rapids, constant and rough, thundered in my ears, setting my whole body on edge, the vibrations of that power dancing in my head, my body like a dishrag. I was limp and spent, but my mind was suddenly a kaleidoscope of thoughts, each one leading inevitably to the next, like water over the falls. I saw again the cliff that had risen straight up out of the bedrock by our canoe, jagged and crumbling, a scree of broken rock with boulders at its feet. I saw again something move at the top of the cliff and a flash of purple, caught and held by the sun, just before the boulder had come crashing down.

I lay there and heard the rapids calling my name, whispering death. I saw again the dead body, the pack in the tree, the aching emptiness of the camp, the golden fathomless stare of the cat, the chocolate bar — and the flash of purple where purple shouldn't have been.

"We could have been killed." Ryan's voice was quiet, almost a whisper, and he rolled over and stared at me as he cradled his injured shoulder. His words hung between us, riding the roar of the rapids and magnifying the uneasiness I had felt at that deserted camp into the first tiny germ of fear.

chapter four

"What the hell are you doing in my truck?"

The angry voice bellowed through the woods, and I nearly dropped the radio phone that I was desperately trying to use as I let out an involuntary yelp.

An enormous man stood at the edge of the woods where the trail I had taken, after splitting up with Ryan to find help, had met an old logging road. He was clenching his huge meat cleaver hands, and the tendons in his bull-sized neck stood out like ropes tightened to the splitting point. I did drop the phone then. I could only imagine the angry expression on his huge face because it was covered completely in thick black curly hair, from the enormous mustache to the bushy eyebrows to the hair sweeping over his forehead like a waterfall. The weight of hair on his face alone looked heavier than I am. His small dark eyes looked incongruous in the huge face. Maybe in his genetic code eyes had been considered a perk and he'd cut back to save costs so that the rest of his body could be massive. They glinted at me like mica, as hard, dense, and unfeeling, the thoughts reflected there cold and inflexible, thoughts known only to himself, building up like steam behind his eyes.

I slowly got out of the truck, hands in the air, never taking my eyes off the guy, and very aware of my smaller size. Every movement was slow and deliberate. Like an unwanted stampede of butterflies I felt my body jarred by a shock of madly fluttering fear. If someone had just tried to kill us back there at the rapids, this guy was the perfect candidate. He'd had plenty of time to get back here ahead of us, and he was angry as hell. My thoughts were making me more and more nervous until it occurred to me that if he'd really wanted to kill us it would have made more sense to ambush us on the portage. Why wait until we left the portage for a road and risk having someone else chance upon us? I felt an enormous sense of relief at my own logic, but it was short-lived. I'd forgotten the critical information that he would have assumed we were both dead. I wished to God Ryan and I hadn't split up to look for help.

I leaned against the open door of the truck, more to keep my legs from shaking than anything else, as the behemoth approached me. I thought about turning to run, but he reminded me so much of a bear that illogically I felt that that would just ensure my annihilation.

"Get your bloody hands off my truck," he said in a strangely quiet voice. I preferred the roar. He grabbed the door that lay between us before I had a chance to move away, and I felt his strength through the door as he bumped it into me, catapulting me backwards as I flailed out to keep my balance. He eyed me over the top of the door, his hands gripping the edge of the partly opened window. They were huge with great ugly red newly minted scars slicing up from his fingers through his massive forearms. I looked behind him, hoping to see Ryan. I took a deep breath because that actually works sometimes and backed further away from the truck as he slammed the door shut with such force that the truck shook, and the sound fled down the road with its own echo on its heels.

"Sorry!" I held up my hands again, fear melting my legs into shaking jelly. Terribly undignified, but then my knees always knocked at public speaking contests at school. I pulled myself together and blurted out, "Sorry, but there's been an awful accident …"

The man suddenly moved closer to me and I instinctively stepped back, but he followed and stood towering over me.

"Who the hell do you think you are?" He kicked the stones in front of me with his elephantine foot and they bit into my legs like needles. "You got a lot of nerve. You and your bloody tree-hugging friends." His face was red and sweaty, and I could smell his anger mixed unpleasantly with my own fear. This guy was unpredictable, the rage smouldering behind his eyes, barely under control. Yet he wasn't behaving like a man who wanted to kill me. He was more interested in his truck than in me. This gave me some confidence.

"I don't know who you are, but I sure could use some help right about now." My voice broke on the last word and I hurried on, hoping he hadn't noticed. "I'm sorry about your truck but there's a body up in the bush and I need a phone to call the police. Your truck was the first thing I came across and it has a phone. I need it."

He glowered at me.

"Yeah sure, lady. I've heard 'em all," he said, but his anger spluttered. He was about to say something else, seemed to think better of it, and said instead,

"What body? Where?" His eyes narrowed to pin-points, his anger suddenly turning into sharp-eyed interest, and something more. Was I imagining it? Or did he already know something about the body in the woods?

"It's back up the portage trail, above the falls, maybe a mile. There's a camp up there."

I thought I saw a smile flit across his face, but it was hard to tell with so much of his face hidden by hair. He was standing very still, with his hands held loosely at his sides. Suddenly he raised them and chopped the air with a vicious downward motion that made me leap back, my heart convulsing.

"I don't give a good goddamn about any dead body. You damn screaming greenies can look after your own dead bodies, and if the guy's already dead, it's no emergency, is it?"

I must admit he had a point. He made a sudden move toward me and then froze as he fixed his gaze on something behind me, the expression on his face darkening another dozen shades. I slowly turned my head and saw Ryan running down the road, flanked on either side by a man and a woman. I was so relieved to see him that when he came up and took me by the arm to see if I was okay I nearly slid to the ground, my wobbly knees suddenly proving how much I needed them to hold me up. We stood together and watched as the man who had been with Ryan squared off with my behemoth, although I was interested to see that he took great care not to get within swinging distance of those huge arms.

"Cameron, what the hell are you doing here?" asked the man in a thin, wheezy voice. He was a slight, balding guy who was wearing a shirt several sizes too big for him. Despite the bravado in his words he did not move any closer to the guy. Cameron's eyes narrowed to slits and his fists clenched, but he said nothing.

"This isn't part of your leasing area, it belongs to the university, and we don't take kindly to you trespassing here," said the man.

"*You*! You have the fucking nerve to accuse me of trespassing." Cameron lunged at the man, who anticipated Cameron's reaction and deftly ducked out of the way.

"You stinking son of a cowardly bitch," said Cameron. "Why don't you put your fist where your mouth is?" He lunged again, but the woman, who, though taller than me, barely reached Cameron's chest, stepped between them as if they were two toddlers.

"Cameron, I think it best that you clear out." Her voice was clipped: not rude, just emotionless. Her clear blue eyes were unblinking as they stood looking at each other. I thought some signal passed between them, but the moment was so fleeting that I couldn't be sure.

"It's not a good idea to come around here," she said.

"Is that a threat, *Miz* Mitchell?" said Cameron with a heavy emphasis on the "Ms."

"No, just a friendly piece of advice."

He snorted, and then a slow smile spread across his face like lava across a valley, vindictive and delighted at some thought in his head. He turned to me.

"The only person I know that camps up there is that bastard who started all this. Must be his goddamned body. Serve him bloody well right, the nosey parker, trying to tell us what to do. As if he knows piss-all about forestry. Well, to hell with him and with all of you. I hope you fry in hell and I'll supply the devil with the fuel you lot are trying to martyr."

He spat the words out like a bad taste he was happy to get rid of. He turned and got in his truck, slammed the door with exaggerated force, and floored it, sending gravel spraying out at us as he roared away.

"What the hell was that all about?" I asked, hoping that words might make my knees behave. I looked at the man, whose face had gone several shades paler.

He pinned me with his eyes, wild and sweaty, stumbled around his words, got his tongue in the right spot, and whispered, "What body?"

Ryan, who hadn't heard the question, turned to me and said, "I only just bumped into these two down by the biology station when I heard you yelp. Leslie Mitchell and Don Allenby, Cordi O'Callaghan."

The woman inclined her head, but the man didn't seem to notice the introductions at all.

"Who was that guy?" asked Ryan, jerking his head in the direction of the departing truck.

Don's voice came again, louder, verging on hysteria.

"What body?" He was nervously wringing his hands and the sweat glistened on his forehead.

"His name is Cameron," said Leslie, who glanced worriedly at Don before repeating his question. "What body?"

"A couple of hours ago we found a body up river at the beginning of the portage around the falls. I was about to tell you when we heard my sister yelp. We need to contact the police," said Ryan.

"Oh, Jesus." Don shook his head from side to side with a half moan.

"For god's sake, Don, get a hold of yourself," snapped Leslie. She turned and looked at me. "Where?"

"We found it near the water about a hundred yards from a campsite of some sort."

Don groaned and whimpered. "Oh, God. It's Jake.

It's gotta be Diamond. Oh, Jesus."

"For Pete's sake, pull yourself together," said Leslie, looking curiously at Don.

"That's his campsite up there. He's the only one who stays up there," moaned Don. "He was due back tomorrow. It's not my fault. If he hadn't returned I was to give out the call. We all do that for each other. We go into the bush so often to do our fieldwork. It's mostly crown land. All our study sites are up this way, we're all biologists of some description or other. I work with small mammals: rabbits and things like that. Jake works with large mammals: Canada lynx, sometimes bobcat. Leslie here's a moose woman. And we do a lot of fieldwork. Our base station is the building around the corner, down the road. We use it as a jumping off spot for say a week, a month in the field at a time. Leslie and I ..."

After this long speech he wiped his forehead with his shirtsleeve. "But Jake knew the bush, unbelievable he was. Not a better man than Jake in the bush. How could this happen to him? How could it be Jake? What the hell happened?"

Leslie stopped the flow of words with a chop of her hand.

"For Christ's sake, Don, pipe down. It may not be Jake. It's probably some poor sucker who got lost and panicked. Jake's too much of a bushman to get into trouble, and he's as healthy as an ox. He'll be along to tell us all about it. Besides, whoever it is, there's nothing we can do right now but get through to the police and report it."

She looked at me and Ryan. "There's a CB radio in my car down the road. We can use that. Cell phones don't work up here — too remote."

We walked in silence. Jake Diamond. The name rang some distant bell in my mind. I did of course know of him as a mammalogist, but it was for something else that this little bell tolled.

"It's Jake. I know it is. It's Jake," wailed Don with such sudden conviction it made me uncomfortable. I couldn't help but think that this trembling basket case knew something the rest of us didn't.

chapter five

"What's this I hear about you finding a dead body? In pieces, no less. I'm gone three short weeks and you get yourself into trouble."

I was standing at my office window looking down at the pavement five flights below, feeling like a washed-out watercolour, bits of me fading into the early morning air, thoughts running into each other, creating mud. The early morning sun glinted off the sidewalk below, and the students rushed to make their 9:00 a.m. classes. At the sound of Martha's deep guttural purr I turned in relief. Martha Bathgate literally filled the doorway of my puny office.

"Really, Martha. Who told you he was in pieces?" Martha had a habit of being able to take my mind off myself and aim it at something productive. She was sometimes even able to dispel my sad moods before they spiralled down into darkness. If only I could figure out how she did it, I might be able to prevent depression from ever getting hold of me again. Unlikely, though; I'd fought it all my life.

Martha winked knowingly at me. "I never reveal my sources, you know that. It simply wouldn't do."

I shared Martha with two other assistant profs who didn't rate their own lab techs, let alone decent office space. But I felt lucky: no one could replace Martha, even working for me full-time. She was my technician, secretary, bodyguard against students, friend, and jack-of-all-trades, who happened to remind me of a tennis ball, round and bouncy. Her black curly shoulder-length hair sprang like a wire mop from her head — cut page-boy fashion it made her face even rounder. Her features were tiny and, although almost eclipsed by the excess weight, they were beautiful, as though designed for fat and not for lean, and her age seemed to have hovered around forty-five for years. In fact, no one even knew her real age. Everything else about her was round as well: round pudgy hands, round belly and legs, short and squat, and now her mouth pursed into a round O. She made me think of the snowmen Ryan and I used to make: three round balls for the body, round raisins for the mouth, and small bright black eyes set against a white face.

"I'm right though? About the pieces? But where in the name of God is Dumoine? That's where you found him, isn't it? I've missed all the news reports, except yesterday's. Fill me in. There was no Canadian news in Bermuda." It was a demand. Martha was the only person I had ever met who knew everything about everyone before they did, without being resented for it. I didn't even try to keep the smile out of my voice. Gossip was Martha's lifeblood, but at least she went to great pains to get it right.

"Dumoine. It's up the Ottawa River about two and a half hours from here on the Quebec side. It's a medium-sized town, and the local police were supremely suspicious of the whole mess. Apparently dead bodies just don't pop up routinely there, the implication being that they pop up routinely everywhere else. They asked me if I was sure it was a human body, if 'perchance' it might not be a dead moose or deer."

"As if you couldn't tell the difference!" huffed Martha indignantly. She was nothing if not loyal.

"To be fair, they've had some woman calling in all kinds of false alarms over the years, dead gophers that look like dead babies, the ribs of a cat mistaken for human remains. How can you mistake a dead gopher for a baby? Anyway, they had no end of stories from her. They thought I was her. It seems our voices sound alike." I spread out my hands in mock self-defence. "When I finally chiselled a word into the conversation and told them that this body was wearing a man's size-ten boots, they advised me that they'd be along. We waited hours it seems — since the body was dead and in a remote area there was no huge hurry. Someone else had said the same thing earlier. Rather crass, I thought. In the end, they didn't need us, to our great relief. The two biologists waiting with us knew by our description exactly where the body was and they made an ID of sorts."

"Two biologists? Anyone we know?"

"I'd heard of them, because some profs from here have collaborated with some of the profs at their university, Pontiac it's called, but I hadn't met them before. A lot of their study sites are up near Dumoine. They have a biology station up there."

I should have known a short answer like that would not satisfy Martha. She put her hands on her hips and waited with eyebrows raised, until I was forced to continue.

"They were a rum pair, two mammalogists — Leslie Mitchell and Don Allenby. They didn't do much talking while we waited for the cops, but then I suppose they were worried it was their colleague lying up there in the bush. Rightly so, it now seems. The cops took down our names and addresses and thanked us and then turfed us out. Allenby escorted them up to the campsite."

"That's it then? No inquest, nothing? You don't have to get up there and tell your grisly story and get mis-quoted in the papers and bring the top university brass down on you?"

Martha had a running battle with the newspapers. She was convinced they all lied through their pens and hid behind their editors when the accusations started to fly.

"They did the autopsy at the little university in Dumoine. The cops called and said there would be no inquest as it was pretty straightforward. Autopsy results concluded it was death by bear. A blow to the back of the head and neck eventually killed him. It was not a quick death, though. The rest of the mess was mauling. Case closed."

"Nasty way to go. Being mauled by a bear, and no one to hear your calls." Martha shivered and then added, "It must have been one of these rogue bears that come sneaking up on decent folk and, without so much as a by-your-leave, swat them like pestering flies."

"That's what the conservation guy thinks. Apparently a team of wildlife enforcers went up there to shoot the poor devil. They're not going to trap this one and move him somewhere else, not after he's killed a man."

"Damn right," said Martha with an indignant look spreading over her face.

"C'mon, Martha. Most black bears are more afraid of us than we are of them, but a rogue bear, one that attacks without provocation, is different. Too bad they give all black bears a bad name."

"Yeah, well, no one in their right mind would want a *rogue* bear in their backyard, and with so many crazy canoeists like you gallivanting through those woods, there's no safe place for a rogue bear anymore. Too dangerous. Once a man-killer always a man-killer, I say."

I didn't say anything. I had had a sudden unpleasant jolting in my stomach as I thought back to the open tins, the food in the campsite, the pack up the tree. I was thinking of the way the sun had fallen across the body, its rays peaceful and warm, quiet and soft, beauty in such horror. The unease was back, and I suddenly realized why. I hadn't seen any sign of any bears in that area. I thought about the chocolate bar still in the tent and the full cans of food and drink unmarked by any teeth or claws. There should have been signs that a bear had been there. There hadn't been: no claw marks, no garbage dragged from the campsite, no droppings, no drag marks, no signs at the mess tent or near the food pack, nothing to indicate a bear had been there except for the horror of the body. But if it had never been there, then how or where had Diamond been killed by a bear?

I brushed the thoughts from my mind. I didn't have time for them, and besides, it didn't concern me, curious as it was. I glanced out the window. Students of all descriptions were flinging a Frisbee about the grassed lawn across the street. I could see the library to the west and beyond it the Ottawa River framed by a stunning electric blue sky. The city sprawled off to the right and Gatineau, Québec, lay across the river. I liked to pretend that I could make out the Eardley Escarpment where my little log cabin lay snuggled in the most beautiful of valleys within the Outaouais. Wishful thinking though. I didn't live *that* close.

"So who was this poor guy?" Martha brought me back to the present.

"We didn't learn anything at all up in the bush. But when we came back and the police phoned to tell me who it was and ask more questions, I did a literature search on him."

"You mean you actually got that old computer to work for you?" I ignored her. Martha could make the computer turn somersaults for her but I seemed to paralyze it and funny things happened. I wasn't about to admit to Martha that I had had to ask the computer guy to help me.

"He was a mammalogy professor at Pontiac University — a well-known and it seems well-liked mammalogist. He's a cat man. He's studied all the North American cats and been to Africa studying cheetahs and helped with breeding of endangered species. He was studying the Canada lynx. I ran his name through my database and it lit up like a neon light. The guy's written dozens of papers on various mammals. Quite a wonder boy. Lectured all over the world and has written several well-reviewed books about the cats of Canada. His name crops up at least twice a month in all the major newspapers."

"Was he also a columnist or something?" asked Martha.

"Actually, no. He's at the other end of the media stick. He gets written about. He's a real wilderness warrior. Couldn't abide any destruction of anything natural and wild. A real hard-line environmentalist. He's leading the fight to have logging banned up in the area around Dumoine."

Martha said excitedly, "You mean the guy with the black curly hair and deep sexy voice that was on all the newscasts a month or so ago?"

I looked at the news clippings piled on top of my desk, rifled through it, and pulled out a piece with Jake Diamond's photo and looked at the curly black hair and warm smile.

"He's the one who single-handedly defied the loggers, erected a barricade to stop the logging trucks, and mobilized the masses. It's been an unpleasant and heated battle. A lot of bad words on all sides, I gather."

I paused, momentarily discomfited, remembering the light in Cameron's eye as it slowly dawned on him that the body might be Diamond's. It had been a very unpleasant moment to watch joy in another man's eye at the mention of death. Here certainly was no friend. Leslie had been so cold, so matter-of-fact, and Don had simply been what? Upset? Horrified? No, that wasn't it. What, then? Frightened? That was it, frightened, but for himself or someone else? Maybe he was just afraid of bears. Academic, really, but I hated it when things didn't fit neatly. I couldn't get the thought out of my head that something weird was happening here.

"I gather Diamond won an injunction to stop the logging and it was overturned. They erected a barricade last month to stop the beginning of the logging. They set up a camp. Dozens of protesters, including children. There were a lot of arrests, and when the injunction was overturned, there was some sabotage of equipment so the loggers can't start until next month and they are fuming mad. No one's taking up his battle and the loggers are gearing up. They plan to start on the east side of Dumoine right away. The north side is slated for cutting next fall."

"Not a few people would have welcomed Diamond's death," noted Martha, echoing exactly what I had been studiously avoiding thinking.

I looked up quickly. The words sent shivers down my spine. I shuddered, remembering our near miss. That flash of purple, was it just a figment of my imagination or had someone really tried to kill us? And if so, why? Had it had something to do with Diamond's death?"

But Ryan and I were still alive, and no one had tried again. It made no sense. Thank God, I had kept my suspicions to myself. No use looking stupid if you don't have to.

"Well, that's all right then." Martha's voice brought me back with a jolt. *If I keep daydreaming like this I'll be jolted out of existence*, I thought.

"What's all right?"

"This bear business. All tidied up, neat as a pin; you've survived, case is closed, as they say, and we can move on to the important things in life such as your insects."

God, if only it were that simple. Martha cleared her throat, an ominous rumble. She glanced over the mess in my office, her sharp, penetrating eyes searching among the bottles and vials on the desk.

"Surely, Cordi, this isn't all you got then, is it?" She waved at the vials and bottles in disgust.

I shook my head. "Everything's up in the lab, but it doesn't amount to even this much." I sighed. One day's collection salvaged from two weeks of work. If I hadn't known just how depressing it all was, I could have read it easily from Martha's face.

"Lord love you, Cordi. That's not enough for even one new lab, my dear, let alone any new experiments you might have cooking." She studied my face closely. "What happened?" she asked softly.

I let my anger slide away from me, but I knew it wouldn't evaporate. It would just go to ground until I hauled it out again, but at least it was being bumped by other thoughts.

"I did get some live larvae. Most of them are in the lab," I said. "I'm hoping we can get them to pupate and then identify what they are, see how long it takes, show their habitat, and try to incorporate that into a lab. Maybe the students will take a proprietary interest in their charges and not get bored."

"What happened to the rest?"

"Two wonderful weeks' worth. We crashed the canoe in the last set of rapids. We hadn't intended to run them, but we accidentally got caught in them." Involuntarily I saw again the boulder, the blur of something purple, and Ryan crashing into the canoe. I brushed aside the images.

"Most of my collection was strapped under the stern and bow seats. We found only pieces of it below the falls. All I came out with was the stuff I collected that last day, and that's only because I left the day's collection at the end of the portage when we went back for the canoe. I don't see how I'm going to get this course working for me. I'm hoping some great thought will jump out at me, rescue me from oblivion." I didn't put much faith in my thoughts, though.

Those insects had taken me the best part of my two-week vacation to collect. We'd crawled over cliffs, shimmied down into caves, swept fields and trees, and raided the maggots off dead animals in search of the unusual and the mundane. Dozens of little kill jars and live jars, each with a tiny card noting date, location, and habitat in which the critters had been found, had been squirrelled away in my storage case. All gone, shattered by the rocks, I thought angrily, all but the ones inadvertently taken from Diamond's corpse.

Martha put on her holier-than-thou expression, nose in the air. "Well it serves you right, gallivanting down suicidal rivers miles from nowhere. Really, how do you accidentally get caught in a rapid anyway? I can't think how you ever got it into that head of yours to go into wild country like that. Why, you'd think you had a death wish," she said, as though her reputation had just been put on the line.

She had seldom ventured into the wilderness in her life. The closest thing to it she had ever seen was my farm and the parks in Ottawa. An earthen path was a monstrous thing; give her good old cement and asphalt and she was happy.

I smiled, remembering the near miss in the rapids. Martha, for once, wasn't far off the mark, even though her sentiment was all ass-backwards, but if I told her the truth she would smother me in sympathy and dire warnings. I preferred being bawled out to suffocating.

"I know, I know, Martha," I said lowering my voice in a conspiratorial whisper, "but some of the best insects are up there, miles from nowhere, in the deepest darkest corners of the Canadian wilderness where bears and wolves and bobcats and dead bodies lurk around every corner and you take your life in your hands just venturing into the woods."

"Oooh, you see? I told you. Too effing dangerous. Sheer stupidity."

Martha took everything at face value, believed everything. Watching her as I told her my story, I could relive it through Martha's facial features. They rose and fell and plummeted and bucked with the rapids, grew round and menacing with the sweeper, grew blank and then widened in fear with the falling of the boulder (I omitted the possibility that someone had hurled it at us and longed to know what facial expression would have gone with that), and finally grew exhausted as she mentally hauled herself out alongside me and Ryan at the end of the rapids.

It was exhausting to watch, but at the end she collected her features, remoulded them into a business-like form, added a frown, and said, "Just what do you suppose we're going to do about course material, with all your insects at the bottom of the river or wherever they go when they dump in a rapids. Classes start in less than two months and I have no specimens to set up your labs."

"We'll have to phone around, find out if some colleagues have some extra unsorted material, and I'll have to scramble and do some more collecting. I'm sure someone would happily lend us some material, especially if we tell them we'll sort the insects from the leaf litter and identify them. "

Martha grimaced. Sorting was not pleasant work.

"Worst case scenario we can use some of Jefferson's collection, but they're not in very good shape." I sighed. "I just don't have time to go on another field trip, with all my experiments needing to be written up. The Dean is on my case pressing me for papers. Publish or perish, as they say." I was eager to get at my research. *Animal Behaviour* wanted more analysis before they'd accept my paper on what male praying mantids might gain from their lopsided encounters with their cannibalistic mates.

"We'll have to get the lab material somehow," I said.

"You don't sound convinced."

"Well, I don't want to have to admit I have nothing new and use the old collections, do I? Not unless I want to get the ass end of the lab next year too, and miss out on a chance at tenure by showing them that I can't breathe new life into a hemorrhaging course."

Seeing Martha's face, I realized I'd said too much. It was one thing to believe your career is stagnating. It was quite another to advertise that fact to your staff. Dreadful idea — too demoralizing, even if I believed everything I said, and Martha knew it. I added hastily, "Oh, it's not that. I'm just disappointed. There were a couple of spiders that I collected that were really rather exciting."

Martha curled her upper lip and hooded her eyes in a look of sheer disgust.

"They're not that ugly Martha, really," I laughed, but it was true that I had never seen anything like those spiders before. Now I wouldn't get the chance to find out if anybody else had seen them either.

"I'd best be phoning around then," Martha said. In a flurry of activity, totally at odds with her considerable bulk, she corralled some vials and jars from my desk and started to leave. I watched in amusement as her face began a one-act play. The features moulded and changed into dawning realization of something, and the something became quite horrendous until her features once again puckered in a kind of silent scream of revolt. She stopped suddenly and looked back at me, her face spewing disgust.

"Those larvae in the lab, they're not from ..." I raised my hands in self-defence. Martha's face grew more disgusted still. Shifting like an ocean wave battering against the sand it ebbed and waned as her thoughts raced through her head, changing her features like the skin of a chameleon. I really believed that her features might disintegrate in imitation of what she was thinking. "Oh, lord save me, Cordi, how can you do these things?"

I shrugged, stifled a smile. "Two of them are on the far wall in the two cages by the sink. The rest are in the common lab. There wasn't room in mine." Not surprising, I thought — my lab was almost as small as my office. I was always having to beg for space from my colleagues who seemed to have gobs of it ... but then, they all had the perks that go with tenure. Martha marshalled her features back into a more or less normal position and waddled out of my office.

I looked at the mail piled high on the desk, sorted through it quickly — nothing from the NSERC grants people yet. God, how they kept me waiting and hoping, second-guessing myself and my competence ten times a day. I was almost out of funds, and without the grant I wouldn't be able to fund a graduate student next fall, and without a graduate student, the department might not be interested in granting me another year. Jesus, life could be a bitch. I stashed all the mail in a big box for some future free moment, and then I returned a dozen calls and put off the lecture planning people another two weeks — how could I give them the synopsis of my course when I had no material? I'd have to fudge it and hope the Dean didn't call me in and grill me.

I gazed out the window, wondering how to pick up my career, feeling the dark cobwebby entrails of depression reaching out for me. My heart lurched at the horrible feeling, and I struggled to rid the thoughts from my head. I'd never get tenure if I couldn't control my periodic depressions.

There was a quick step and heavy breathing, and I was thankful for an interruption until the round, wrecked face of Martha reappeared in the room. I read disaster in every nuance of the wobbling, shivering flesh on her face.

"Jesus, Martha, what happened to you? You look like a squashed spider."

It was true. Every ounce of flesh on her face seemed to be sagging into a puddle and her skin was as white as milk. Martha took in a great deep breath and grew rounder, like a balloon. "It's your lab, Cordi." It came out in a screech that set my nerves to grinding.

"What is it? What's happened?" I asked, moving quickly around my desk, the pit of my stomach lurching like a tugboat in a jar full of hurricanes.

"I think you'd better come see for yourself." I took one last look at Martha's face as it seemed to metamorphose into even greater doom and raced out of my office, taking the stairs two at a time. There was no one in the long corridor. The doors were closed on all sides and the institutional tiles on the floor sparkled in the overhead fluorescent lighting. My door was the sixth from the end, on the right.

It was ajar, and even before I reached it, I smelled it. *What is it about smell and disaster these days?* I thought calmly, in that unreality before reality hits. I walked in.

Everything seemed to be in its place, nothing wrong except for the heavy reek of insecticide. It was everywhere — the air was glutinous with it. "This isn't happening," I said, trying to will it so. "It's not happening." I moved in a daze from cage to cage. Insect after insect, dead. The mice and salamanders seemed okay, but who knew what the chemical would have done to my controlled conditions? All garbage now. Thank God I wasn't in the middle of any mantid experiment.

Nothing could stop the deadly work of the insecticide. I moved from cage to cage unbelieving, touching the cages, looking in. But at least my data was safe. The insects could be replaced. I turned to my laptop computer to boot it up, but I didn't get far. The keyboard was drenched in some sort of fluid that had spread throughout the computer. A horrible feeling crept through me as I bent to sniff the keyboard. Formaldehyde. It was swimming in formaldehyde. Like an automaton I turned on the computer, but nothing happened. I remembered the death sentence handed out to the computer of a friend of mine, who had once spilled a glass of red wine on her computer. All my files gone. My raw data, gone. But I had backups. A pain in the ass to get them reinstalled, but at least I had them.

Or did I?

I turned from the room, took the stairs on the run, and raced into my office to the drawer where I kept my computer backup disks. I yanked it open and stared at the empty drawer. No disks. I pulled it all the way out and flung it on the floor, getting a precarious sense of relief from watching it splinter and shatter. *Not very well made*, I thought, in that strange displacing calm that disaster spawns. With a sinking heart, I remembered doing a backup the previous week and asking my grad student to put them in my office when the backup was done. But he'd lost his key to my office and had left the disks in the lab. I raced back upstairs and flung open every drawer and cupboard, but there were no disks. I turned in desperation to the computer and started madly pushing buttons, looking for a miracle I knew I wasn't going to get. What can I say? I'm an indecisive fatalist. Sometimes.

It was some time before I was aware that Martha was standing in the doorway, with a handkerchief draped decorously over her nose.

"Who would want to do this to you Cordi?" she whispered. "In all my years here I've never seen anything like it. Nothing exciting ever happens around here, and then suddenly, in the space of weeks, you find a dead body, nearly die, and have your lab gratuitously fumigated?"

I kicked the drawer with my foot. "Whoever it was, I've got to find them. I've got to get those disks back." After months of lethargy induced by one of my black moods, it felt good to feel so motivated, even if it was out of fear.

"But, Cordi, what makes you think they'll still have the disks?"

I looked at Martha, giving the butterflies in my stomach a ride worthy of a sailboat in six-metre waves.

I took a deep breath to calm the waves and swallowed hard. I thought I was a pessimist, but this horrible thought had miraculously eluded me.

"Because if they don't, I'm history."

"You sure are, my dear Cordi."

The voice grated every nerve in my body as I turned to face Jim Hilson. He walked in without being invited and casually picked up one of the fumigated cages.

"Oh, Cordi, this is just dreadful. Now you won't be able to publish any papers." He looked at me ruefully. You're going to need a bit of luck, Cordi, to get out of this mess." He smiled then and replaced the fumigated cage. "Cheers," he said. And then he was gone. Just like that.

chapter six

I spent the rest of the afternoon in the zoology building with the security people and police, bottling up my anger and panic and trying to appear stoic, when I actually felt totally destroyed. The harried diminutive blond female cop was very pleasant but not encouraging.

"The lock on the lab door was jimmied, but whoever did this had access to the main door or came in during normal hours and hid somewhere until later."

"That could have been anyone," I moaned. "All faculty members and grad students have a key to the main door, and people come in and out at all hours of the day and night to check on their experiments."

"So technically anyone on staff could have let themselves in without being noticed?"

I nodded, but I realized it was worse than that. "The building is open from nine to five and there is no security guard at the main door." I couldn't help wondering how Jim had found out so quickly. Could he have done this? Was he that set on eliminating me as the competition, or had he coincidentally been in the hallway and smelled the insecticide? Odd, though, since his lab was one floor below mine.

"So, anyone could have come in, waited until after hours, killed your bugs, stolen your disks, and then left at night. No note. No one's claimed responsibility, no fingerprints. Is there any reason to suspect an animal rights group?"

"With insects?" I asked incredulously. "Do you realize how much most people detest insects? You have to be cuddly, furry, soft, and photogenic before the animal rights activists get hot under the collar. If this is linked to them I'll eat candied ants for breakfast."

Finally the police left and I reluctantly turned the lab over to Martha to clean out and get the cages ready for new material. *What new material?* I thought. All my research from the last month was gone because I had failed to print a paper backup for a month, and much of my raw data was lost going back years. I'd need months just to sort through my paper records and design more experiments to replace the lost data for the *Animal Behaviour* paper if I couldn't find the disks. It would be at least a year, if I was lucky, before I could publish again. And I knew what that would do to my chances at tenure. I shuddered at the thought. I had no choice. I had to find the disks or go down trying. I started ruminating on all the things that could go wrong and then realized that I had to do something to keep my dark thoughts at bay or I wouldn't get anywhere at all. But it wasn't easy — it never is.

I'd started sorting out what experiments I might be able to salvage from the paper records in my office when Martha poked her head in.

"I was cleaning out the cages after you left and found something really strange."

My ears buzzed at the sound of her words. Martha and strange were anathema. I didn't think the word was even in her vocabulary. God, what else could happen to me today? *Let me count the ways*, I thought.

"I took all the dead insects and put them in separate jars according to their cage numbers, just as you'd asked me to do, but when I came to do the two mesh cages of larvae there weren't any."

"No cages?"

"No. No larvae in the cages. They were completely empty. Not a single larva, none at all."

"You mean all the cages with larvae? The ones I brought back from the canoe trip?" Something twigged in my mind.

"That's right. The ones from you know what," she said with one of her meaningful looks, "as well as all the larvae from your succession experiments. Only the larvae were touched, and whoever it was was very, very careful. They didn't miss a single larva. My guess is they dumped the contents of each cage into a bag and then swilled out the cages."

"Why would they do that?"

"Maybe they figured you wouldn't try to catalogue all those dead insects, that you'd just count your losses, pitch them all, and start again, that you'd never notice the larvae were missing."

I thought for a moment. "But why would they want me to think that?"

I just might have done that too, but I needed those samples for the lab work because of the lost collection on the river. But why would they be interested in the larvae at all? Who could possibly get anything from destroying those larvae? What was so important about the larvae that they had been stolen, and why had the rest of my insects been fumigated?

"Maybe someone's found a cure for cancer in blowfly larvae." Martha caught my venomous glance. "Just kidding."

"What about my pickled larvae, in the jars near the door?"

"They're all there except for the two I labelled 'Dumoine.' They've vanished."

"Only the stuff from the canoe trip. What about the live larvae in the other room?"

"They're still there. It was the first thing I checked."

"Put new labels on them will you, Martha? I don't want them to go missing. They might hold the answer to this whole mess."

"What do you mean by that?"

"I'm not sure, but whoever did this was interested in the insects I brought back from Dumoine, and some of those came from Diamond's body. Maybe there's a link: dead body, a ransacked lab, stolen insects and disks. No bookie would bet on odds that this is all coincidence. There's got to be a link among the insects, the body, and my stolen disks." *Not to mention a probable attempt on my life*, I thought morosely. Martha opened her mouth.

"Don't say it again, Martha. I don't want to hear it. Whoever it was could have dumped formaldehyde on top of my disks just as they did with the laptop. They didn't. They stole them instead, so there's a chance they're still around." I was angry and a little bit scared, if I had the guts to admit it, which I knew I didn't. At least not to Martha, anyway. I couldn't bear the thought of what it would do to Martha's face to know I was scared.

"But, Cordi, the cops have nothing to go on. They're not optimistic they can find out who did it. No one saw or heard anything."

I heard myself in her words. She was usually the optimist, me the pessimist, but I couldn't afford to give credence to my pessimistic thoughts. Hearing them coming at me from Martha almost dissolved my resolve, but then I thought about what would happen to me if I didn't fight and I rallied my wits.

"I don't care what the cops say. I'm damned if I'm going to let someone screw my career without going down fighting. I've worked too bloody hard to see it slipping through my fingers."

Martha cleared her throat and looked at me.

"Now what?" I asked, feeling like my balloon had just been pricked and I was mentally hunting around for the ragged bits of wet rubber to try and put it back together again.

"I know it's a bad time, but the editor of *Animal Behaviour* emailed asking about your revisions."

"Oh, Jeeesus, Martha. Stall him. Tell him I'm working on some last-minute stuff. Don't let on that I've got no data! I need more time." I pulled my hair. "I can't lose this. It's too important a publication, and if I don't publish, the team in Calgary will surely beat me to it, not to mention kissing my job goodbye. He says they've already approached him but I'm first as long as I can deliver. Damn it to bloody hell. Why is it always me?"

After Martha left I tried to compose a letter to the funding people explaining why my quarterly report would be late, asking for more time. But I couldn't concentrate. My mind kept wandering back to my ransacked lab. What was so important about the larvae and my disks? To put me off the scent? What scent? I sat, stocking feet propped on my desk, thinking about it, and then took the rest of the day off, I was so discouraged by it all. I needed to talk to Ryan. Even that was discouraging. I had to make do with my brother, ever since Luke had left.

Not that I didn't appreciate bouncing ideas off Ryan, but he had his own family and I was aware that they came first. I wanted another Luke, or did I just need another Luke to lean on? Depressing thought, because Luke had actually been a bit of a jerk and a lot of a prima donna. Surely next time I could want a companion that I didn't need? Had that ever happened? Stop thinking!

I grabbed a cold juice from among all the frozen specimens in the little fridge in my office. I needed activity to keep my thoughts at bay until I could bounce them off Ryan, before they bounced me into more and darker thoughts. I scooted out of my office, hoping to get across the Champlain Bridge to Aylmer before the federal civil servants flocked out of work and created a half-hour wait.

Usually I loved the drive past Aylmer, where the country really began and the tree-clad cliffs of the Eardley Escarpment rose above the river valley, which once had been a shallow inland sea. But my thoughts blocked out the beauty of the land and I saw it only vaguely through my self-doubts. Twenty-five minutes later on the straight two-lane highway I crested a hilltop and the Ottawa River spilled across to the horizon, and for a precious moment my thoughts deserted me as I took in the sparkling water that beckoned me. Shortly after, I turned right onto a dirt road that weaved past several houses and then through an old farm gate into the valley that had been my home off and on all my life.

At the crest of the hill I stopped the car, determined to get a grip on myself. It was my elixir after a long day's work. Spread out at my feet were rolling fields planted with corn and hay, stretching to the escarpment, which swung up over my head. The barns stood at the end of the road by the cornfields. The old stone farmhouse where I had grown up, and where Ryan and his family now lived, was catching the late afternoon sun, rosy and warm. My little cabin lay out of sight, out behind the barns.

I wheeled my car in past the farmhouse and pulled up in front of the dairy barn. Ryan's car was parked there, although he usually parked in back near the entrance to his office. I got out as the hum of crickets, the heat of summer, the feeling of the dried earth, and the smell of manure and hay mingled in the air with my thoughts. As if they needed fertilizing, I thought sourly — there were enough of them already.

I opened the heavy wooden door and walked into the darkness of the barn down a long narrow corridor, then through a second swinging door into the barn proper. Three lines of fifteen stalls ran the length of the barn and the cows were all in and ready for milking, their impatient lowing matching the full stretch of their udders.

I caught sight of Ryan on the far side, hauling the milking equipment to a cow, the black snake-like tubes with the shiny vacuum cylinders looking like a modern-day Medusa.

"Hiya. Where's Mac?" I was amazed at how normal my voice sounded. My whole career was ready to whirl down the drain and here I was asking about Mac. I looked down the aisles for the tall, thin, rake-like figure of Macgregor with his mane of milk white hair. He'd run the farm since my parents had retired to Ottawa and France, but recently Ryan had been doing more.

Ryan had the milking stool strapped around his waist so that when he stooped to collar the teats he had something to lean against and save his knees. I watched as he pulled on the long black tubes and expertly hooked the milking unit onto the cow's udder. I'm not sure I'll ever feel comfortable with this vacuum pump stuff. I'm always afraid I'll suck off the cows' teats when I do it. Being a woman, it kind of makes my skin crawl to see those teatcups clamped down like that. The whole thing was so different from when I was a kid and my parents had hand-milked the cows. I sometimes missed the sweet warmth of the cow against my shoulder and cheek, the pull of the teats, the spray of the milk. When I had finally learned how to do it, the milking had been mesmerizing and strangely relaxing: sitting on a wooden stool about where Ryan was now, my head leaning against the cow, eyes shut, the milk rhythmically splashing into the bucket. That gentle noise was now replaced by the hum of vacuum suction. I looked at the cows and felt sorry that none of them had ever felt a human hand-milking them.

"Where's Mac?" I asked again.

"He's got some kind of flu bug again."

Mac had seemed less vital recently and I realized with alarm that he must be pushing seventy-five. What would we do without him? Ryan couldn't run the operation on his own. He was too often away on business, and Rose, his wife, had two preschoolers to care for. The thought left me cold, yet life is defined by death. If we lived forever, life could not be the same. Death gave it meaning, where immortality could not. Death made it leaner, meaner, infinitely more exciting, because every second was precious. God. Even eternity was weighing on me today. Where the hell did these thoughts come from?

Now that I was here with Ryan I suddenly felt tongue-tied, my thoughts everywhere but where they needed to be. Problem was I didn't know where to start. I wondered if my theory was just crazy nonsense, and I didn't want to hear Ryan tell me as much. I was so easily deflated when I was in this kind of mood. But a theory was better than the alternative — nothing — and I couldn't sit around waiting for the police: they'd as much as told me they couldn't do anything.

Ryan disconnected the tubes, disinfected the cow's teats, and moved to the next cow. After he'd hooked her up he leaned against the barn wall and grinned at me. "How's the city?" Ryan seldom had occasion to go into Ottawa. He had a lab and a darkroom behind the barn, and with a fax machine and computer he was able to conduct much of his business from home, run the farm, and have lunch with his family all at the same time. I hesitated, and Ryan looked up and saw the worried look on my face.

"What's up, Cor?"

I fiddled with the ear of the cow Ryan had been milking. It flipped its head and tried to nuzzle my fingers. "Some jerk broke into my lab and killed all my insects."

"Oh lord." Ryan looked at me, searching my face. He reached out for me, held me close. "I'm sorry, Cor. All that work."

The warmth of Ryan's body made me want to melt into it and forget all my troubles. Hugs had that effect on me. Horrified, I felt tears stinging my eyes and pulled away, turning my back to Ryan. All I needed now was to cry like a blithering idiot.

"Why would anybody want to do that?" said Ryan, jumping into the awkward silence I had created. "I can understand it if you worked with cute cuddly things and some bozos thought you were mistreating them, but insects? Who would ever dream of championing insects?"

I struggled to get my voice out of the bubbly crackly stage that preceded full-fledged tears and said nothing.

"Can you salvage any of your experiments?" Ever the practical Ryan.

"That wasn't the worst of it, Ryan." I paused and turned to him. "They took all my backup disks and drenched the computer in formaldehyde, wiping out all my data — maybe three years of work, four papers — all my backups. The computer tech people aren't holding out much hope and neither are the cops. Whoever it was did a good job, wore gloves and all those spy-type things."

Ryan's jaw sank down around his knees. "But you have paper backup?" He looked down at my face. "Oh no, Cordi," he whispered. "Tell me it isn't so."

I looked down at my feet.

"No paper backup for some of my raw data," I said bitterly, "and the disks were in the lab too."

"Dear God, Cordi. What are you going to do?"

I could have hugged him for not reminding me how many times he had told me about making sure I had backup. Even so, I couldn't still the urge to defend myself.

"I thought I had it all organized. The backup disks were in my office far away from the lab in case of any accident. I guess I should have brought a copy home."

"What happened?"

"When I was backing up last week — you know how slow it can be — I asked Greg if he'd turn off the computer, put away the disks in my office, and lock up when it was finished. Unfortunately my office was locked and he didn't have my key, so he took the disks back up to the lab and put them in the drawer under the computer, meaning to return them to my office this week. He forgot, and I never noticed."

"Can you salvage anything?"

"Yeah, but I've lost most of my raw data. And I need it to do revisions for *Animal Behaviour*. They may give up on me. The Dean won't be pleased either. He's under pressure to have his staff perform, and having me basically lose maybe a year's work puts me behind the line for publishing. I can't understand why all this happened in the first place."

Ryan scrunched up his brow, the worry lines tickling his eyes.

"Oh damn! The cow!" He leapt into action. The tubes were trying to suck out the milk that was no longer there, and the cow was doing a bit of a jig. Ryan scooted around darting in to pull the tubes off, and I found I couldn't help laughing. Ryan emerged from the side of the cow looking sheepish.

"At least I made you laugh," he said as he moved down to the next cow. "But I don't see it, Cordi. Maybe they mistook your lab for someone else's. Are any of your colleagues in biology or entomology doing any controversial stuff that environmentalists or animal rights activists might be offended by? Even bugs are getting their sympathy these days."

I hesitated and ran my hand down the backside of the cow, who was moving about restlessly, her udder painfully distended as Ryan moved in with the tubes. He'd been late in starting the milking.

"Ryan, there's no reason for it that I can see. No animal rights activist would come hounding me when there are other, more photogenic critters to stalk."

"Have you failed any student lately? Or what about Hilson?"

I shook my head, "No. I don't think he has the guts to take things that far. And I haven't failed anyone who'd be a likely candidate. No, there's simply no reason for it that I can see unless it has something to do with this Jake Diamond guy."

Ryan looked bewildered, reached for some words, hesitated, reached for others, and finally said, "Diamond. That's our dead body, eh?"

"Yeah, turns out he was the guy causing all the trouble up there over the logging, a guy with a quick temper apparently." I filled Ryan in on Diamond's biography, or what I knew of it, and then told him about the larvae and how only the specimens from Dumoine had been taken.

"So, in the space of a week we find a dead body, almost get killed, and then your troubles begin. The dead larvae from the canoe trip are stolen along with all your disks, some of which had data from the trip already entered." He looked at me for confirmation. I nodded. "Also your hard drive is toast."

"That's right," I said, "and the only link that I can see is the larvae. They came from Diamond's body. So it must to be related to Diamond's death, my disks, the larvae. He seems to have made a few enemies, Ryan, especially among the loggers. There are a number of people out there who might be quite happy he is dead." Ryan looked at me in astonishment.

"His death was an accident, Cordi," he said, reading my mind and not liking what he saw.

"Was it?" I asked.

chapter seven

Ryan slammed the gearshift back down to second and braked as the grey Jeep ahead of him came to a sudden stop.

"How the hell can you go through this every day?"

I looked up from reading the newspaper and eyeballed the snaking line of rush hour cars ahead of us on the Champlain Bridge. I thought things were actually moving along quite smoothly.

"You get used to it, even look forward to it." I said. "I've learned to shut out the traffic, think about other things, plan my day. It's only when some jerk starts honking that I get rattled. I mean, what are you supposed to do? Ram all the cars off the bridge to let the sod by?"

"It's a thought," said Ryan through gritted teeth.

"Yeah, right." I said. "And where would that get you? I used to daydream about all sorts of ways to vent my frustration but it only made me angrier when the daydream was over and I realized nothing had changed. The same jerk was still trying to turn left in a 'no turn' lane."

Ryan glared at me as if it were my fault and revved the car in exasperation. He hated going into Ottawa and usually begged a ride with me when he had business in town, so that he would have some company. I would drop him off where he wanted to go — the film lab today — and he would meet me at my office after work.

"Hey, look at this! I rated another piece in the paper. The same guy that interviewed me last week and wrote that piece about my accidentally collecting the larvae. The reporter thought it was gross and would sell papers." I thought it made me look like a fool, but I didn't know how to tell him it was off the record without looking worse. I mean, anyone who hadn't seen the body bits would wonder how I could mistake a human being for a wild animal. Ryan was preoccupied with the driving so I read the article to myself. This time he'd added all kinds of gossipy stuff including some of the items found in the tent — sleeping bag, camera, film canister, chocolate bar. Why would he do that?

Ryan honked the horn at some guy ahead of us who hadn't moved ahead fast enough. My voice trailed off as my thoughts took over and we drove the rest of the way in silence.

By the time Ryan had driven himself to the film lab, rush hour was over and I had no trouble zipping down the Queensway to work. I stopped by the computer store where I'd dropped off my computer the day after the theft to check on it, but the news was bad. They hadn't been able to salvage anything.

"What did you do to it? It stinks," asked the totally unsympathetic store clerk, making me feel like a jerk. I paid the bill and took the computer back with me, feeling absolutely rotten-to-the-core stupid. Why could these guys make me feel like that? Secretly I hoped the jerk was wrong and the computer would one day spew out all my data. Fat chance. By the time I pulled in to work the staff parking lot was full — some dingbat had parked in my spot under the oak and I had to cruise the streets looking for a place to park. I spiralled out further and further, feeling like a vulture caught in an updraft, when down was where it wanted to go. In the end I had to hoof it for ten minutes.

The zoology building was a utilitarian six-storey affair that paid no homage to any school of architecture, except box-like boredom. Even the brickwork was an anemic yellow. Maybe it had been cheaper than the rust red variety. At least it wasn't like the architectural monstrosity of the library across the road. That looked like something out of a sci-fi plot.

I crossed the small quadrangle of grass and weeds, with its token tree cordoned off from harm by a three-foot-high fence, and took the five flights of steps two at a time to my office. Half an hour late and so much to do. Damn. I rushed in through the tiny outer foyer of my office to find Martha drinking coffee with a blond bombshell. The comparison between the two was ludicrous, like an elephant and a gazelle. The bombshell rose swiftly to her feet and I turned to Martha for some explanation. As far as I knew I had no appointments this morning. And I didn't want any either. I didn't feel like talking to anyone.

"Lord love you, lady. Where have you been, Dr. O'Callaghan? I told her half an hour ago you'd be here in two minutes. This poor woman is swamped with my gut-rot coffee and is too polite to say no every time I fill up her cup."

The bombshell made ineffective noises through her perfect teeth, as if she was embarrassed, but not really.

She was taller than I am and very, very thin. She wore burnt orange pants that fitted her like a glove and a silk blouse with a navy blazer. Very elegant. She made me feel positively inelegant in my faded navy cords and T-shirt with frogs hopping all over it. She wore her frizzled hair shoulder length and her watery pale blue eyes looked unfocused as she turned to me. Her round, full lips were shaped like the period beneath the exclamation mark of her straight nose. Her anorexic eyebrows were dyed jet black. She was very heavily made up, sporting every colour of the rainbow on her face, except the natural ones. Around her neck was a stunning silver pendant and embedded in it was a small curved tooth. I looked pointedly at Martha for an explanation or introduction or something.

"Oh yeah. Right. Sorry. This is Lianna Cole, Dr. O'Callaghan." We shook hands and I was surprised at the strength of the handshake; I actually had to keep from grimacing as I matched her pressure and felt my ring jam into my hand. She hadn't looked the type. I had pegged her as the dishrag variety. Martha said nothing more — she either didn't know why the woman was here or was quite content to let the two of us work it out, hoping for an extra tad of gossip.

"What can I do for you?" I asked.

Lianna glanced over at Martha, who stood there looking at the two of us with a big expectant smile on her face. She looked positively predatory. Martha could sense gossip and scandal the way an ant can sense sugar.

"Come on into my office," I said, and led the way past Martha, who gave me the hairy eyeball.

Lianna followed, picking her way through the pile of papers on the floor in the doorway. I cursed under my breath and pulled off a stack of file folders from the only guest chair in the room. My grimy lab coat lay sprawled on the floor, and I was suddenly aware of how messy it must look, but I was determined not to apologize for the mess. I sat on my desk, wondering if my hair looked as wind-blown as it felt.

"Sorry about the mess." I bit my lip. Damn. "What can I do for you?"

Lianna Cole rummaged in her purse and took out a cigarette, her surprisingly short, chubby fingers gripping it like a vise.

"Do you mind?" she said as she raised it to her round red lips. I was reminded of all the cigarette butts I saw in the parking lot, so many with red lipstick. I could see the grey choking smoke swirling through the trachea and bronchi to the tiny alveoli and capillaries. Positively revolting.

"Yeah, sorry, but I do mind, unless of course you want to take over my laundry bill and buy me an air ionizer to clean up after you've left."

Whoa Cordi — you're way out of line here, I thought, surprised at myself, as I watched the confusion spreading over her face. She wasn't used to hearing no to that particular question, and I wasn't used to saying it. I felt rotten, but even so, I didn't say anything to make it easier for her, and wondered why. I guess I was just in a foul mood.

Lianna tossed the cigarette into her purse, closed it, and, tight-lipped, said, "Maybe I've come to the wrong place. I'm not so sure you can help me."

I bit my lip and refrained from saying, "Just because I don't like smoking?" and said instead, "Well, I won't know unless you tell me." Why was this woman getting under my skin?

She stared at me for what seemed like an eternity, and then made up her mind.

"Jake Diamond was my husband."

Oh boy. What an insensitive jerk. Too late, I now saw that the finely sculpted face looked puffy; the carefully applied makeup didn't quite hide the shadows under her eyes, and the blush, expertly applied, didn't hide the extreme pallor of the rest of her face. She was struggling for emotional control. Or was she?

I wildly searched for the right words, but couldn't find them, and said nothing instead, surprised again by my own belligerence. I'm not normally rude, and certainly not to strangers. Like everyone, I usually like to make a good first impression.

Lianna took a deep breath and said, "I kept my family name when we married. He used to kid me that I was the only woman he knew that didn't want to exchange Cole for a Diamond." She laughed, a lonely, haunting sound that made me squirm. Cole for a Diamond. Jeeesus.

"I understand that you found the, um, that you found …" Her voice cracked and her hands nervously fiddled with her necklace. Hauling my eyes away from the necklace, I finally rallied to the niceties of human etiquette.

"Yes, that's right. We were on a canoe trip and found his camp. We didn't know who it was until later. I'm so sorry," I added lamely.

Lianna held up her hands in a gesture of helplessness. "Look. I'm not here to hear your rendition of how you found the body. I'm here because Jake accidentally took my diary with him and I sort of want it back."

"Haven't the police contacted you about his belongings?" I asked.

"The police finally released everything to me. But there was no diary. I called them but they knew nothing about it — said they'd never seen a diary."

"It must have been lost," I said, trying to remember if I'd seen it. "The cops must have misplaced it."

"I don't think so," said Lianna. "I mean the cops, anyway. They did double-check for me. And why would they lie?"

"What's this got to do with me?"

"You were there, before the cops got to the scene. Was it there?"

My interest quickened. "What did it look like?"

"It was about the size of a deck of cards, hard black cover with bright orange tape on both sides, so that I wouldn't misplace it easily."

I thought back to the inside of the tent, saw the empty canister, the sleeping bag where I had thought a body would rear up and bite me. I saw an image of a small black book with an orange slash poking out from under the tent, but the name on it had not been Lianna's. I hesitated, then said, "I think there was a small black book of some kind, but I didn't look at it." It had been there and yet it wasn't when the cops arrived. What had happened to it? What was going on here?

"Look, Lianna, it was likely lost in the shuffle," I added. She looked at me curiously and I ploughed ahead. "There was a lot of stuff the police took. They could easily have lost it, or more likely misplaced it. I'm sure it will turn up. Why is it so important?"

"You can ask that? I've just lost the man I spent fourteen wonderful years with and you ask me why I want my diary of some of those years?"

"I didn't mean to sound callous but ..." *Jesus, I did mean to be callous*, I thought. And why this reluctance to tell her everything I knew? And why hadn't she asked me about their cat — presumably it was hers too? And it was still lost out there in the woods, as far as I knew. We'd forgotten about it in our haste to get back.

"Look, I don't see that there's anything I can do," I

said, hoping my lies weren't as transparent to her as they were to me.

Liana stared at me, and then gathered up her bag. "It was there. You saw it. You said so. Maybe you took it."

The words hung between us like a red flag and I said. "Look, I have no idea ..."

But Lianna suddenly lashed out at me. "No idea, my ass. I had hoped you could help, but I can see there's no point."

"Perhaps I can help you if you explain why you insist that it is your diary. The book I saw had Diamond's name on it."

She looked at me, her eyes widening and narrowing like a camera focusing. Her anger vanished and she seemed to shrink back into a vulnerable snakelike bundle in the chair.

"He once asked me that if I outlived him, would I please burn all his black books, without reading them."

I raised my eyebrows at her and Lianna hurriedly continued.

"He sometimes read bits of his diaries to me, about other people, and he could be pretty cruel — truthful, but then truth can be cruel, crueller still if the person is no longer around to soften the written words. I just wanted to carry out his wishes." Her eyes flickered past me but refused to meet my eyes. She dabbed them with a handkerchief.

"Look, all I can tell you is that I saw a black book in his tent, so the police must be mistaken. You'd better ask them again."

After Lianna had gone I stood by the window fiddling with the blind, my eyes unfocused, thoughts swirling. Things were getting decidedly suspicious. No signs of bear, the possible attempt on our lives, my fumigated insects, no larvae, the loss of my disks, and now the mysterious disappearance of a small black book that I had seen with my own eyes, and Lianna's sudden vehemence when I remembered the book but didn't know where it was. Suppose there was something suspicious about Diamond's death? More to it than a bear? But what? Suppose that was the link? Someone was hiding something, and whatever it was, it had to do with Diamond's death.

I looked down over the quad and saw Lianna walking briskly toward a row of parked cars. I watched as she unlocked the driver's door of a candy apple red Porsche and roared out of the parking space, cutting off a cyclist who raised his fist at her as she sped away.

I sighed and went in search of Martha. I found her in my lab cutting liver to feed the newly arrived larvae and others, which I'd begged from a colleague.

"One of the larvae from you know where has pupated." Martha raised her plump forefinger and pointed, the look on her face almost palpable — if a face could roll its eyes, Martha's face was doing so now.

I moved down to the cage in question and stood staring inside. I read the label. One of the grubs from Diamond's body. The ones salvaged from the lab next door where I'd left them the night of the fumigation. I looked inside. The fly was settled on a hunk of liver, its wings still clinging to its body. I'd pickle it and identify it later. Something twigged in my mind and I looked at the label again, remembering the pine forest where I had collected the grubs. Surely it wasn't possible? But I remembered distinctly the cedar twigs collected with the larvae and the cedar embedded in Diamond's wounds.

"Well, I'll be dammed," I whispered. What the hell was going on here?

I stared at the newly pupated insect and realized I was out of my depth.

chapter eight

I hauled down my entomology and forestry texts and spent the next couple of hours immersed in them. Ryan called to say he had a ride back with Mac, who had come into town for a doctor's appointment, so I was able to stay until I found what I was looking for. I finally called it a day at 7:00 p.m. Now I needed Ryan as a springboard for the theory forming like a wasp's nest in my mind.

I pulled in by the barn and saw Ryan dismantling a cedar rail fence, making the most of the long daylight hours. I walked over and leaned on the fence watching him. I decided to be blunt and came straight to my point.

"Jake Diamond's body was moved after he died."

"So what?" said Ryan.

"But it's weird, Ryan,"

"Why? It's really no big deal. So the bear dragged him a short distance. There's nothing ominous about that."

"It was moved a long way, Ryan. At least a mile and a half."

"So the poor guy hauled himself all that way trying to find help before he died."

I don't know what I was expecting his reaction to be, but his lack of interest to this point was disheartening. I needed to find a reason for my stolen disks before I could hope to find a lead. I was pretty sure I had that lead, but I wanted support.

"You think he could have crossed a river and walked over a mile in rotten terrain while mortally wounded?"

Ryan raised his eyebrows at that and finally looked at me with a modicum of interest.

"And," I added, "you show me a bear that would do that and I'll make my name in zoology. It'd be a rogue bear in more ways than one."

"How in the name of God do you know it was moved that far?" asked Ryan.

"There was no bear sign in the area where he was found."

"No bear sign my ass. You saw the body."

"Yeah, sure, but I think the bear killed him somewhere else. There were open tins of food and a chocolate bar in the tent, for heaven's sake, and you tell me a bear wouldn't return and ransack that? There were no droppings, no claw marks on any of the trees. We would have seen something. But there's more. I did some research in the library. Larvae on a dead body can tell people a lot of things. Have you ever heard of forensic entomology?"

Ryan raised his eyes heavenward. "Oh lord, Cordi, I can guess."

"I spent the afternoon in the library reading all I could about it. Did you know that forensic entomology is the study of insects and crime? You can sometimes pinpoint time of death, where the person died, and if they died inside or outside by the larvae and insects found on the body."

"That's gross, Cordi."

"It's kind of neat, really. If some guy accused of murder claims he found the victim outside and the bugs show he died inside, bingo!"

Ryan said nothing.

"Okay, okay. So it's gross, but once a person dies, especially if there is a lot of blood, flies are attracted to the scene and lay their eggs in the body. Every insect species has a different incubation period and you can tell by how long it takes them to develop into full-grown larvae just when the person died. Not only that, but only insects endemic to the area where the body is found should ever be found on the body unless it's been moved."

"So?" Ryan wrinkled up his nose in disgust. "I hope there's a point to this, Cordi."

"One of the larvae that I collected from Diamond's body pupated today. I haven't identified it yet and it may not tell me anything, but the cedar twig it was on when I collected it tells me a whole lot."

Ryan interrupted me.

"Whoa, wait a minute Cordi. I thought all the larvae were destroyed?"

I told him about the larvae in my colleague's lab.

"Okay, so how does any of this tell us his body was moved?"

"Because there were no cedars anywhere near that body, Ryan. We were in a white pine forest."

Ryan let out a long, low whistle. "No cedar. God, you're right."

"I checked the vegetation maps for the area, went over them meticulously, and the closest cedar forest of any consequence starts upriver about a mile or so from where he was found."

Ryan still wouldn't give up.

"Okay, so he got cedar twigs stuck in his clothes. I mean, he was in the bush for weeks before he died."

"Not deeply embedded like that. They were deep inside, as if he'd been rolling around in the stuff and the bear's claws or teeth had driven them in."

Ryan had stopped working on the fence and was deep in thought.

"Ryan, isn't it possible that my lab was fumigated and my data destroyed to get rid of any evidence that Diamond's body had been moved?"

"Whoa, Cordi. That won't work. No one knew you had larvae in the first place, except me and Martha."

"That's not true. Remember? It was in the papers that I was a zoologist and had collected some grubs from the body before I knew it was human. The reporter thought it was a good gross slant and that he could get some mileage out of it."

"Yeah, Cordi, but why would anyone want to hide the fact that the body had been moved in the first place?"

Good question. We wrestled in silence with our thoughts as I helped him wrestle the split rail into position.

"I don't think it was the first time they tried to get the larvae, either," I said quietly.

"What do you mean, Cordi?"

"When that boulder sent us down the river. I'm sure it was no wild animal that sent that flying."

"What?" Ryan wiped his brow and looked at me.

"I saw a flash of purple just before the boulder fell. What wild animal that you know wears purple?"

Ryan continued to stare at me and finally found his tongue. "You saw it too? It looked like somebody's shirt or sleeve," he said quietly. "But I thought it was my imagination. I mean, why would anybody do that?"

"I couldn't believe it myself," I said. "There was no reason for someone to push a boulder at us — until now. I think whoever was hiding on that cliff thought I was carrying all the larvae with me. They must have watched us taking specimens and understood the significance of that. I still had my collecting pack with me, remember, but I'd emptied it at the far end to make it lighter. They wouldn't have known that."

"Jesus, Cordi. That means someone tried to kill us." He said it as a statement, and there was no mistaking the emotion in his voice.

"Whoever it was must have thought they'd destroyed the larvae until they read the newspaper article, and shortly after they struck again."

"So you're saying that whoever it was who sent us into those rapids did it because of some bugs? What are you getting at, Cordi?" Ryan's voice made me feel as though I ought to admit myself to the nearest psychiatric hospital.

"Sounds crazy, but not because of the insects. Because of what the insects might tell us. Remember what I told you about forensic entomology? What if the insects said Diamond died three weeks sooner than the coroner's report? Or that he died inside a concrete bunker and not outside in the woods?"

"Isn't that pretty extreme? How would you get a bear inside a concrete bunker for God's sake? Remember, he was killed by a bear, so what does it matter if he was moved or not? The cops are interested in who did the deed and they already know that."

"Do they?"

Ryan laid down the cedar rail he was preparing to put into place and stared at me.

"So what you're saying is that Diamond died in a cedar forest and somebody went to a lot of trouble to move the body afterwards, back to his permanent campsite."

"Exactly. But why do it? What possible purpose could it serve?"

"Maybe someone was with him when the bear attacked and panicked and couldn't help him. Maybe someone tried to help him, carried him, and got as far as the campsite and then panicked again when they realized he was dead. Now they're just too frightened and ashamed to come forward."

I thought back to Don's behaviour and wondered if Ryan's theory could apply.

"But why fumigate my insects then?"

"Suppose whoever it was didn't want the body found in the area where Diamond actually died and they were afraid your larvae would expose them?"

"Expose what, though? What could there be about an area that makes it important enough for someone to move a body such a distance and then nearly kill us to kill the grubs? And then come back to finish them off in my lab?"

Ryan said nothing.

"I don't know, Ryan. All I do know is that I need to find out more about the circumstances surrounding Diamond's death."

"Cordi, I don't like that look on your face. What are you planning?"

"I guess I'll have to call the coroner and pump him for information, and then go up there for a couple days and see if I can locate this cedar forest."

"So you think that whoever took your disks is connected in some way to Diamond's death?

"I'm sure of it, Ryan, and it's my only lead. I can't let this go now. I've got too much at stake. So what about it? Will you do a search and get the coroner's name for me?"

We walked down to the barn to a small side door and up into what had once been a small hayloft and was now Ryan's office and darkroom.

Ryan tapped away at the computer keys, a nice soft whirring sound that I always thought sounded so much more intelligent, urgent, and critical than the old pounding of a typewriter key.

"He's in here somewhere," said Ryan as he accessed the news database. "I don't know why you don't just phone the cops and ask for his name."

"Because they'll want to know why and I'm no good at lying, and they'll think I'm nuts if I tell them my theory."

"They'd have a right to think you're nuts, and what makes you think the coroner in charge of this case will be any more receptive to you?"

I shrugged, my stomach already in knots over what I might say to him. I walked over to the window and looked out across the fields. Ryan's office had a beautiful view of the escarpment, and at this time of day, with the sun turned to gold on the cornstalks, it looked like a piece of a paradise.

"He's an academic. Maybe I can appeal to that side of him."

The quiet pinging went on. Ryan was into the newspaper database now, scanning the papers from the day after we had found the body. While Ryan worked on his computer I rummaged through our camping gear. It was gathering mould in the corner of his mudroom where we kept all our camping gear and where we'd just dumped our packs after our trip. I began sorting through it and making a pile of laundry. We'd both studiously ignored it, hoping the other would clean them out and throw the sweaty clothes into the laundry. I sighed as I pulled out sleeping bags and clothes. I separated them into two piles, "dirty" and "okay for another year." I picked up my khaki pants, every pocket bulging. I threw out all the garbage and checked the other non-garbage pockets, pulling out my knife and a wad of scrunched-up blue paper. At first I couldn't remember what it was, and I unscrunched it carefully. It was covered in doodles and scribbles. It had been smeared by the rain and the rapids into almost illegible handwriting. I could make out what looked like the word "antlers." Then someone had scribbled and circled a few lines; there was something that looked like "red welt ock" followed by three numbers and something that looked like "NV."

I shrugged and tossed it in with the other garbage.

"Here it is." Ryan's voice interrupted my thoughts and I came over and stood behind him, peering at the black letters on the Macintosh screen.

"Duncan MacPherson."

chapter nine

It was some time before I actually got through to Dr. MacPherson, partly because I dreaded the call but also because once I got my nerve up and realized I had no choice, protective secretaries at the anatomy lab at the university and at the Coroner's Office in Dumoine gave me the runaround. Finally I pleaded an emergency involving life and death and used the "Dr." before my name without mentioning that I was not a medical doctor.

I introduced myself over the phone as Dr. Cordi O'Callaghan, but before I could tell him why I was calling he said, in a deep, throaty burr, "Cordi O'Callaghan? We've met."

"We have?" I racked my brains but the name was not familiar at all. How embarrassing.

"At the butterflies and moths convention, Albuquerque. I showed you my luna moth job."

Memory flooded back. There was only one guy who had had a beautiful, green-yellow luna moth with its spectacular 4.5-inch wingspan and two long elegant tails.

"Right! I remember you. You're the one …" I stumbled to a halt, the unspoken words hanging in the silence worse than if I'd said them.

"That's right," he finished, chuckling. "The one with a nose to rival Pinocchio."

Oh God, I thought. Why was I always putting my foot in it?

"I'm sorry, I didn't mean —"

"It's all right. It is an identifying characteristic, after all."

It sure was, I thought. I couldn't remember anything else about him except his nose! It dominated his entire body!

"What can I do for you? Something about Jake Diamond, I presume? You were the one to find the body, weren't you?"

"Yes, that's right. I'd forgotten the police would have told you that. I'd like to get some information from you about the autopsy results, if that's okay."

His voice dropped an octave, became guarded, cautious, professional. "Surely you know that that information is confidential unless, between friends, there's a damn good reason it shouldn't be. Is there?"

Oh God, I thought. This isn't going to work. My mind went blank and then, in disbelief, I heard myself say, "I think his death might not be as straightforward as it sounds."

There was a long silence. I could hear him breathing at the other end as we both took in the implications of what I had said. I thought he was going to hang up, and it served me right, too, for putting my cards on the table right away, but instead, surprisingly, his voice warmed ... and was there just possibly a trace of amusement in it?

"I think perhaps we had better meet, my girl. Tomorrow? Nine a.m?"

"I can manage that, thanks," I said, biting off the "my boy" before it got past my tongue. It wouldn't do to alienate him.

"Would you mind bringing your butterfly keys? I have a butterfly I'd like you to identify."

I smiled as I hung up. So that was it, was it? *You scratch my back, I scratch yours*, I thought.

The following day it was pouring rain and windy as hell. It took me just under two hours to get from my farm to Dumoine and then another twenty minutes to locate the anatomy building, which for some reason wasn't on the university campus, which housed one of Canada's first northern medical schools. There was nowhere nearby to park, and my raincoat and light canvas hat just weren't enough to keep the wet from running down my neck as I walked back from my parked car. The rain was horizontal and my shoes were squelching by the time I reached the building.

The pathology department was in an old turn-of-the-century stone building near the centre of town. I walked up the wide stone steps and through the large wooden doors. It was an imposing building, built with grace and built to last. I didn't bother looking for the elevator. It was only three flights up and I hated the cramped feel of elevators anyway.

On the third floor I walked down the corridor looking for room 303. As I neared the end of the hall I could hear the quiet murmur of voices. The door to 303 was open and the murmurs were coming from there.

I peered around the door. The room was huge, with tall lead-paned windows climbing to the vaulted ceiling, the massive stone arches pink from the granite from which they were built. There were perhaps eighty students gathered in groups of four around tables draped with white cloths. They were whispering in the quiet, almost clandestine atmosphere. The sickly sweet smell of formaldehyde permeated everything.

I juddered to a halt when I realized, with a sickening gag, that all those shrouded forms were cadavers. If he'd wanted to unnerve me he had certainly succeeded. My eyes clung to the figure closest to me with uneasy fascination, as if looking at just one would make it seem better. I'd never been in a human anatomy lab before, with dozens of still, wrinkled figures lying prone on all those tables. Some were still partially draped where the students hadn't moved on with their scalpels, others lay exposed, the white shroud missing and their pasty, leathery, wrinkled bodies half dissected.

I pulled my eyes away from the surreal scene and reached out for the doorframe to steady myself. There was a tall sturdily built man seated at a desk just inside the door, his back to me. When I'd regained my equilibrium I cleared my throat, and he turned around.

No mistaking him. The nose stood out like a huge tuber someone had unkindly stuck to his face. I forced myself to look at his eyes, grey-blue; his grey-silver hair, almost non-existent; his mouth, behind a thick grizzled beard, all paling into insignificance next to that gargantuan nose. If anyone could claim the right to cosmetic surgery this man could. I marvelled at the character of a man who could go through life literally thumbing his nose at it all and not letting it bother him.

He must be one hell of a self-confident old bugger, I thought, to continually parry the looks of strangers and remain as oblivious as he appeared to be. Perhaps he had adopted his nose as a kind of trademark, an expression of himself. It certainly was unique.

He rose quickly, agilely, stretching out his hand in greeting. He was a big man. He had the look of someone who had once been all muscle, taut, tight, and bull-doggish, a professional athlete, but now the discipline of daily workouts had been too much for him and his muscle had softened to fat.

"Come in, come in," he said with a grin, the words low, almost whispered, in a voice studiously kept under control. It was a rich deep voice, straining at the invisible brakes that forced it out as a whisper. He reached out his massive paw, and I watched in fascination as my hand completely disappeared in his.

"We can talk in my office. Don't want to disturb the young 'uns." He waved his free arm vaguely in the direction of his students while still bear-pawing me, and I wondered if I'd ever see my hand again. I'd released the pressure several times, but when he didn't respond I pressed again and then went limp. He didn't seem to notice, but eventually, he gave me back my hand.

As he led me back through the lab to his office I studiously kept my eyes anywhere but on those shrouded figures. The sickening smell of formaldehyde had never been so horrid. The anatomy labs I had supervised, with dead rabbits and cats, didn't quite smell like this. I felt dizzy. Having never seen a dead human body before this year I was certainly getting my fill these last few weeks.

We walked past shelves of books and coat hooks with lab coats covered in God knows what, to a small glassed-in area on three sides that was strategically placed to overlook the entire lab. Like a commander at the head of his troops, he commanded a full view of all the medical students.

He held the door open for me and watched in amusement as I finally gave up to some inner need and looked up over the room of students, quietly going about the business of dissection.

"They seem so ... so ..." I couldn't find the words to describe the cool, casual way in which the students were conducting themselves, compared to the stomach-writhing mess I was going through. He was watching me with an amused quirk to his smile.

"Relaxed? Calm? Nonchalant?"

"Yeah, that's it." I turned back, glad not to have to view all those silent, shrouded figures.

"You think so?" Duncan grinned mischievously. "They're keyed up tighter than a wound-up toy soldier. Watch this."

As he spoke he picked up a metal ruler from his desktop, held it between his two fingers, stepped out the door, and let the ruler drop to the floor with a clatter. Small as the noise was, every student in the room jumped involuntarily, like a pre-programmed glitch in a computer or birds changing course in mid-flight, all in unison, and then, guiltily, as if jumping like that were an embarrassment, they went back to their dissection, pretending that nothing had happened.

I watched in sick fascination as one student threw something at another and yelled a little too loudly and a little too forced, "Have a heart, my friend." *Dear God, was that really a heart?* I thought. The following eruption of laughter sounded forced, as if by laughing at death its finality could somehow be diminished. Perhaps they needed some way of kidding themselves in order to get through it.

Duncan's grin was almost as big as his nose.

"They hold it in very well — most of the time," he chuckled. "Have to, but when you're that keyed up —

these are all first-year med students — you can't hide your anxiety when something startles you, no matter how many crass jokes you make to hide your feelings. I've been teaching anatomy students two days a week for twenty-five years and that trick has never failed, even when I warn them I'm going to try it when they least expect it. It's the ones that tell the raunchiest jokes that jump the highest. I could probably do a personality study on that — he who jumps highest is least likely to have come to terms with death. Doing the same thing in the lecture hall doesn't even get their attention."

I wondered what would happen to the poor wretches if Duncan dropped a stack of books instead of a ruler. Did first-year med students know how to give cardiopulmonary resuscitation?

He opened the door for me and motioned me inside, gently closing the door behind him. His office was small, almost as small as mine, but meticulously tidy. Every surface was piled with a neat stack of books or file folders, a computer, printer, telephone, and bookshelves of anatomy and pathology texts and forensics. A photo of Duncan in military dress stood on the windowsill. What war was that, I wondered.

There was one other chair besides Duncan MacPherson's plush upholstered affair — a hard, straight-backed, unpadded, uncomfortable-looking thing designed to keep visiting to a minimum. He grinned when he saw me looking at it.

"My students would stay in here gabbing forever if they had a comfortable spot to place their butts. Now, my girl, tell me why you think his death isn't so straightforward. An old man like myself could use some lively spice in my life." The lilt of laughter in his words softened the intent. The last words were full of challenging amusement.

I said, "What would you say if I told you Diamond's body had been moved after he died?"

Duncan shrugged. "Not much. Bears are strong. They can drag a carcass."

"This was over a mile of rough terrain and across a river to boot."

Duncan raised his eyebrows questioningly. "That, I admit, dear girl, is a bit of an aberration. You'd better explain how you think you know all this."

"When my brother, Ryan, and I discovered the body there was no sign of any bears having been in the area. I remember it niggled in my mind at the time, especially since there were tins of sardines, food, and drink at the campsite, even a candy bar in the tent."

"You mean any self-respecting bear in the area would have been expected to pillage the food pack and take the chocolate bar from the tent?"

"That's right. Bears are omnivores, they'll eat anything, and their sense of smell is infamous. Just a tube of toothpaste left in a tent has been known to draw a bear."

"But there was no bear sign."

"No, there was no bear sign."

I then told him about my discovery of cedar twigs in Diamond's wounds, the pupating larvae, the location of the closest cedar forest, and the theft of my disks. When I had finished, he said, "The autopsy did reveal cedar twigs in his wounds, so I can corroborate that part of your story. He certainly didn't pick them up on a stroll through the woods. They were driven in by the bear's claws."

I nodded. So far so good. "The topographical maps indicate that the nearest cedar grove to where Diamond was found is a good mile away and on the other side of the river. So I think he was moved at least that far by someone who, for some unknown reason, didn't want his body found where he died."

"Intriguing. But not enough to open the case. And hardly an indication that his death was not as straight-forward as it appeared. Your words, not mine. Pure conjecture. No proof." Again that trace of amusement tinged his voice, but his face was perfectly composed, or was it because I couldn't see anything else but the nose?

"My career is at stake if I don't find my disks. I'm sure they're related in some way to Diamond's death ..." I paused, and out it came totally unbidden. "At least I didn't say he was murdered."

Duncan drummed his fingers on the hard metal desk and grinned.

"Was he?"

I was taken aback. I had the sneaky feeling that MacPherson was pulling my leg, yet hearing the word was like making it real, and I realized that I had been skirting around the idea for days, without facing it.

"Of course not. The bear got him, right? You did the autopsy?"

"Yes, it was definitely a bear that got him." I could feel his interest start to wane then, and I needed to jumpstart it back into action in a hurry. I told him about the attempt on my life and that I thought it was because whoever did it wanted to destroy the somehow incriminating larvae.

"Sounds pretty far-fetched to me," said MacPherson. I felt the wind go out of my sails and cursed myself that I could feel like giving up because of something some stranger with nothing at stake had just said to me.

"Did you have the larvae on you at the time?" he asked.

"That's the funny part," I said, desperate to recapture my momentum. It scared me that I could lose it so easily. "I've gone over it a dozen times in my head. All my collection was strapped under the seats of the canoe, and normally I carry my day's collection with me in a container in my backpack. However, that day I took out the full container and left it at the end of the portage, replacing it with an empty one in case I came across something of interest."

"So, if someone had been waiting at the beginning of the portage they wouldn't have seen you switch the containers?"

I nodded. "They must have seen me collecting the larvae from Diamond's body and were waiting for the chance to destroy them. When they saw me getting into the canoe to bail it they seized their chance. I was still wearing the backpack when we got caught by the current."

"Let me get this straight," said Duncan. "Your lab was broken into about two weeks after you got back?"

"That's right."

"How did they know? And if they knew why wouldn't they have broken in sooner to destroy the insects? Why wait two weeks, especially after they had shown no qualms about killing you?"

"Because that's when it was reported in the papers that I still had some larvae from the body. When I called the cops they weren't interested. The case was closed. Whoever it was obviously thought the larvae were lost in the canoe. Most of them were."

"So. You think you might be able to find something in the autopsy results that would help you?"

I nodded.

"You know I can't let you look at them."

We looked at each other across his black metal desk. Duncan rose, and my heart sank, but as I got up he raised his hand.

"Perhaps, my girl, you should take a look around my office while I go and help my students." His hand absently tapped a brown folder on his desktop as he winked and left the room.

I watched him go, and manually thrust my jaw back up from where it had fallen. I eagerly reached for the folder. The autopsy results were filed neatly and marked "Diamond" with the date of the autopsy and a large red stamp saying "confidential." I was going to owe MacPherson more than the ID of one lousy butterfly.

Everything was included in the file: a copy of the police report and a list of all the items found at the campsite, including those found in the backpack.

I ran through them. One empty film canister had been found, but the camera had been empty. A deck of cards, a couple of pencils, one sleeping bag, bright orange. One chocolate bar. No mention of the diary anywhere. Interesting. The food pack had contained dried staples and fresh vegetables, carrots, potatoes, dried meats, sugar, flour, nuts, raisins, cook pots, even Diamond's toothpaste and brush. Curious, that. I wondered again why an experienced camper like Diamond would be careful enough to haul his toothpaste out of a bear's reach and then leave a chocolate bar in the tent and opened tin cans of beans and sardines lying about the site.

I flipped through the file to the coroner's report. The page was a sea of tight red ink, but the writing was totally illegible and highly technical. I could make out the odd word but nothing providing any continuity. Why hadn't he typed it on a computer?

"Solved it yet?" Duncan's big voice crashed into the little office.

I looked up and gave him my best hangdog look. "I can't read your writing. Would you mind translating for me in a nutshell what you found?"

"My dear girl, if you think that dew-eyed hound dog look is going to persuade me to help, you already know me better than you think," he guffawed. "My writing's not that bad, but those are just my original notes. The computer copy is with my secretary." He picked up his notes and flipped through them. "Diamond died from loss of blood. He was severely mauled, but none of the wounds alone would have killed him. He bled to death."

"Was there anything else?"

"Let's see. Hmmm. He had taken some kind of sleeping pill, nothing really unusual ..."

His finger moved down through the jumble of words. "Ah, right. Here. This was a bit of a puzzler. We couldn't explain it, but it wasn't sufficient to keep the case open. We also found evidence of a strong tranquilizer in his blood."

"What's that mean?"

"Apparently he used tranquilizer guns in his work to put down his study subjects so he could radio-collar them. Looks as though, in his panic, he managed to get the tranquilizer gun but either it wasn't soon enough or he was unable to jab the bear. The theory goes that he finally used it on himself to ease the pain. He certainly would have been in monstrous pain before the loss of blood mercifully let him lose consciousness. Awkward position, though."

"What do you mean?"

"The puncture mark was in his right shoulder, with the needle partly broken off in his arm. Strange. It's a difficult place to jab yourself, especially if you are right-handed, but not impossible, I guess, with a bear pinning you down. The police concluded that the bear must have jerked Diamond at the wrong moment and the gun went off, hitting Diamond instead of the bear. They never found the tranquilizer gun, though, when they searched his campsite."

That's not surprising if he wasn't killed where he was found, I thought. "How did he get the gun, load it, and use it in the short time it takes a bear to charge?"

"He must have already had it loaded up for its real purpose and grabbed it when the bear charged. He could even have been after the bear, following it to put it down for his research. Apparently he has done that before. Radio-collared bears, although his main line of research is cats."

I grunted and pointed at the report. "Were there any other marks on him?"

Duncan laughed. "He was mauled by a bear, girl. Of course there were."

"I mean not made by a bear," I said.

Duncan looked at me shrewdly, nodded his head.

"You're sharp, my girl, very sharp, but no. Just the usual cuts and scrapes and bug bites that you'd find on a man in the bush."

I mulled this over in my mind while Duncan continued to talk.

"None of this offers any insight into why any one would move the body, assuming you are correct, of course. If the body were discovered why not raise the alarm right there, let the police know? Why move it downriver and let some strangers trip over the remains?"

"My guess is that somebody's hiding something and it looks as though Diamond got mixed up in it somehow."

"Why not just hide the evidence and leave the body then?"

"Because somehow the evidence is linked to the place of death itself?"

Duncan poked some eraser droppings around on his memo pad, corralling them into a neat pile.

"I'm afraid it's all speculation. None of this merits reopening the case, so if you intend to go gallivanting around asking questions, getting people's backs up by insinuating murder where murder may not exist, I'd be very careful. The cops would not take kindly to it."

"I have to get my disks back," I said in quiet desperation. I hated how wobbly my resolve was. I had to keep reminding myself that going forward was better than going backward. I had everything to lose by doing nothing, but there was no guarantee that finding out the circumstances surrounding Diamond's death would get me my disks back. But I had no other leads. I had to find out what happened.

Duncan looked at me with a half smile, as if he were reading the positive side of my thoughts.

"I'd do the same if I were in your shoes. Let me know how you get along."

He grinned at me, pulled on his nose with his thumb and forefinger, and rose from his chair.

"Now, about my butterfly ..."

chapter ten

"So what did the coroner say?"

I looked up from my desk to see Martha poking her head in the door from the outer office.

"How the hell did you know that I talked to the coroner?"

Martha smiled. "Nothing gets past me. Actually you doodled on that pad by your phone. 'See Coroner re: Diamond's death.'"

I quickly looked at the pad and thought I'd have to be more careful about what I doodled.

"After all, what with your larvae disappearing and what you told me about your discovery that the body was moved, in combo with that memo, I put two and two together. Let's have all the gory details."

I rolled my eyes at the ceiling. Nothing for it but to tell Martha all about my meeting.

"So now what?" she asked when I was done.

"So now, I'm going to go talk to all his colleagues, for starters, and see what happens, see if any of them can lead me to my disks." I dreaded having to talk to all these people, in case I found myself stuck in that godawful darkness of one of my mood swings on the morning I had arranged to meet one of them. Depression has a habit of incapacitating its victim. I was thankful it was summer: more than likely I'd be okay. It was usually the winter months that haunted me, made worse by the fact that I seemed powerless to head it off. Maybe I needed to see a professional, but the thought made me feel ill and I hurriedly relegated it to the back of my mind with a lot of other baggage.

It was four long days before I could get away from the university and drive out to Dumoine. On the morning of that day I woke up relieved to find that I was in a good mood — no fear, no dread, no despair, just normal anxiety about whether I would ever find my disks or not.

No saving angel had delivered them to me with a note of apology for having taken them. The cops had no new leads and more or less said, "We'll call you," which of course meant my case had now been placed in the unimportant file, probably had never been in any other file.

I left the farm as the sun was spreading over the Eardley Escarpment, rimming it with soft golden tones and the first pale hint of the leaves changing. The cows were mooing, their udders full to bursting, calling Mac to come and give them relief as I drove out the farm gates and turned northwest on Highway 148. I stopped in Shawville for gas and a bottle of water. Not much had changed in the years since I'd come here as a girl and shown my calf at the Shawville Fair. Pretty heady times for a 4-H kid way smaller than the calf, who basically walked me around the arena while I made a show of trying to be in charge. It didn't help that Ryan and his friends were hooting and hollering like banshees. I'd showed them all, though, when I won first prize. And I'd gone back, year after year, because it was a fantastic agricultural fair to compete at. And because I liked the petting zoo.

Two hours later I pulled into the grounds of Pontiac University in front of the zoology building in Dumoine. For a small campus in the country it was remarkably stark, as if the developer had chosen to ignore aesthetics. The results showed, raw and ugly. There were few trees and no effort had been made to have the buildings fit into their surroundings. They looked like a bunch of pill boxes in need of medication themselves.

I pulled open the heavy glass doors of the two-storey zoology building, which shared its space with psychology and human resources. The familiar sweet, musty smell of formaldehyde, dirty cages, and disinfectant swept over me. Zoology buildings the world over smelled like this, I thought: urine and feces, scent glands, and formaldehyde — a veritable cocktail of smells. In the foyer, hanging from the ceiling, was a huge metal spider's web with the resident spider, ass to ceiling, hunkered down looking as though it was waiting for some poor unsuspecting undergrad to commit to biology. A young man pushing a tray filled with glass flasks and Petri dishes walked briskly through the foyer.

"Where can I find the zoology office?" I called after him.

"Follow the typing," he said and then he was gone, the rattle of the Petri dishes slowly being replaced by the distinctive soft tapping of a computer. I followed the sound down to a door splattered with a thousand notices for seminars and meetings, most of which seemed to have already happened.

There was no sign of anyone in the main office, but the *tap tap* was coming from behind a portable wall.

"Anyone home?"

The tapping stopped abruptly, and seconds later a blue-eyed, red-haired, diminutive woman in a tight black skirt and pink spandex shirt flounced around the corner. I wondered how she had ever got the skirt on. It looked like paint. I felt my own worn pants, comfortable, practical, and wondered how this woman could stand high heels and tight skirts. It was certainly a rarity in any zoology building I had ever been in. If she was here for a degree, maybe it was a bachelors and not in zoology. I reeled back at my own chauvinism.

"What can I do for you?" she asked in a high-pitched, squeaky kind of voice that made me want to oil it.

Before I could answer she said, "I'm just filling in for one of the secs — she's sick, my master's research is stymied, and I need the cash so I offered, but there's hardly time to eat. You should see the letters these guys want done. Been six days now and I'm getting good at it."

"Can you tell me where I can find Don Allenby or Leslie Mitchell?" I asked.

She shot me a suspicious look, and the smile on her face grew brittle.

"If you're the press or the police we —"

"No, actually I'm not. I'm just visiting. I'm a zoologist from Sussex University."

"Oh, well, in that case no probs. Don Allenby's my supervisor. He's in room 202. Mitchell moved into 105 although how she can stand to do that so soon after …" she hesitated, blushed.

"After what?"

"Well, you know. Surely you've heard about it in the papers. Made Dumoine quite famous."

"You mean Jake Diamond?"

"Oh, gruesome story there, isn't it? I mean ..." she glanced hurriedly at me. "I mean, they say he died fast, like, I think, at least they say ..."

"What a way to go."

"Yeah, but sort of like him, you know? Ever the macho man. Oh, such a great guy though. I had him for the course on animal form and function. Funny man and sexy as hell."

"Did you know him well?"

"Ha. Would have loved that. Nah. He was just a prof. I got to know him a bit because I'm a grad student of his colleague, Don Allenby. They worked together on a bunch of papers, you know."

"You mean they collaborated?"

"Yeah, I guess. Diamond was a cat man and Don is small mammals. They teamed up sometimes on those predator-prey jobs — you know, linking the number of predators to the number of prey and that sort of stuff. Diamond's name always came first. I always wondered about that. Guess Diamond felt he had to be first author. Had an ego the size of an elephant. Lots of profs around like to take all the credit, you know, but at least he did a lot of the work. Some profs do zip all. Their graduate students do it all and then the profs take all the praise. Oops, sorry."

"Sounds like he could have had a bunch of enemies."

She looked up suddenly, surprised.

"Nah. Not Diamond. Everyone liked him. I'm pretty sure. Except Davies, of course, but Davies doesn't much like anyone at all."

I gave her a quizzical look.

"Guess you haven't been around here before if you don't know Davies. He calls himself the dean of the zoology department such as it is here, only four profs, you know. We're a small operation. The student rumour mill has it they hated each other's guts."

"Why?"

The woman laughed. "Diamond was a free spirit, you know what I mean? He was classy, like, and didn't care what Davies thought of his lectures so long as the students liked them. Like the time he taught us the mechanics of flight. He brought in a whole slew of mechanical birds and he had them flapping all over the lecture hall. It was great. Then Davies walks in and everybody shuts up. He's kind of a dried-up little man. He kinda looks around and eye-balls Diamond with his fierce little flinty eyes and just as he's about to say something — God, we would have given a lot to know what he was going to say — a little whirly-bird bashed into his bald head and everyone started laughing. Davies was furious and he stalked out like a scorched rooster. After that there were lots of rumours that he was actively trying to get rid of Diamond. Hard to do when Diamond had tenure but, well, there you go. Guess Davies won't need to worry anymore, eh?"

"Davies doesn't sound like the kind of guy who would have liked his profs getting involved in stuff like logging protests and things like that," I noted.

"You can say that again. He wants to be president of the university here, not just dean of science, and I think he feels Diamond was preventing that from happening. He was furious about Diamond's high profile in this logging spree, said it harmed the reputation of the university — meaning his reputation. Oooeee was that fun. Manning the barricades. It was like one great big ..."

She stopped in mid-sentence as footsteps sounded in the hall. She glanced at me, suddenly anxious. "Don't tell anyone I said any of this, will you?" She turned and raced back to her typing as a gaggle of students entered the office on some mission or other.

I walked down to the end of a long tiled corridor, peering at the doors as I went. Each door had a glass pane in it, but most of the occupants had carefully blocked them with pictures of animals or pithy sayings.

Unlike the other offices, whose doors were closed, the door to room 202 was open. I knocked and walked in.

Allenby was sitting at a desk surrounded by papers and looked up quickly as I came in. He didn't look much better than when I had last seen him in the bush, except that his clothes fitted him and were immaculate and his crisp white shirt highlighted the extreme pallor of his face.

"Dr. Allenby. I'm Cordi O'Callaghan." I held out my hand. "We met up in Dumoine. I stumbled across the body."

"Oh yes," he said uncertainly. "Yes, I remember now. Come in, come in." He didn't get up to shake my hand because he hadn't seen the gesture. Not surprising since the man hadn't looked at me since his first quick preoccupied glance. He remained behind his desk as if it could defend him from my presence.

"Did we arrange to meet? I didn't ask you to come, did I?" he said, looking at a point somewhere way off to the left of my ear.

"May I sit?" I asked.

Finally he looked at me and smiled. "Oh, yes, sorry, do."

I studied him for a moment trying to evaluate how much to tell him.

I decided to keep it simple and told him that my lab had been fumigated and my disks stolen and suggested there was a possible link between that and Diamond's death.

"What possible link could there be?" he asked.

I told him briefly about the significance of the cedar twigs and my certainty that the body had been moved. I was sure the disappearance of my larvae and my data were related to that one fact.

"I don't know if there's a link. I may simply be on a wild goose chase, but you're a researcher. You can understand what it means to have your data stolen and why I'm grasping at the only straw I can find."

Allenby began shuffling the papers on his desk. His eyes flitted across my face avoiding eye contact. I could see a fine mist of sweat forming on his upper lip. What was he so worried about? Could he have moved the body, and if so, why?

"What do you hope to get from me?" he asked the wall in front of him. I followed his eyes and saw a picture of a young woman and a small girl swinging on a hammock, laughing at the photographer. The little girl was the spitting image of Don.

"I don't know. I'm hoping something will twig. What can you tell me about Diamond?"

"Diamond?" The word rang out like the tolling of a bell and lingered in the air, as if it were the first time Allenby had ever uttered the name. Finally he shifted in his seat, but the silence dragged on. Suddenly Allenby looked directly at me.

"He was a bit of a legend. He knew the bush backwards, could survive on nothing. You know the sort of thing. Give him a knife, a tinder and flint, and some snare wire and fishing line and he could live forever. Sweet irony that he got done in by a bear."

I said nothing. There seemed to be nothing to say.

"We were working on a paper together, a cycle paper on lynx and hare. Hares are my baby, lynx his. Now, I don't mean to be rude but I don't see why any of this should interest you. He's dead, isn't he? Mauled by a bear, so why are you poking about? It won't bring your insects back to life and it's not going to help you get your disks back. It isn't related at all. Just some macabre coincidence."

I didn't say anything, waited. The silence lengthened until Don couldn't stand it any longer.

"He was a good man. Ruthlessly honest in all his dealings, almost to a fault, and when he got behind a cause he gave everything he had to it."

"Like the logging?"

"Yeah," sighed Allenby. "Like the logging. It became a personal vendetta to him." He glanced out the window, as though he were seeing a magnificent pine slowly topple, and then dragged his eyes back to me.

"Jake organized everyone to oppose logging up here in the Dumoine area. It's prime logging country, has been for generations, but the logging companies haven't done much replanting and the clear-cutting of the past has caused a lot of erosion."

"How many of the faculty have study sites up in the area?"

Allenby looked at me and nodded.

"Yes. That's right. We have a biology station up in the area and most of us have some ongoing and long-standing projects up there, either our own or those of our graduate students. If the area is logged, lots of research could go up in smoke. So yes, Diamond did have a very personal reason for fighting the logging companies. He'd been studying lynx and bobcat in the area for fifteen years. So, it was not all altruistic, although he probably would have argued otherwise."

"I understand he organized a barricade to keep the loggers out."

"Yeah. And it worked. Jake was the sort of guy that could inspire you. He was the catalyst. Now he's dead, and no one has taken over his leadership. Without him the cause is winding down. Because of the barricade and the publicity surrounding it we got a temporary injunction, but it didn't last long. Now the loggers are poised to move in and we're without a leader. You see, Jake was one of a kind. He really believed we had to win or the world would collapse. That's what drove him. No one else has quite the same drive."

"Was he well liked?"

"What's that got to do with it?" Allenby raised his thin voice to the stretching point, was about to say something and then thought better of it. Instead his voice dropped and he said, "Yeah. He was well liked by most. He had people who didn't much like him, loggers and people like that, but I don't think he had any real enemies."

"Were you in the area on or around the day he died? Did you see anything that might help me?" He hesitated only a fraction.

"I was out there well east of his site, working on a hare census in a new area. Left for the field before he did, and came out about a week before Leslie and I bumped into you."

"What were you doing up there when I ran into you?"

Allenby stared past me, his round wet eyes unblinking.

"We were manning the barricade with about thirty other people. Didn't you see it?"

I shook my head.

"It's just up the road from the biology station. If you came by the portage, though, you'd bypass it, so I guess that's why you never saw it. We've been using the biology station as a storage spot for food and other supplies."

"Was anyone else with you who was out in the field who might have bumped into Diamond on his last day or seen something that could help me?"

"I don't really know what you're looking for so I can't say. I didn't see him. I generally prefer to do my fieldwork alone. You should check the bio station schedule, though. We have an in/out roster. Everyone signs out and signs in again when they return. We have to record where we're going, who with, and for how long. It's an honour system, but everybody observes it for their own safety. Besides, Davies doesn't take kindly to wasting the budget on emergency rescue operations. They're expensive and if they are unnecessary, well … you understand."

"Where can I find this roster?"

"Dr. Davies keeps all the old ones in the registrar's office. Roberta, my grad student, is helping out there this week. Someone's sick, I think, and she needed the cash. It costs a lot to get a grad degree these days. Go ask her."

"Who else should I talk to?"

"Diamond's grad student, Patrick Whyte, might be able to tell you something. He sometimes went out in the field with Diamond, but I don't think he went on this last trip. Anyway, Diamond and I weren't that close, just work colleagues. I was far too conservative for his liking and not athletic enough. You should also speak to Leslie. They were friends once."

His voice suddenly sounded hollow and empty.

"Look. I'm sorry. I have a load of work. Leslie's new office is just down the hall. Diamond's grad student is in the lab, room 205. But he won't be there right now. He's demonstrating a lab. But you'd better speak to Davies. He gets furious when things happen around here that he doesn't know about."

I stepped thankfully out of his office and went back up to see Roberta. Allenby had unnerved me and I wasn't sure why. The *tap tapping* was still going on, and I popped my head around the barrier. She jumped.

"Sorry, didn't mean to scare you, but Don said there was a roster for the biology station that I could take a look at."

"Oh sure. You mean the 'come look for me if I don't show' book? It's over here."

She led me across the cluttered space to a large desk heaped with magazines; above it was a huge topographical map with red pins scattered about. I waved my hand toward it while she got out the roster and put it on the table in front of me.

"Are these all the study sites for the faculty?"

"Yep. You got it. The little red pins mean people in the field right now. All those other little pins of various colours mean study sites.

There were strings linking together all the blue pins, all the yellow, and so forth, so at a glance you could see all the study sites.

"Who's yellow?"

"That's Don. He works in the area east and south of the bio station."

"You're Don's student, right?"

"That's right. Just finishing up my master's. Roberta Smith. I'm doing a population study on hares, but most of my fieldwork is done. I'm glad of that. I don't really like the bush. But he's up there almost as much as Diamond."

I remembered the picture of the woman and the little girl.

"What about his family? How does he juggle his time with them?"

She frowned.

"Oh no. Don't you know?"

"Know what?"

"He doesn't really have a family anymore."

"But the picture in his office?"

"Yeah, his wife and kid. Really sad."

I felt sick, anticipated what was coming. Waited.

"That picture was taken just before his wife died, five years ago now, I think. It was a godawful accident. They were driving home one night. Don fell asleep at the wheel, or so they say. They barrelled through a stop sign and were flattened by a truck. His wife died instantly, and the kid, who was only four years old at the time, is now a vegetable. But Don won't give up hope that she'll get well. The poor man was wracked with guilt and has spent every blessed penny and gone into debt giving her the best care in a private nursing home. He still talks about the day she'll come home, but we all know she never will. He won't face up to that, poor man. He'd do anything for the poor kid."

I tried to say something, anything, but what do you say to a story like that?

"He changed after that. Never the same again, they say. Some men can get over their grief, but his daughter is always there to remind him, I guess. He moonlights at other jobs to help pay for the poor kid. Shows, too. His work here is suffering, and Davies is sitting on him pretty hard."

Again, I had absolutely nothing to say. All I could think of was the pain the man had gone through.

"But it's not all bad. He and Diamond have just done a paper together, but Diamond wanted to postpone publication for some reason, so it's on hold. Don was really disappointed — so was I, because my name is going to be on it too. Diamond wouldn't tell Don why, just asked him to be patient. When the paper gets published it will give Don a boost and hopefully help to get him some more funding. At first Diamond really was doing him a favour collaborating like that, but then Don's data turned out to be good, so I guess Diamond was right to take him on. Surprised everyone, though, because Don's work hadn't been very good since the accident. Sloppy, you know." She shrugged and said, "Diamond was a good man. He didn't deserve such an awful death." Roberta hastily wiped her eyes with her sleeve, and I wondered if the tears were for Diamond or Don.

I stood there like an idiot trying to think of something to say, but there really wasn't anything that would make her feel better. I gave her some time to get herself back together again and then gently asked, "Does Don have a semi-permanent camp like Diamond's?"

She shook her head. "Only Diamond did." She said slowly, "You see, he loved the bush. Often went up just to write his reports and to get away from his students. Even if he had no fieldwork to do. Sometimes I think he started doing it to get away from his wife. Often he'd go up just for a night, mark some papers, and come back in time for afternoon lectures. I used to have a bird, 'cause I demonstrated his comparative anatomy class and I was always afraid he'd miss classes."

"That's a hell of a portage to get to his place for just an overnighter."

I was remembering the rain-mucked steep cliff paths and treacherous footing Ryan and I had stumbled over in our haste to get help. Even in excellent shape it wasn't your average sort of daily walk.

"Oh, that route. You been there? Canoeist, right?"

I nodded. "It was a bitch."

She laughed. "Yeah, only the canoeists take that route. Diamond hardly ever used it, and no one at the station did.

There's another path, only a quarter-mile from the road through the forest. Easy footing. He'd drive up, park his car just out of sight in the bush, and walk in. Take him ten minutes at most. And he was real close to the barricade. He set it up just on the road between the biology station turn off and his portage. Very convenient for him. He sometimes slept at his camp when he was on the barricade."

"You were part of that group, right?"

"What? The barricade? Oh sure. It was a hoot. We'd all go up as often as we could, take our sleeping bags and stuff. Diamond made sure there was all kinds of food and stuff, and his friend Shannon oversaw all the cooking. Just like camp."

"Is the barricade still up?"

"It's on hold. We got an injunction before Diamond died, but it was overturned. I don't think we'll stop the logging now, especially now that Diamond is gone. He was the leader."

"Did the rest of the faculty support the cause?"

"A lot of us did, but Davies was furious. Diamond's graduate student, Patrick Whyte, wasn't too enamoured with it either. Not sure why. He's usually a gung-ho environmentalist, but then he's been working his butt off to get his thesis done by Christmas so he's not had much time to get involved, I guess."

She didn't sound very convinced.

"He and Diamond actually had a vicious row over the barricade. Patrick thought it was stupid and would just make things worse, but there was no swaying Diamond. He was a stubborn son of a bitch. Even Davies had no effect on him. He just railroaded over everyone when he thought something was right."

I picked up the roster and began flipping through it.

"I have to get back to work," she said. "Just leave the roster on the table when you're finished, 'kay?"

I thanked her and turned my attention to the roster. Fifteen minutes later I had it all. Diamond had died sometime on the eleventh of July, four days before he was due back. Leslie had signed out on July 5, returning July 13, the day before Ryan and I had stumbled upon the body. Don and Roberta had left July 8, returning July 11. Patrick had signed out from July 7 to July 11. Even Eric Davies had been out in the bush July 10 to 12 along with two grad students. And who knew how many people were manning the barricade a mere ten-minute walk from where Diamond's body was found at his camp?

With so many people in the bush the week Diamond died, why had it taken so long for his body to be discovered?

chapter eleven

I found Leslie in among a whole truckload of boxes in Diamond's old office. His name was still on the door, and the snarling face of a Canada lynx growled out at me. I knocked, and a moment later Leslie appeared at the door eating an apple. Her black closely cropped hair made her face look quite masculine, but the rest of her was definitely a woman.

"Well, so we meet again."

"Looks like you got promoted?"

"Yeah. Soon to be full professor from associate. But what a way to do it, eh? Over Diamond's dead body. Nothing like taking over the responsibilities of a dead man." I was startled by the bitterness in her voice, but then she smiled and I thought maybe I had been mistaken.

"We never properly introduced ourselves back up there in the woods. Leslie Mitchell." She hastily switched the apple to her left hand, wiped her right hand on her pants, and held it out to me.

"Cordi O'Callaghan," I said as I gripped her hand in mine. I winced at the strength of it. This was getting to be ridiculous. Had everyone learned that a limp grip labelled you a wimp? The harder you squeeze the more important you are?

"Come on in," she said and led me into the chaos of her office. There were boxes everywhere, all in various stages of being unpacked.

She knelt down in front of a box and started rifling through its contents.

"You're an entomologist aren't you?" she asked.

"A zoologist, really, but I often work with insects."

"And you've lost all your specimens, as well as your disks." She looked up at me, and seeing my surprised look she laughed. "This is a small university. Nothing is private here, and we stick by each other. Don just phoned to warn me you were coming around."

She sat back on her heels, a file folder in each hand.

"Being a zoologist I know what it's like to lose data or have an experiment go wrong and the hopes of tenure with it. I gather you were hoping to recover the disks. What makes you think they'd still be around?"

"Hope. Desperation. I don't know. They weren't trashed at my office. They were physically removed, so I have some hope they're still around, that whoever took them realizes what they mean and won't destroy them. There's nothing on them that would be the least bit useful to anyone but me."

The words hung in the air. The silence lengthened. She dropped the folders back into the box.

"Not even to another zoologist or entomologist?"

I paused, startled by her question. I hadn't really given that possibility much thought. What if someone had wanted my data to beat me to publication and the stolen disks had nothing to do with Diamond? Ridiculous. My work just wasn't important enough, even if there was another team working on it. If I had some new breakthrough, then it would be different, but ...

"Not interesting enough," I said, and felt a pang of anger that my work really wasn't something someone would want to steal.

"That doesn't mean it isn't interesting to someone else," she said. "What were you working on, besides the larvae?"

"Basic taxonomy. Nothing earth-shattering. Some succession work and some stuff with praying mantids. I can't see that anyone would be interested, except me."

"You're probably right."

I tried not to look hurt at this cryptic dismissal of my work.

"It was only a suggestion, but maybe you should be looking somewhere else besides here. Why do you think Diamond's death is related to the theft of your disks anyway?"

"Don seems to have told you everything."

Leslie rocked on her heels.

"Yeah, well, he said you had some crazy idea that the larvae you found on Diamond's body indicated that he had been moved a long way from where he died. Even if your accidental attempt at forensic entomology can tell you that, what the hell does it mean? It makes no sense. I mean, why would anyone want to move his body somewhere else? It's ludicrous."

She yanked another box over to her side and rummaged inside.

"Because his death might not be what it seems."

Leslie slowly turned to look at me, her face blank and unreadable. "What's that supposed to mean?"

When I didn't answer she waved her hand impatiently.

"You can't get more straightforward than being killed by a bear. You really are desperate, aren't you? Sounds as though you're grasping at straws. Can't say I blame you, though," she added.

I watched as she emptied out the box and started sorting out the papers that had been in it. Finally, as I had hoped, she broke the silence.

"Did you ever actually meet Diamond?"

"No. I knew of his work, of course, but I never met him."

"Yeah, well, he was well-liked by most people. He'll be sorely missed. If you're suggesting his death was anything but a horrible accident ..."

"I'm not suggesting that, but was there anything Diamond was doing that could have made people angry enough or frightened enough to explain why his body was moved?"

"You mean like a sick prank or something? If you look hard enough everyone has enemies. But Diamond just got really careless. His campsite was a literal siren call of food. The cops said he even left a Mars bar in his tent, for God's sake."

She shrugged, and I waited, hoping for more.

"What do you want me to say? He got careless. I've been there, know what it's like. But this time I got the consolation prize. I got his job. Lousy way to get it, and people calling me callous behind my back. What do they expect me to do? Say no to a promotion I've sought all my life? Sure, we were rivals — no secret there. I wanted his job. God knows I deserved it. But I didn't want it this way. I've just learned the hard way to take what I can get in a deck stacked in favour of men. You got tenure?"

"No."

"See? And you're not likely to even have a chance at getting it without your disks, right?"

The look on my face must have said it all.

"What research are you working on?" I asked, wanting to get the spotlight off me. I hated it when my questions came back at me.

"Oh, I'm quite eclectic. Move around and fill in the gaps left by my colleagues. Some taxonomy. I've worked with parasites and planaria, and done some studies with mice. I've spent the last few years working on moose and their predators, and a new project that I hope will prove very interesting."

"What's that?"

"Don't have enough data to go public yet or know for sure if the hypothesis will stand, so I'd rather not say just yet." She smiled. She was actually quite pretty when her face lit up like that.

"It's a new angle, may not pan out … but I have to wait and organize the data before I make it public. You know how it is with us scientists. Paranoid that someone else will beat us to it."

The phone rang, and Leslie grabbed for it.

"Mitchell here." I watched as she threw me a grimace and said into the phone, "Really Davies, don't you have anything better to do than that? I'll get it to you as soon as I have a moment. Yeah, she's here. Why? You want me to send her over? Okay. No problem. I'll tell her."

She hung up the phone and stared through me.

"Odious little man, that Davies. Always skulking about trying to dig up dirt. Seems to hate us all. Can't imagine what turns a man to hate so much." She refocused her eyes on me and said, "He wants to see you. Two doors down and on the left."

She turned back to her boxes and I started to leave, then hesitated.

"Why did it take so long for Diamond's body to be discovered? Surely someone from the biology station would have gone up to his camp?"

"He never encouraged anyone to go up there. In fact, he actively discouraged anyone unless it was a dire emergency. We left him to his own devices. Didn't make any difference to us. Even his women never went up there. It was his sacred turf. He guarded it like a cornered sow. We simply respected that, and by the time you found his body he wasn't due out for another day."

I thanked Leslie for answering my questions, but as I left, I hesitated in the hall outside her door, aware that something she had said had twigged something important somewhere in my mind. Problem was I couldn't quite grasp what it had been before it was gone.

I followed Leslie's instructions and found Davies sitting at his desk. He was a small man, no taller than I was, in his early sixties with a halo of white hair punctuating a bright red dome and a bristly, charcoal grey Groucho mustache. He was flipping through some files in the open drawer of a desk, but when he saw me he jumped to his feet and scurried around his desk to meet me at the door. He did rather give the impression of a rooster with his bald red head and jerky movements.

"You must be Dr. O'Callaghan." His voice was cold but surprisingly beautiful with a deep, lilting, musical sound at odds with his size. He could have had a career in radio. He didn't offer his hand or ask me in, so I stood in the doorway and waited. "May I ask you what you think you're doing going around asking questions you have no business asking?"

Taken aback, I began to explain about my disks, but he impatiently waved me to silence.

"Yes, yes, your disks and larvae and things." He dismissed my entire career with a wave of his hand. "Don filled me in on it all, and I want it to stop. I can't have you in here wasting my people's time. We've had enough from the police and the press. If you need anything please come to me."

He was invading my personal space, herding me before him and out of his doorway and into the hall.

"Perhaps I can help you sometime, but not today. As you can see I am extremely busy." With that, he withdrew his business card, handed it to me, and quietly closed the door behind him.

I stood in the hall a moment wondering why he felt so threatened. I debated precisely two seconds about going behind his back to see Patrick Whyte. But I was on a roll, my confidence level at an all-time high, and I wasn't about to waste it — I never seemed to be able to count on it being there for me, so it was a real bonus. I needed it now, and I had it, so I cruised down the hallway and found a back stairway up to the second-floor labs, hoping Davies wouldn't appear out of nowhere to scream at me. I peered into one lab and was directed down the hall to another whose door was wide open. Through it I could hear a male voice raised in anger.

"Yes, well, keep out of my damn business. I can speak to whomever I want. It's a free world," said the voice and then I heard a telephone slamming down.

I waited a discreet few seconds so that he wouldn't think I'd overheard and then knocked on the open door. He was standing by the window looking out, and at the sound of my knock he jumped and turned around. Evidently he was making another phone call because he gripped the phone in his hand and I noticed his knuckles were white. He was very tall, maybe 6' 5", and well built, and his thick, unruly blond hair swept over his forehead like a tidal wave. His eyes were a soft, deep, clear cobalt blue, and as he turned them on me I felt myself involuntarily melting into them. We stared at each other in silence for some moments, and then he waved at me to sit down. Disconcerted I sat down rather suddenly as he barked some orders into the phone and hung up, having never taken his eyes off me.

"Photo lab's always getting things mixed up" he said. "I asked them for black and white prints and they've given me colour. What can I do for you?" He smiled. You could get lost in a smile like that, I thought, momentarily sidetracked.

"My name's Cordi O'Callaghan," I said, when I finally found my voice. "I wanted to ask you some questions ..." I hesitated, unsure how to proceed.

"So you're Dr. O'Callaghan, eh? Tough luck about your insects."

I looked at him and then laughed nervously. "Davies?"

"It was in the paper, and dear Davies just phoned to tell me not to talk to you. So, tell me why I should?" His eyes danced in amusement and watched me closely.

I gave him a brief outline of what had happened with my insects and disks and he seemed genuinely interested, so I asked him how well he had known Diamond.

"Well enough. He was a bit of a prick, to tell you the truth. Don't get me wrong, I'm sorry he's dead, but he and I never really hit it off." He moved over to a jumble of folders on a desk. "Mind if we talk while I work?"

He folded himself like a jackknife into a chair and began sorting through the mess. I sat and watched.

"Quite a mess, eh? It's not usually like this. It's Diamond's main work area — was, I should say. He did most of his work here. Always kept it neat as a pin, but somebody came in a week or so ago and rifled through it.

I haven't had a chance to clean it up yet. Whoever it was spent a lot of time here by the looks of it — all his files have been searched. Don't know what they were looking for, but they sure left a mess behind. Now I have the job of going through it, tidying it all up, and seeing what sort of papers we can publish for him posthumously."

"Did you call security?"

Patrick looked up in surprise. "Why would I do that?" he asked.

"In case something was stolen."

Patrick laughed, a deep rich chortle that was infectious.

"Nothing to steal here, but lots over there, and nothing's gone, as far as I can see." He waved his hand around the room and made his point. I could see three computers, microscopes, and all manner of equipment.

"What about the computer? Any files missing?" He looked at me quickly and frowned.

"I never thought of that. I'll have to check, but I haven't noticed anything missing."

"You're his PhD student, is that right?"

"Yes." He smoothed out his frown. "I've been working with him for two years now looking at parasites on Canada lynx. He does most of the fieldwork and I do the lab stuff."

"What was he working on up in the bush before he died?"

"I don't know for sure. He said it was follow-up stuff on his lynx population experiments, that he needed to get a tad more data, but he'd already put in six weeks up there earlier in the spring with our pilot, Jeff, following our radio-tagged lynx. At first I thought he was goofing off, three weeks and all, when he had a lot to do here, but everyone needs a holiday and it was so peaceful without him hanging around me like a leech."

"What changed your mind?"

"I got the impression that he was either working on something new or had a new angle on something old. He seemed quite excited about it, but then he always overreacted to everything. I did get the impression that it might have been a new project or maybe something to do with the logging, but he never said and I wasn't about to ask. We all keep things close to our chests when it's something new. No one wants to be scooped."

I felt a pang of resentment. First Leslie, now Diamond. Why couldn't I find something new?

"You didn't like him."

"No, I didn't."

He ended the sentence as if he was ending the conversation, but I persevered.

"I understand you two didn't see eye to eye over this logging business."

Patrick looked up quickly and fixed me with a frown that made his eyebrows merge into one long bushy slash. I much preferred the smile.

"We had our differences. He was a real firebrand radical when it came to the logging issue. He had to win at all costs. I thought he was an asshole and not harmless. He was a dangerous man. Intelligent but with a real temper, and he had a real problem with women. He did try to treat them as equals, but they shone out of his eyes as sex symbols — with no brains. If you've ever met his wife you'll get my drift, although I must say his current girlfriend isn't so bad. Guess he's getting better at picking them."

"He's got a girlfriend? Does his wife know?"

"Does his wife know? Are you kidding? Everybody knew. The wife was filing for divorce. He'd been through half the department here. The man chased anything in a skirt. He wasn't a cruel man — just horny."

I thought about Lianna's tear-streaked face. Perhaps not such a grief-stricken widow as she had seemed, pretending to rein in emotions that weren't there. Good actor though. I had to wonder why. To get the black book? Why was it so important?

"Who's his girlfriend?"

"You mean his current one?"

"Yes." God, how many had he had, I thought, suddenly feeling sorry for Lianna in spite of myself.

"Shannon. Healthy, shy little thing, not like his usual mannequins. She was in here the other day picking up some stuff from his office. Pretty broken up about it, I'll say that for her. Not like the wife. They had a hell of a fight here. Met in the hall outside his office."

"What happened?"

"They lost it. What a ruckus. They were screeching so loudly and the swear words were colouring the air blue. Something about Diamond's property and will, but why Shannon should be hoping to get it is beyond me. Wife's entitled to everything unless he left a will saying otherwise. Anyway, it was pretty ugly, and Davies nearly burst a gut trying to get them out before the students heard any more. Quite comical, actually. He looked just like a sheepdog trying to herd his sheep."

"Had she and Diamond been together long?"

"Year, year and a half, I'd say. No more, anyway. I must say, he seemed quite happy with her. She'd be able to tell you more about Diamond than any of us if you're willing to be patient. She's in Ottawa. Lives on McLeod, I think. Diamond commuted on weekends. I can give you her number if you like."

I nodded. Patrick rummaged through a desk, then wrote down the number on a scrap of paper and handed it to me. I noticed his fingers were long and slender and he wore a single ring on his right hand, a grey star sapphire that showed dull in the false light of his office.

"You should talk to Leslie, too. Do you know her?" he asked as I took the paper from him. He didn't let his half go right away, and I wasn't sure what to do. I shook my head and looked up at him, feeling like a fool as I hung onto my half of the little piece of paper.

He smiled and suddenly let go. I squirreled the piece of paper away and said, "I was just talking to her."

"Good," he said. "She can tell you a lot, I'm sure." He laughed and shook his head. "They loved to hate each other, those two. He got tenure and she didn't. Apparently they were equally qualified, but there was only one tenured position open. They say she was very bitter and vindictive. Claims it was sexist. Who knows? Happened before I was here. She's got his job now and tenure will follow I'm sure. Damned happy about it, I should say. Poor taste though. Wouldn't put it past her to have been smiling at the funeral."

I picked up a small tooth on top of the desk, twirled it in my hands. It looked like the tooth of a carnivore.

"What's this?"

"That's a Canada lynx tooth. Diamond collected a lot of samples whenever he could, and he had an extensive tooth collection that he prized. All the cats from all over the world: lion, cougar, jaguar, cheetah ... He nearly knocked the lights out of one of the loggers at a meeting when he broke the chain around Diamond's neck and flung it across the room. It was one of his precious teeth, and nobody lays a finger on his precious teeth without permission. There's a film of that meeting. You should take a look at it if you want to see what Diamond was like. Quite entertaining."

"What meeting was that?"

"An information meeting about the logging up near Dumoine. It got quite emotional."

"How can I get a copy of that film?"

"I'll set up a showing for you at the media centre here if you want."

"I'd like that. It could be useful," I said. I put the tooth back on the desk. "Did Diamond usually take photos when he went out on his trips?"

"Yes. He always had his camera with him just in case."

"What about this last trip? Anything turned up?"

He looked at me curiously, and I noticed that his blue eyes were flecked with black motes that made them appear fathomless.

"Nothing's turned up here that I know of, but then the police are probably sitting on it still."

"They didn't find any film."

He frowned but said nothing.

"Did you ever go on any of his field trips?"

"Yes. He hated company, but he usually needed it when he was tranquilizing the cats to put a radio collar on, and that's when I'd get my samples — you know, you're a zoologist — vials of ticks and stuff. Anyway, I always shot the dart — he hated to do that."

"Isn't that out of character? I would have thought he would be the sort of macho man who would hunt."

"No, he hated weapons of any kind. He blinded a kid in one eye with a BB gun when he was eight. Apparently they were in the woods alone and the kid screamed and there was blood everywhere and he kind of lost it. It made him sick. As I said he was a sensitive man, at least when it came to anything inherently violent. I can't help but like that in the man. But he was too damn stubborn. Thought he was right all the time. Trouble was he was bright enough that he usually was.

Anyway, I would shoot the darts and then I'd help with the radio tracking equipment."

"How easy would it be to accidentally shoot yourself with a tranquilizer gun?" Patrick looked at me and turned his head to one side. God, he was a nice-looking man. I mentally kicked my thoughts to scatter them out of my mind. They were too damn distracting. The effect this perfect stranger was having on me was unnerving.

"What kind of question's that?" He shuffled some papers uneasily and cleared his throat. "Not easy, but I suppose it could happen. It's a gun really, and the ammo is a dart that shoots out. The impact of the dart in the animal's hide releases the tranquilizer. Still, you'd have to be pretty dumb or fantastically careless or accident-prone to do that unintentionally."

chapter twelve

When I got to work first thing the next morning I geared myself up and phoned Shannon Johnson, Diamond's girlfriend, but all I got was a chirpy voice saying she and Diamond were out and to leave a message. Jeez, Diamond had been dead for at least three weeks by my reckoning and she hadn't changed the message? Creepy. I left my name and number and explained the reason for my call and suggested a meeting after work.

I called a list of entomologists Martha had come up with and shamelessly pumped them for information about their courses: what they had found worked and what didn't. It was discouraging. Most of them had enrollment way down and grant money in the air, except the ones working for agriculture, and they had gobs of money.

I spent the rest of my day doing research in the library and missed the call from Shannon, but Martha confirmed that the date was on — or at least that's what she thought she'd gleaned from the garbled conversation.

I left work early, shopped along Elgin Street, and bought a good sturdy rope hammock that I'd been dying to get. The kind with the wide wooden spreaders. Then I walked down Elgin to McLeod and Shannon's apartment. It was an old apartment building on the corner across from the Victoria Museum — a five-storey red brick affair with a wide central staircase going up to the second floor. I walked up the flight of stairs and found apartment 2. There was a little card identifying the occupants as Diamond and Johnson.

I knocked on the door and waited a long time before it opened and a tall blond-haired woman in a fashionable two-piece suit stared out at me. I wondered why Patrick had called her small until I remembered how tall he was. Anyone under six feet must have seemed small to him. Shannon stood a good three inches taller than I did. Her green eyes were puffy and red and her tiny features were the colour of sorrow — ash grey. There was a slight resemblance to Lianna, but this woman had more warmth. She kept wringing her fingers and looking behind her. I introduced myself, but Shannon ignored my hand and didn't invite me in. She just stood there and stared at me and then said in a curiously emotionless voice, "I don't understand why you think I can help you, why you think a bunch of stolen disks have anything to do with Jake."

Her voice was soggy, her green eyes flat and dull, as she waited for some cue from me.

"I don't know that it does, but Jake's the only lead I have to go on."

Shannon stood in the doorway fiddling nervously with the doorknob until I had the strongest desire to grab her hand and pull it away from the damn knob.

I repeated what I had said on the phone, all about my disks and Diamond. When I finished there was an uncomfortable silence as Shannon struggled with some inner battle and gripped the doorknob like a lifeline. She kept shooting looks at me and as quickly looked away, making up her mind a dozen times and changing it until I finally said, "Look, maybe now isn't the best time."

At that Shannon made up her mind.

"No, no I think it's okay. I suppose you'd better come in." She pulled open the door and let me in, then quickly closed and bolted the door behind her.

I followed her down a short, indigo blue hallway into a very large room. It had lovely high ceilings and large windows overlooking the museum, and the windowsills were wide enough to sit on, except that they were full of plants. The windows were open and a gentle breeze was blowing the pale peach curtains inward. There were boxes of books, some computer disks and file folders in the centre of the room, and papers spread over every surface. The back of a red velvet sofa had been slashed and the stuffing was all over the floor. Three pictures leaned against the wall, one of a lynx and two of Diamond and Shannon, with the glass shattered and the photos ripped.

"Oh, it's kind of a mess," she said, which I thought was rather an understatement. "Someone broke in and trashed the place sometime this morning. The police only just left."

It was quite a mess. Diamond certainly seemed to have left a lot of paperwork behind him that interested someone. First his office ransacked and now his home. I wondered if he and his wife still kept a house together and if it had been searched too.

"I came home for lunch and found stuff flung everywhere. It's horrible. It's taken all afternoon to clean it up and figure out what's missing. Just a bunch of vandals the police say. Why do people do these things?" I didn't like the sound of her voice, a tight, bare-knuckled type of voice, on the verge of control and the abyss beyond.

"Look, maybe I'd better come back another day. It's not a good time for you."

She answered so quickly and with such vehemence that it made me start because it seemed so out of character. "It's the perfect time. You can help me clean up while we talk." She looked at me and softened her voice. "I sure could use the help." She handed me a plastic bag and indicated a pile of papers in the corner. I picked my way through the mess and began stuffing papers into the bag.

"What did they steal?" I asked.

"Nothing important as far as I can see," she said. "All our valuable stuff is here: the stereo, VCR, computer …"

I had sidled my way over to the computer, and the distinctive smell, though weak, made my skin crawl. The computer was covered with the same stuff that had wiped my own computer clean.

I looked around and saw her staring at me. "You didn't keep any important records on this computer, did you?"

"We used to, but the computer had total system failure once and Jake never trusted it again. He used it only for small stuff anyway. He'd bring home his current work on those disks and feed them in. He never left any of his work on the computer, just games and things like that."

"Any of your work?"

"Me? No. I don't know anything about computers. I like a pen and paper better. I never used it." I wondered if she knew what the formaldehyde had done to the computer — surely she could smell it — but I didn't have the heart to bring it up. She'd find out soon enough, if it was important. "Do you know what was he working on? His grad student said he was excited about something. Any idea what it was?"

"No." She hesitated. "But Patrick's right. He was kind of excited about something, but when I asked, all he would say was that it was important and he wanted to surprise me."

I idly started looking at the labels on the disks — all games of one kind or another, no data, no personal stuff.

"Was anything stolen, anything at all?"

"Yes. About two months before Jake died he brought back a little box filled with some mammal teeth and fur, said it had something to do with his lynx studies. You know about his lynx studies?" I nodded. "He sometimes brought stuff like that home, not often but sometimes, and only the really good specimens. He kept them in a box in his desk over there. Most of what he collected he gave to Patrick to catalogue, but sometimes, if a tooth was particularly good, he'd bring it back for himself."

Her hand went to her neck and I saw she was wearing a necklace with a single tooth, embedded in silver, dangling from a silver chain.

She saw my eyes glance at her necklace and dropped her hand and smiled.

"This tooth is … was … his Florida Panthers' tooth, he said."

I raised my eyebrows in question.

"He liked to collect the teeth of all the sports teams named after cats, professional and amateur — Ottawa Lynx, Florida Panthers, Cincinnati Bengals, Bobcaygeon Bobcats, Dumoine Pumas — you name it, he collected them and turned them into necklaces."

I remembered Lianna's necklace and the much smaller tooth she wore. I wondered what cat that had been and what team it had represented. What a strange man. Most men give rings or earrings, but Diamond obviously handed out the canine teeth of felines to his women. Talk about being hooked on his profession.

"He gave me this just before he went into the bush. He had one just like it. They came from Florida and New Brunswick."

His and hers necklaces, I thought with a shiver. *Yuck*.

"Anyway his collection is gone — he was very proud of it. Seems like a dumb thing to steal but there was a lot of silver too. The police figure that's why it was taken, for the silver he used to make the necklaces."

She stood there fiddling with her necklace for a long time.

"They say you found him." Her voice cracked, and she sat down suddenly amid a pile of file folders and the stuffing from the sofa, which poofed up around her like dandelion fluff.

"Why'd it have to happen to him?" Her voice sailed too high and shattered, and I found myself looking around the messy room for a Kleenex and going to the kitchen for a glass of water. Shannon struggled to hold back the tears and gulped the water I brought to her.

"Sorry, I can't help it. I still can't believe he's gone. I can't believe it happened. Jake was the best woodsman I ever knew. He kept a flare gun by his head every night before turning in just in case he needed it for bears or other wild animals. The cops didn't mention that he'd fired the flare. It just doesn't fit. He'd have had time to fire the flare. No one could surprise Jake. He had eyes in the back of his head. He would have fired the flare."

"But it was a rogue bear, a crazy bear, Shannon," I said with a conviction I wasn't sure was justified. "A rogue bear is unpredictable. It could have been stalking him. Perhaps he just didn't wake up in time," I said, trying to remember if there had been a flare gun listed in the police report.

"Jake would wake up if a grasshopper tried to sneak by him; he was that light a sleeper. Honest to God. An owl couldn't sneak by that man. There's no way he could have been surprised by a stupid bear. Even a rogue bear or whatever it is you call it. He would have had some warning, some feeling that there was something bloody wrong. I've seen him wake in the tent and listen for fifteen minutes until a bear, silent and stealthy, walked into our camp one night. He knew. Don't ask me how the hell he did, but he knew and he was ready for it with the flare gun. He didn't have to hear it first. He could sense it with some sort of sixth sense. He would have put up a fight."

"But suppose he'd taken a sleeping pill or something like that? Maybe a shot of scotch even. It could make him groggy. It would be harder to wake up, make him sleepier." I was remembering the coroner's report. The guy was certainly under enough stress with the logging to have resorted to something that would let him sleep.

"A sleeping pill? Jake? A sleeping pill? Christ, you obviously don't" — she suppressed a sob, swallowing it — "didn't know Jake. He never took any pills at all, no medication, not even vitamins. He was not just a planet environmentalist, he was a body environmentalist too. And who would ever take a sleeping pill in the bush anyway? No. He'd have woken in time to do something, even if he'd had a drink or two. I'm sure of it. Besides, he had Paulie."

"Polly?"

"His cat. Never went anywhere without little Paulie. Beautiful black velvet cat with liquid gold eyes. Loyal little devil. It belonged to Jake's nephew but got run over by a car. The parents wanted to put it down but the nephew appealed to his Uncle Jake. The vet had to amputate one leg but the cat adapted remarkably well and Jake began to admire it for its tenacity. In the end he kept it. She stuck to Jake like a burr. She went with him every time they went into the bush. Nothing got by Paulie. Nothing. She'd have wakened him even if he were in a coma." She looked up and saw the expression on my face.

"You know something," she said eagerly. "What?"

"There was a black three-legged cat around the day we found Diamond."

"That was Paulie!" she said excitedly. "Where is she? Have you got her? Is she okay?"

I shook my head. "It disappeared and we never saw it again."

The eagerness in her face faded and she murmured something about posting a reward.

"Look," I said, trying to bring the subject back to Diamond, "even a seasoned woodsman can get careless sometimes, and that's all it would take if a rogue bear was around. He was careless enough to leave a chocolate bar in the tent. He could have misplaced his flare gun too, or lost it along the portage."

Shannon's head jerked up and she stared at me, open-mouthed. "Are you crazy? No way. He found out he was allergic to chocolate, months ago. Migraine headaches. But he didn't like to tell anybody. He thought he had to be macho and all that. He hated to think he had any weaknesses. But even if he was sneaking it on the sly, he'd never leave food in the tent. He made me empty my pockets of candy wrappers and burn them before we got into the tent, he was that meticulous. Drove me crazy. He knew what bears could do and he never did anything to entice them. He never kept food in the tent, even toothpaste, and he always strung up the food pack well out of reach of animals. And I can't imagine him ever losing that flare gun. He's had it more than twenty years and it's saved his neck a dozen times or more."

"Suppose he did lose the flare gun? Would he have resorted to using his tranquilizer gun in an emergency?"

She nodded. "Yeah, sure, if he had time to load it and all, but it's not something you can do quickly, and besides, he didn't have his trank gun with him this last trip."

I looked at her in surprise.

"How do you know?"

"Because it's in my car. He forgot it there when I drove him to work the day he went into the bush. I didn't notice it until last week."

I tried to swallow the implications of this new revelation. If Jake hadn't taken out the tranquilizer gun, then whose dart had hit him?

"Could he have picked up another one at his office?"

"It wouldn't have occurred to him. He'd already packed it, you see, but he needed something from the pack and we were in such a hurry and he asked me if I could find it, and, well, I guess in my haste the tranquilizer gun case got left behind."

So where did the dart come from that was found in Jake's body, I wondered. Someone must have been with him when he died, but who? Shannon got up and dumped a green garbage bag full of stuff by the sofa and then handed me another bag.

"I know it's crazy," she said. "He was killed by a bear, but somehow I still can't believe that." She was looking like she was going to crumple again, so I quickly changed the subject.

"Were there any disks stolen?"

"You mean like yours? I don't know. As I said he didn't keep any disks here except ... Yeah, hang on a moment. This might help you." She got up, picked up her purse, and rummaged in it until she finally surfaced with a disk.

"He gave me this just before he went into the bush. Asked me to take it to a printer and print out the injunction stuff on it for him and keep it in my purse until he got back. He was afraid the loggers might get hold of it and learn his game plans, I guess. He'd have done anything to stop the logging up there. He loved that place. And how he envied those guys on the west coast — you know, the ones who saved the forest because of a rare owl that lived there? He and his family used to camp up in Dumoine when he was a kid. Anyway, I printed out the injunction stuff for him — it's still at work. You're welcome to the disk, though. It's no good to me anymore."

She handed me the disk. I placed it in my inside jacket pocket and then stood up to go. Shannon accompanied me to the door, grabbing onto the doorknob once again.

I turned on the threshold and said, "Jake Diamond's wife came to see me last week."

Shannon tensed every muscle and clenched her fists around the knob, but she said nothing.

"She wanted to know about a black diary of hers that she says Diamond mistakenly took. She thought maybe I'd seen it when I first found Diamond as it hadn't shown up in the police report and wasn't among his effects. Do you know anything about it and why she'd think he had it?"

Shannon ground her teeth and went pale and trembly. The doorknob rattled in her hand.

"You'd think she'd be happy with the insurance policy she had on his life. A million bucks is nothing to sneer at. I know it made Diamond horribly nervous. People kill for less than that. She wants everything of Diamond's right down to his camera and all the beautiful pictures he took of his lynx and bobcats. His stuff's not worth much, God knows, but it means a lot to me to have those things, and I know she just wants them to shut me out. Diamond said he would leave all his things to me. He wrote another will in his black diary, and we got two acquaintances to witness it. He wanted me to have those pictures, to have all his things, not that bitch. She really told you that black book was hers?"

"The black book isn't hers?" I asked innocently.

"No, of course it isn't. I don't know or really care what she told you. The truth is that he wrote another will."

"Isn't that a little odd, not going through a lawyer?"

"Not really. Jake said it's perfectly legal as long as it's witnessed and it's handwritten. It all happened because the night before he was due to go into the bush he read an article in the paper about separated couples, and what to do to make sure you don't get screwed financially. Well, it said the first thing to do is to change your will because if you die all your stuff goes to the wife, not to me. So he scribbled it all down in his black book and we got it witnessed by his friends. He was going to put it in the safe deposit box but he didn't. I checked. It isn't there."

"And you have no idea where it is?"

"It must have gone into the bush with him. I haven't seen it, but my brother, he's a lawyer, he told Lianna's lawyer about it. Her lawyer then confirmed its existence with the witnesses, and told me that unless I can find the will, the will favouring Lianna stands."

Suddenly her green eyes widened and she looked right through me. "Holy God. The bloody bitch. Do you think that's why my place was ransacked?"

chapter thirteen

W hen I got into work the next day I met Martha in the hall staggering under a pile of books as she tried to open the office door with no free hands. I didn't make it in time to catch the pile as it toppled over. I leafed through Jemima Puddle-duck as Martha picked up Winnie the Pooh and Brer Rabbit. Martha was not married and she'd never talked of any children.

"Martha, what are you doing with these?" I asked.

"The local daycare needs some more books, so I scrounged up some of these from the students here," she said with a shrug.

We walked into her outer office and I dumped the books on Martha's desk and let out a big sigh. Martha cannot stand big sighs followed by silence, so I knew I had her attention.

"This thing's getting stranger and stranger, Martha.

I can't figure it out. Nothing fits." I quickly filled her in on my conversation with Shannon.

When I was through Martha chortled and said, "When I was a kid I used to do those big thousand-piece jigsaw puzzles."

I looked at Martha in exasperation. What the hell was she going on about?

"It was a wonderful feeling getting those last few pieces, but one day my kid sister put one puzzle in the wrong box. One was a mountain scene with a stream and the other was a mountain scene with a stream but all different — same colours. I couldn't get the puzzle. It didn't make sense because I didn't know what the final picture looked like. When I finally realized what had happened I was able to fit the pieces together." Martha's eyes were twinkling like a gurgling mountain stream. "You have to figure out what the problem is before you can start fitting the pieces together," she said triumphantly as she plunked herself down in her chair. I pulled up a stool and straddled it.

"Okay. You find a dead body. Killed by a bear. Someone moves that body from the death scene. There's no forensic entomologist at the scene — except you — so the cops don't collect proof that the body's been moved. You do. Then your life is threatened, your lab is fumigated, and all the insects taken from Diamond are stolen. Coincidence? Unlikely. Someone went to a lot of trouble to prevent you from finding out the body had been moved. That is your first question. Why was the body moved?"

I remained silent, wondering what she would come up with.

"Okay. We know, or at least we're pretty sure because of the tranquilizer gun, that someone was with Diamond when he died. It wasn't his trank gun, and Shannon told you he wouldn't have had a chance to get another. Suppose whoever it was got scared, tried to save Diamond, but accidentally shot him with the trank gun. Then panicked and fled."

"Who moved the body then?"

"They came back and moved the body because the place he died would identify them somehow."

"Why go to all that trouble? Why not just go to the cops with the whole story and muscle it out? It's not a criminal offence to try and help someone."

"Maybe they were too ashamed."

"Yeah, right. It's got to be something more," I said.

"Maybe he was in partnership with someone and they'd discovered something worth a lot of money, a gold mine or something. When the bear attacked them, his partner, after failing to save Diamond, moved the body so that no one would come snooping and find the gold. Then they snatched your disks to cover their tracks."

I was musing on the merits of Martha's theories, particularly the last one, when the phone rang. Martha answered and handed it over to me.

Duncan's voice came booming over the line. "Did you know they found the bear about a day after the body was found?"

"How do you know? I don't remember seeing it in the papers."

"Apparently before they could get a team together to go and comb the area, one of the loggers phoned and said they'd shot a bear near Diamond's permanent camp. The wildlife people went up to take a look but the loggers apparently burned the body to keep other wild animals away. Can you believe it? The wildlife guys were furious and thought maybe it was just an attempt to hide a bear-poaching job, but the loggers' story held and they didn't find a pelt. Apparently one of the loggers had recently been raked by the bear and his friends had saved him. He had the scars to prove it. Of course, it was too late to be able to prove it was the bear that got Diamond, but the wildlife guys were convinced by the scars. Two rogue bears in one area is hard to stomach."

When I didn't say anything to this piece of news Duncan asked, "Are you still there?"

"Yeah, sorry, I was just thinking about something else. Was there a flare gun among Diamond's belongings?"

"Hang on a sec." I could hear a file cabinet opening and the rustling of papers and then he was back on the line.

"Let's see ... No, no flare gun. Should there have been?"

"Apparently, yes. When I talked to his girlfriend she said he never went into the bush without his flare gun."

"Nope. There was no flare gun found, but there was something else you didn't see which might convince you that perhaps you're blowing things way out of proportion."

At least he'd softened it with the word *perhaps*, I thought as he continued.

"Seems Diamond was quite careless. One of my report pages was with my secretary the day you came. Diamond's trousers were drenched in fish oil — not the kind found with fresh fish. This was an oil, like sardines, which would fit with what you said about sardine cans being found there."

My mind raced back to that lonely and deserted campsite, and I said in puzzlement, "Yes, but why would a man who hauls up his food pack, complete with toothpaste, wear trousers saturated with fish oil that is bound to be a dinner gong for any bear in the area?"

"So he ate sardines for dinner and spilled it. Do it all the time myself. Those tins are such a bitch to open."

I shook my head at the phone. "Doesn't make sense.

He comes across as an experienced camper. He knew the dangers. Why didn't he wash his pants?"

"Maybe he didn't have another pair." When I snorted, Duncan changed tack.

"There's no accounting for people's lapses. Haven't you ever forgotten to look both ways before crossing the street and narrowly missed getting flattened? Awful yeasty feeling in your mouth when it happens."

After we disconnected I stood in my office staring at the wall thinking about Diamond, then roused myself, said goodbye to Martha, and headed off to the library. I didn't get away from work until prime rush hour. I sat stuck on the bridge over the Ottawa River and watched four kayaks darting in and out of the rapids while I thought about forensic entomology, which, of course, directed my thoughts toward Jake Diamond and my disks.

What had really happened to him up there in the woods? Had there really been someone with him that day? Had they shot the dart at the bear to try to save Diamond and jabbed him instead? Were they partners in some illegal scheme that forced the partner to move the body? Was there an illegal still up there in the woods, or were they poaching and didn't want the police to find the evidence? Was that why the body was moved? And if so, how was this going to help me find my disks? I had to find out if there had been someone with Diamond when he died. If there was, I prayed they'd be able to lead me to my disks, if I played my cards well enough. Problem was, I wasn't sure if I held any cards at all.

Clouds were rolling in from the west and it had started to rain as I pulled my car up in front of the barn and jumped out. Ryan's motorbike was parked outside his studio, and the red light wasn't on — he wasn't in the darkroom. Great. I could try to get him to help me with the disk Shannon had given me. I took the metal stairs two at a time and rapped on the door before barging in.

Ryan gingerly took the disk from me and turned it over in his hands as if it was contaminated.

"Cordi, who else has this disk been conversing with?"

"Oh, for heaven's sake, Ryan, how would I know? You have a virus detector, don't you? Besides, it's a Mac."

He grunted, and reluctantly pushed the disk into his hard drive. The computer hummed and hawed but no bells and whistles came up alerting us to some nasty infection being transported by the disk. When the disk's icon, labelled "Stuff," had mounted on the computer Ryan double-clicked on it. There was one folder on the disk, named "Logging."

Ryan opened the folder. It contained files of all Diamond's logging information, briefs, letters, and records of all logging events up in the Dumoine area for the past forty years. There was also a file that turned out to contain his calendar of events for the past year, some articles on data falsification, and some letters to colleagues.

"Let's check his calendar," I said, hoping something would jump out and make everything right again, but knowing it wouldn't. Why couldn't I be an optimist like Martha?

Diamond had been meticulous at keeping track of all his appointments, times and dates. Ryan went back to March and started scrolling from there.

"Ryan, stop!"

I took the mouse from him and scrolled back and forth, highlighting two separate entries a month apart. The first said, "Speak with Don re: paper. Is Roberta involved?" The second, a month later, said, "Clear day for

Don and the Dean re: ethics, paper." The second entry was scheduled for five days after Diamond died.

"What do you suppose that means?" said Ryan.

"Don Allenby and Diamond were collaborating on a paper together. Roberta told me Diamond had asked Don to postpone publication. He was very disappointed and so was Roberta because she will be one of the authors — quite a plum for a master's student."

"You think there was something wrong with the paper? Diamond's got a folder here on data falsification and other illegal activities. Holy shit, that'd ruin Allenby's career if he made up his data. Maybe it's the student?"

Ryan clicked open the essay, which talked about how the public trust had been undermined by scientists faking their data, but that it was essential to be sure before accusing someone because their careers could be ruined.

"Jesus, Cor, if one of his students falsified data, no one would touch them again. That breast cancer study in Montreal by some guy — I can't remember his name now. Remember how it played in the media? Data falsification is career-ending. If this guy's student was doing something shady and Diamond found out, then his death has been very beneficial for her. Fake data. You'd be dead in the water."

I took the mouse from Ryan's hand and scrolled through the documents.

"He's got stuff here on that fish in the Mediterranean," I said. "The one they said was extinct, until some fisherman landed a live, breathing specimen."

I continued searching the files.

"He's got a whole folder on all his old papers. Jesus, he was prolific. Look: artificial insemination of captive cats, predator-prey relations, pregnancy in lynx, an overview paper on extinct and endangered species ... Hey, here's something on the Puerto Rican crested toad.

They thought it was extinct, too, until a toad hopped out of a crevice one day. Remember that?"

I idly wondered how many more species, thought to be gone forever, would prove us wrong, just like the toad and the fish. I clicked on a file labelled "Lynx," but the computer beeped and prompted us for a password.

"Wonder what's so special about that one?"

Ryan shrugged, and I went back to Diamond's calendar and began scanning all the months before his death.

"Take a look at this."

I pointed at the screen.

"He had regular meetings with a guy named Jeff. Look at that — three, four times a month, but the entries end in May."

"I thought you said his helper's a guy by the name of Patrick, not Jeff."

I reached for Ryan's phone in my growing excitement, forgetting any fears I might have had about a cold call, and called Patrick, but I got no answer, so, since I was on a roll, I tried Shannon. She answered on the sixth ring.

I went straight to the point.

"Diamond was apparently going to meet with the Dean. He had an appointment five days after he died. It looks as though it had something to do with one of Don's students. Do you know anything about it?"

"Um, I don't know. I mean, I'm not sure. Jake was really upset about something — maybe it was Dr. Allenby. I don't know, but whatever it was, I don't think it was really great, you know what I mean? He wouldn't eat my lemon meringue pie one night — can you believe it? He always loved it, but he said he was so angry about a paper he couldn't touch anything."

"Do you know what paper it was?"

"Paper? What? Oh. Oh, I see. He never told me much. Could have been any paper. He marked lots, and he wrote some stuff himself that got published in those magazines no one reads but the scientists. God, they're really boring, but you see, I didn't find his work really interesting, so I don't really know." She paused and then added sadly, "I guess I should have taken more interest."

I made some reassuring noises and then asked her if she knew if Jeff was the same guy Patrick had mentioned to me.

"Yeah, sure. Jeff was a pilot friend of Jake's. Actually, he introduced us. Jeff was an old flame of mine, sort of. I used to go up to his lodge near Dumoine and help with the cooking. I met Jake there. He liked to come and see Jeff's birds and stuff."

"Birds?"

"Yeah, Jeff bred wild birds — rare ones — and other animals, too. He had lots of land and Jake loved to go up there. He died last month, in a fire. Broke Jake up. Me too."

"They were good friends?"

"Oh yes. They were real buddies, and Jeff also helped Jake with his biology stuff."

"What do you mean?"

"Well, being a pilot and all, Jeff took Jake out to kind of fly over where Jake wanted him to."

"You mean aerial surveillance?"

"Yeah, that's it. I think they'd fly over his study site looking for the cats with all this special equipment."

"Did you ever go with him?"

"He never asked me. Not that I would have gone. I'm kinda afraid of heights, but he could have asked."

"There's a locked file named 'Lynx' on the disk you gave me. Do you know anything about it?"

"Sounds like his research file, although why it'd be on his logging disk, I don't know. He always password-protected his research files. He usually kept his research at the university."

"Do you know if he had any favourite passwords?"

Shannon laughed. "Yeah, sure. It pissed him off that he even had to use a password for his documents. He never really believed it was necessary, but he did it anyway because Davies was on his case about security and stuff." There was silence at the end of the line, and then she said, "He made it as easy for himself as he could. He almost always used his mother's name, Leah, with a two-digit number after it. Sometimes he used his cat's name, Paulie, or other family names ... I figured I'd really made it when he trusted me enough to tell me. I'm the only one who knows, besides Patrick. Anyway I'd try the Leah one first and try numbers from eleven to ninety-nine. He never used three digits. If that doesn't work, ask Patrick. He should know."

I wrote the names on a piece of paper and handed it to Ryan.

"One last question: Did Diamond like sardines?"

There was a long pause and then, "Sardines? Yeah, he loved sardines."

"Were they part of his diet in the bush?"

"Hardly. Not when he could get fresh fish from the lake. Sardines are so smelly — they attract too many animals. He wouldn't likely touch them out there with a ten-foot pole." There was a pause and then she asked, "Why, were there sardines in the tent too?"

"Not in the tent, no." Thoughts were tumbling around in my mind taking shape, coalescing. I rang off, and as I stood there lost in thought, Ryan exclaimed, "Bingo. We got it! Leah22."

There were six main folders labelled "lynx/cat" with a three-digit number after each one and another main file labelled "wild card." There were reams of data in each of the cat files detailing everything about the lynx, including pregnancy. The notes were meticulous and boring. The measurements and physical characteristics of each cat were recorded at the top: weight, length, length of pregnancy, and so on, and all with the nauseating detail of a thorough researcher. It was mind-numbing and a little chastising. My research was not this thorough. But at least he was human. I noticed that he'd forgotten to record the weight and length for the sixth cat. In one of the folders there was a paper on captive breeding and artificial insemination techniques for lynx and a reference to four captive reared cats — Dana, Simba, Sian, and Myth — who were bred successfully, it seemed. I smiled. So Diamond had had a sentimental streak. He'd given these cats names rather than numbers. Another folder titled "radio-collaring" had the notes and observations and surveillance records on six cats. All cats had been under surveillance from at least May on, except one from April on. I skimmed through dates of surveillance and rough maps with dots all over them, wondering what I was looking for. A pattern? An indication of what he was doing just before he died?

On impulse I put a call into Patrick again and this time got him on the first attempt. The sound of his voice sent shockwaves through me, and I realized my hands were shaking. Disconcerted, I stammered out my hellos and identified myself, silently cursing my sudden attack of nerves. Or was it nerves?

"I've just got into a disk of Diamond's that Shannon gave me and I wanted to ask you some questions I couldn't answer."

"Fire away." I tried to picture him on the other end of the line. Was he smiling? I wished I had something to say that wasn't just business, but I couldn't think of a thing in my muddled state of mind, so I asked him what I had called to ask him in the first place.

"You said the other day that you accompany Diamond on his tagging expeditions. Do you also accompany him on surveillance flights and ground surveillance to track the animals' movements?" God, I sounded so bloody official. What was he thinking of me?

"No. Not usually. It's very time-consuming, but I do help sometimes. We radio-collared the last cat in May. Let me just boot up here and check." I heard the telltale ping of a computer turning on and shortly after Patrick was back, "Yup, May. I helped him with that and went out on surveillance a couple of times in late April and early May but then he said he didn't need me for any surveillance in May and June anymore and I was happy with that. I had a lot of my own work." He paused, his tone suddenly guarded. "Why are you interested in this?"

I wished I could see his eyes. I couldn't read anything from his voice.

"I'm wondering if whatever he was working on just before his death might have something to do with why his body was moved and why my larvae were killed and my disks stolen."

Patrick grunted into the phone but politely said nothing. I cleared my throat, wondering what I was looking for, knowing he was wondering that too. "Diamond's data lists six cats that were surveyed in the six months before his death. Do you —"

Patrick interrupted, "What was on that disk Shannon gave you?"

The sharpness of his tone put me on the defensive, and I felt the beginnings of panic welling up inside me that surprised me. I really didn't want this guy angry at me. I wanted him to like me.

"What she told me was on it: all his logging stuff. But then there was also a folder on his research."

"I think we'd better meet. Before I answer any of

your questions I want to see that disk. At the same time I can show you the film."

There was nothing for it but to agree. The coldness of his voice made it clear that I'd get no further on the phone. We arranged to meet in two days' time at his lab.

I hung up, part of me pleased that I would see him again, part of me frustrated because he had every right to the disk and the information on it and I didn't. Part of me upset because I hadn't liked the coldness in his voice and I wanted to warm it up in the worst way. This guy was really affecting me.

Ryan was in the darkroom, so I fooled around, trying to find the password for the last folder. I tried Leah all the way to 99 and then repeated it with the name of Diamond's cat, Polly. No luck. Ryan came out of the darkroom with some negatives and laid them out on his light table as I was making a copy of the disk.

"What did you lose?" I asked, dreading the response. I'd delayed asking the question for so long I was sure it would be all bad.

"What?"

"You know, the film you lost at the rapids. How many pictures did you lose? Ballpark damage."

"I didn't lose any." His words echoed off my thoughts like a boomerang and came winging back at me with menacing meaning.

"What do you mean you didn't lose any?"

"I checked my records and every shot I took is accounted for."

I stared at Ryan. He took meticulous records of each of his pictures, noting the f-stop, ASA, lighting, everything, all neatly numbered, and he wasn't missing any?

"Then that film that we found?"

"Wasn't mine," said Ryan.

chapter fourteen

"This throws a whole new light on things, doesn't it?" I said as I watched Martha deftly cutting up some pieces of liver.

"I mean, whose film was it if it wasn't Ryan's? Can you tell me that? Do you think someone wanted it badly enough to try to kill us for it?"

"Doesn't make sense, Cordi. Besides, the film was lost in the rapids."

"What if there was something incriminating on it and someone just wanted to destroy it? Sounds better than being a martyr to a bunch of insects, doesn't it?"

Martha looked up with interest. "You mean your close call had nothing to do with the larvae?"

"I'm not saying that exactly. I thought at first that it was the larvae, but maybe it was the film. The police report gibes with what I saw: there was an empty film canister and the camera was empty. That means at least one film is missing. The film we found wasn't in a canister, and if the film had something incriminating on it, it might have been enough for someone who saw us find it to dump our canoe to get rid of it, not aiming to kill us but just to get rid of the film."

Martha wiped her hands on her apron and said, "Alternately they could have had the same motive concerning the larvae, although the film seems more plausible, I admit. So you think they lost it and saw you pick it up? If you're right then the film had something on it that someone wanted to keep secret."

"We'll never know, will we?"

"Maybe Diamond was blackmailing someone — you know, sex pictures and stuff."

I raised my eyebrows. "Now there's an original thought."

"It's a time-honoured one anyway," quipped Martha.

I spent the day working on my various papers. Patrick Whyte called while I was out for lunch and left a message with Martha saying he had made arrangements to show me the film at 10:00 a.m. and could I meet him then. I cursed myself for not being around when he called, and then immediately cursed myself for feeling the way I did. Which was what exactly?

Next morning I woke feeling vulnerable and scared and hoped to God my autumn darkness, which had struck every year without fail for all my adult life, was not falling prematurely. I had too much to do, but it was all I could do to drag myself out of bed, the horribly familiar feeling threatening me like a hit man. At my worst, in the depths of winter, there were times when a hit man would have been better than the blackness that enveloped me like a straitjacket. I felt a little better once I was up. I usually did, and the edge to my mood softened. It was too soon for my worst months. I clung to that hope and took a long hot shower to wash the deadness from my thoughts. As a result I was half an hour late leaving and cursed myself for the lost time. I had really wanted to make sure I got to Whyte's lab in plenty of time to talk to Don before I had to view the films, but my initiative had deserted me and I arrived at the campus wishing I were anywhere else.

I wheeled my car into the parking lot of the zoology building and reluctantly got out. I rummaged around in the back for a box of Kleenex — something had blown into town and I was plugged up with hay fever. I had forgotten to bring any antihistamine, and I didn't feel like going to a drugstore with everything else I had to do in the mood I was in. I could put up with the hay fever for a spell, as long as I had Kleenex.

As I walked toward the zoology building I noticed a bunch of handwritten signs plastered along the walkway into the building with a picture of a familiar black cat with yellow eyes. In huge print the sign asked: "Have you seen Paulie? $$$ Reward $$$. Call Shannon." So Shannon must have decided she ought to do something for Diamond's cat. I must say, even I felt guilty about leaving the poor thing in the bush, but I had had other things on my mind at the time and I had told Leslie and Don. I'd presumed they would do something. I caught sight of Davies and, like some guilty kid, hid behind a parked car and waited until he had disappeared into the building before I headed toward Patrick's lab. In the foyer I saw Don and nearly let him get away before I found my resolve and called out to him. He stopped and waited for me to catch up to him.

"Got a cold in this weather?" he asked as I approached him in a sneezing fit.

"Just hay fever."

"My mother had hay fever. She said the worst of it was that she would get so plugged up that she couldn't smell the flowers. And she loved flowers."

"She's right. You can't smell a thing during hay fever season."

"I'm on my way to a lecture. Let's walk and you can tell me what you want," he said, as he turned and headed toward the zoology building.

I said to his back, "There was something in Diamond's calendar about you and the Dean. Can you ..."

Don stopped suddenly and faced me, so that I almost bumped into him.

"How did you know about that?" he whispered. His eyes flicked over my face like the darting tongue of a snake, searching randomly for God knows what.

"Well, Shannon gave me Diamond's research disk ..."

Don was suddenly as still as ice, staring openmouthed at me, his eyes frighteningly still. As I watched they grew rounder and rounder until the whites looked as though they would split and spill all over the blue of his irises.

"Shannon. Diamond told Shannon? But he promised me," croaked Don. "Oh God. Listen, I was desperate. I didn't do anything really bad, just a few figures here and there." He looked around nervously. "You can't pin anything on me. The data's gone. No one can prove I faked anything. For God's sake, my little girl ..."

I tried to keep the surprise from showing on my face as my thoughts tumbled around. He'd faked the data? Jesus, what a bombshell. And I'd thought it was Roberta. He stood to lose everything if Diamond had made that meeting. But he hadn't. I suddenly saw things quite clearly and heard my voice, as if detached from my body, say coolly, "You faked data on your joint paper and now

Diamond's dead. You stood to lose everything if he'd lived, didn't you?"

Don looked at me in growing horror. "I didn't do it. I'm allergic to sardines. Can't you see it's a lie? Why would I bait him? I'm not ..."

He stopped suddenly. His eyes were darting around like bingo balls bulging out of his head.

"Oh no," he said in a stunted whisper.

He looked wildly around him like a cornered animal, the sweat running freely on his forehead, his hands twisting together like the talons of an eagle on its prey.

"You've got to believe me," he said frantically, turning his back on some approaching students and putting his hand up to shield his face. He said nothing until they had passed, and then he grabbed me by the shoulder.

"We can't talk here. Can you come to my house this evening? Eight o'clock?" He dropped his hand, suddenly aware that he was gripping me too hard. He fished around in his coat pocket and pulled out a business card. He hastily wrote his home address on it, his hand trembling, and stuffed it into my hand.

"Please don't talk to anyone about this until I've had a chance to talk with you. You go around crying bloody murder and you'll get someone killed."

He turned abruptly and left, leaving me to ponder what he'd just told me.

I stuffed the card into my pants pocket and, glancing at my watch, headed off to Whyte's and Diamond's lab, deep in thought. I hung around in the foyer for a spell, gearing myself up until it was 10:00. Roberta didn't hear me come in. I almost didn't recognize her because she was wearing jeans and a T-shirt. Maybe the tight skirt and heels had just been an aberration or she had had a date that night and no time to go home and change. She was leafing through some stuff on Patrick's desk. When I cleared my throat she jumped and said, "Christ, you scared the shit out of me." She waved at the desk. "I was just looking for some papers ..." Her voice petered out, and I wondered why she felt she had to make an excuse to me. She must have wondered that herself because she suddenly said, "What are you doing here again, anyway?"

"Patrick said he'd meet me and show me a film of the logging meeting," I said, hoping he hadn't forgotten his meeting with me.

She quickly moved away from his desk and said, "You'll have fun watching that, all right. A real soap opera that was. But I just talked to Patrick on the phone. He's not coming in today. Sure you got the right date?"

I nodded. And felt like a fool. Nothing like being stood up in public.

"Well, I think you'd better phone him."

She gave me the number, but all I got was voice mail.

"Does he live near here?" I asked.

"Yeah. Just down near the library. I've never been there myself, but it should be easy to find. Don't tell him I told you, though. He hates visitors."

Great, I thought. *Nothing could boost my confidence like hearing that.* I watched her scrawling Patrick's address on a waste piece of paper. I wondered just how much she had been involved in Don's deception. She had collected some of his data. Surely she couldn't have done that without knowing it was false. It would have ruined her career if she had knowingly participated.

"I understand Don and Diamond were going before the Dean just before Diamond died. Do you know why?"

Roberta's hand stopped in mid-air. Her eyes widened in surprise — or was it fear? — but she regained her composure quickly and handed me the address, saying, "Sorry, I don't know anything about that. Look, I've got a lecture. Bye."

I watched her as she ran down the hallway, wondering how much of a lie I had just heard and how much truth.

I dawdled along the three blocks to Whyte's house trying to still my nerves at seeing him again by telling myself he couldn't be interested in me if he'd forgotten about our appointment. And why the hell would he be interested in me anyway? Jeez, I was really down on myself today — I couldn't seem to please myself no matter what I did. I found myself standing in front of a tiny, rundown house with a white picket fence set well back from all the other houses. There was a huge apple tree overhanging the front door, and although the pink paint was flaking off the door and windows, the house at least looked neat.

I opened the screen door, raised the heavy metal knocker, and hesitated. Once it fell, I was committed. I let it go. Its thud rumbled through the house like thunder.

After a short wait the door opened slowly and gingerly. An elderly woman with rheumy eyes gazed out through the screen. She was wearing two startling pink barrettes that were losing the battle of keeping her snow white hair out of her eyes.

"Who are you? What do you want? We don't need any fish today, do you hear?" she said in a flat monotone.

"I'm not selling fish," I said with a smile. Did he still live with his mother?

"Well, we don't want any more of those damned chocolate bars either. I think everybody plays hockey around here, don't you? Always looking for money to keep their ice cold. Why don't they just play in the winter as God intended?" She began to close the door.

"Mrs. Whyte?"

The door stopped closing and slowly reopened as the old lady peered again around the door.

"No, dearie, I wouldn't be seen dead with that wretched man's name attached to me. I go by the name I was born with: Santander. Pity my son won't change, but then he didn't hate his father quite as much as I do. Do you realize what a selfish, whining, snivelling, log-splitting son of a ..."

She started at the sound of Patrick's voice calling gently from the bowels of the house. "Mother, Mother, what are you doing?" She looked at me conspiratorially.

I smiled uncertainly. "I have a meeting with Patrick Whyte, please."

"Oh, you don't want to go upset my little Pattie." Again, the old woman started to close the door. "He's busy now on his electric computer. There's a sweetie. Run along home and play."

I started to protest and then heard Patrick's voice again, "Mum, what are you doing? You know you're not supposed to go answering the door. I'll take care of it. You go back to your room."

The voice was strong, solicitous, and made my knees go weak, but when its owner jerked the door wide he stopped, suddenly embarrassed. Was it because he had forgotten about me or was it because of his mother?

His mother cackled in the hallway. "Your girlfriend called me Mrs. Whyte, Pattie. What a rotten nasty man he was ..."

"Mother. Nobody's interested in Dad," he said gently. "Leave it be. You know it just upsets you. And she's not my girlfriend." He gently guided his mother back into the house as she called over her shoulder to me.

"You don't want to go upset my little Pattie. He's got his work to do. He's got a paper route, all by himself, and only eleven too. He's gonna be really wealthy one day."

"I'm sorry. Perhaps I shouldn't have come," I said, when Patrick returned.

He shrugged as if to say the harm was done.

"It's one of her bad days," he said. "She just forgets sometimes what day it is." He looked at me, as if waiting for me to contradict him. I wanted to say something that would make him realize that I understood, make him realize what a terrific person I was, but of course I couldn't find the words. Probably because I didn't really understand what he was going through.

"You wanted to see Diamond's disk before showing me the film? We were to meet at your lab but you weren't there, so ..." I trailed off.

"Oh jeez, I'm sorry. I completely forgot." He glanced back over his shoulder, flicking the hair out of his eyes. "I forgot. Give me five and I'll be right with you."

I stood in the foyer peering into the dark interior, feeling embarrassed. But why should I feel embarrassed? He was the one who had forgotten. I could hear Mrs. Santander's voice floating querulously back to me. "But Pattie, I don't want Mrs. Brickman again. I don't like her. You know I don't, Pattie."

It was some time before Patrick came back, ruffling his hand through his hair and sucking on his lower lip.

"Let's go," he said.

I had to jog to keep up with his rapid walk across a small park, down a residential street, and out onto the campus. He didn't say anything, and the silence was excruciating. Finally, I just said the second thing that came into my head. The first thing was X-rated.

"Who took care of Diamond's film?" I asked.

Without a hesitation in his stride he said, "I did. He'd dump everything on my desk and get me to take it to the lab."

"Did he take very many pictures when he was in the field?"

Patrick laughed. "It depends on what you mean by many. Jake was a photoholic. He took pictures the way most people eat potato chips — non-stop."

"What about pictures from that last field trip? Did any turn up?"

"Yeah, that was odd. There were none, at least nothing's arrived at the lab. I suppose Lianna might have them. I hadn't thought to ask her."

"As I told you, the cops say there were no films at all. No unexposed film either."

"Odd. He must have lost them, I guess. It's been known to happen before. He once put all his exposed film in a jacket pocket and then lost the jacket. "

"Did he usually keep the canisters to put the exposed film back in? Or did he toss them?"

"Always kept them. He wasn't like most of us, who usually lose a canister or two. His exposed film always went back into a canister. You do ask a lot of questions, don't you?" But at least he said it with a smile.

I thought back to the film Ryan had found. It hadn't been in a canister, and that could mean only one thing: if the film was Diamond's, it had been taken out of his camera by someone else. But why?

When we got to Patrick's lab I handed him the disk and he popped it in.

I pointed to the folders and said, "There were six cats."

Patrick shook his head and began searching through the files. "Can't be right. We only collared five."

He punched some keys and said, "No, that's wrong. Diamond's got an old folder mixed up in his current things. He was always doing that sort of thing. It's impossible, you see. We lost the sixth radio collar a year ago — we had only six because they're worth a small fortune. One of the lynx disappeared, and the signal stopped transmitting. We never did find the collar, much to Davies' annoyance."

"But look, one of them appears to have been tagged in March," I said and reached over to take the mouse from him. Our hands touched, and I looked up to see him smiling at me, his eyes dancing and my heart swirling. I looked away in confusion. He took his hand away.

"No way. He never tagged on his own, never. We tagged five cats in April and May. This sixth cat is from last year. We radio-tagged six cats last May, so he's mixed up his folders somehow with them."

He punched in some numbers and checked the date. There was no year. No wonder Diamond mixed them up. I wondered if he forgot to date his data often.

Patrick stood up, towering over me, and I suddenly felt his strength as he looked down at me, aware for the first time of just how small I was compared with him. Disconcerted by the force of this revelation and the softness of his eyes, I tried to concentrate on all the questions that I wanted to ask him. He walked over to a shabby leather sofa and sat down.

"Have a seat," he said, patting the sofa beside him and smiling. *Jesus, what do I do now?* I thought. Self-consciously, I walked over and sat down, feeling like the Tin Man needing his joints oiled as his eyes followed me the whole way to the sofa. Suddenly all I wanted to do was get away, afraid I would blow whatever I hoped might develop between us by saying something stupid. I was in that kind of mood, but I needed to know what he knew and it was easier to ask questions than to get up and make some feeble excuse about having to go. I was committed. There was no easier way out than to stay. So I pressed on.

"What I wanted to know was where he was flying during May and June and who flies surveillance for you?"

He turned his eyes away from me then and said, "It would have been over his study area, which is huge, but the notes would pinpoint that. He has the co-ordinates keyed in. I have them here, but you must understand that their home range can be quite big, so I really don't see that their movements will help you at all."

I sighed. Big dead end.

"What about Jeff? Who was he?"

"Jeff Reardon? He used to take Diamond out. He owned a small wildlife preserve up near Dumoine and did a bit of breeding of wild animals. Had permits, of course. It was a first-class operation."

He paused, and I could hear a phone ringing in the distance.

"What happened to him?" I asked softly.

"His place burned down in July and took Reardon with it. Everything was lost, all his records, everything. It was a real tragedy. Most of the animals died too. It was a horrible fluke thing. We'd had no rain in weeks — you remember how dry the spring was. There were forest fire alerts out all over the place. And it was too remote for the fire department to get there in time. Lightning hit one of the buildings and there was nothing anyone could do. All the buildings were wood. It was gone in twenty minutes, they say. Reardon died trying to save his animals."

"I'm sorry."

"Yeah, me too. It's a horrible way to die. "

I didn't know what to say to that so I just nodded, and waited a respectful amount of time before asking, "Would Jake have worked with him on artificial insemination?"

"You mean the captive lynx? Absolutely. One of Diamond's females was shot by some goon a few years back, and the three cubs, two females and a male, were left to die, so Diamond took them to Jeff and they were raised semi-wild. They experimented with artificial insemination. Jeff picked up a couple more, a male and female, on a reconnaissance flight in New Brunswick. Another hunter's nervous trigger finger had orphaned them, I gather. Anyway, that gave Diamond and Jeff a lot of cubs to work with, and I think all three females got pregnant. Diamond used to go up there a lot to watch them in their compound and see what difference it made being in captivity and that sort of thing. He spent a lot of time up there this past spring."

"Did you ever go up there and see the cubs?"

"No point. The cubs were strictly off limits to anyone but Diamond and Jeff. Guarding their turf, I guess. Diamond was like that. Fiercely protective of his research. Hated anyone ogling him."

"There's a locked folder on the disk Shannon gave me. Any idea of the password?"

"Locked folder? What's it called?' He rose to check it out on the computer, but then changed his mind and sat back, shifting himself closer to me so that his left thigh pressed against mine.

"Wild card." Somehow I managed to get the word out as my mind lingered on the warmth of his body.

"Doesn't mean anything to me," he said, smiling down at me. "Must be personal, but I'm afraid I can't help you. His passwords were always names — even his bank card number, he turned that into a name — said it was easier to remember. Anyone tell you you have beautiful eyes?"

God, now what do I do? I thought, startled by this sudden change of events. Seeing my confusion he stood up and offered me his hand. I hesitated a fraction of a second and then gave it to him. He pulled me up faster than both of us realized and I stumbled against him. I felt his other arm come around my waist to steady me and I wanted to melt into his arms in the worst way. I looked up into his eyes and got lost in their warmth. He didn't let go of me, but stared into my eyes.

"Who are you, Cordi O'Callaghan?" he asked in a soft voice, as he languidly traced a finger around my mouth. Footsteps sounded down the hall and he gently let go of me, and I screamed inside for what I had been sure I had seen in his eyes. He said, as if nothing had just passed between us, "Let's go see the film." I gathered my senses together and followed him out the door, marvelling at my composure. He led me down a maze of corridors and out into a courtyard. He took my arm then and we walked in silence, my thoughts in turmoil, until we came to a large three-storey old stone building, the only old building on the campus. We walked up the wide stairs, through the massive oak door, and down a long tiled corridor. The walls were warm wood panelling and the high ceilings soared over Patrick's lanky frame. He told me that it was an old courthouse that had been turned into the university's multimedia centre. We stopped at the main desk in a central foyer, and Patrick rang the piercing bell that stood on the desk. A big, burly dishevelled redhead appeared from an inner office.

"Kevin, buddy. Here's the lady that wanted to see the footage of the peace camp meetings — the ones that the students of 101 filmed where Diamond and the loggers nearly came to blows."

Patrick turned to me as Kevin left to retrieve the film and said, "I've got to get back. Are you around for dinner?" I don't know why I said no. It certainly wasn't what I wanted to say but out it came, and he just smiled and said, "Maybe another time then?" I mutely nodded and then he was gone. The ache in my mind that he had ignited grew stronger as I watched him disappear. Why had I said no?

What was I afraid of? Was I on the threshold of something good or something bad? I stood there in the hall twiddling my thumbs and thinking about him. I must have been mistaken about the look he gave me. It must have meant something else. He was really just being polite asking me to dinner. I tried to put him out of my mind. I didn't need this.

"Dr. O'Callaghan!"

I turned with a sinking heart and saw Eric Davies walking briskly toward me, his small frame and hair and red face bristling with purpose. I braced myself for the onslaught. He was at least ten feet away when he held out his hand and sailed in on me, saying, "I think I owe you an apology for my behaviour the other day."

Was this damage control, I wondered, and if so, why?

"It was inexcusable. I do get carried away when it comes to guarding the reputation of my department." He took me by the arm and said, "I hope you won't make any trouble for us here. You know our university doesn't need negative publicity. We don't want anything more in the papers."

I laughed, a meaningless, hollow, social response as I shook my head and he released my arm. "I'm just trying to find my disks, that's all." We stood for some moments in awkward silence.

"Patrick said you were going to look at the film of the information meeting about the logging. I was hoping to catch you before you see it."

"Well, you have. Kevin's just gone to get it," I said.

Davies let out a long, low laugh. "Diamond sure blew that one. The cardinal rule for environmentalists battling the opponent is never, ever lose your temper. Diamond paid for that."

"What do you mean?"

"He lost the chance to reason with these people, to show them that we are intelligent and are willing to work together for solutions. His tantrum — you'll see it in the film — led to the inevitable: the logging company pushing forward and Diamond responding with a barricade and court proceedings. Might have gone that way anyway but who knows?"

I nodded but said nothing.

"And he's made a royal muck-up for the reputation of this university. Just my luck to get a brilliant troublemaker like Diamond. He did good research but he brought a lot of bad press around here with all his harebrained ideas and causes, and I got some of the blame. I could have killed the man but the bear beat me to it. It's always better to solve problems in a rational, reasoned way, and not go off the deep end."

I marvelled at the dichotomy inherent in his last two sentences and the fact that he didn't seem to see it. "Is that what happened between Leslie and Diamond?"

Davies narrowed his eyes and peered at me.

"What are you getting at?"

"I understand Leslie was in competition with Diamond for tenure since they first arrived. Now that Diamond's gone I gather she's a shoe-in to get tenure."

"He was the better man. Oh sure, their qualifications were about the same, but Diamond struck me as a better researcher and he can't get pregnant. Leslie, of course, should have had tenure a long time ago. She was very bitter and took it out on Diamond. She's very good but we have a small budget and not enough tenured positions, so Leslie lost, until now, of course."

"You're not worried she'll get pregnant now?" I asked.

He didn't seem to notice the sarcasm dripping off my voice.

"Oh well, now that we don't have Diamond, we can handle it if it happens, you know?"

"No, I don't know," I said, and then, wanting to avoid controversy, I added, "It couldn't have been pleasant working with them."

"It was a pain in the ass, quite frankly. They had a hell of a row about a month before Diamond died. Leslie was getting more and more bitter about tenure, and we couldn't offer her anything. We suggested she look elsewhere, of course, though we hated to lose her. But everything's tight and there was nothing out there for her that she wanted. Then Diamond was secretly offered a job in government — increased salary and security. Somehow Leslie found out and tried to persuade him to take it but he'd already refused it. Said he liked small-town life."

"Why didn't Leslie apply for the job?"

"That was the source of her anger. She didn't hear about it until it was too late. It was a little bit under the table, I think. They invited him to apply with all the other public servants, guaranteeing him the job. It wasn't well-advertised, and Diamond apparently wasn't about to tell anyone. A bit selfish, I thought, but then he was a selfish man. Anyway, she was livid and he just laughed at her. He really was an asshole where Leslie was concerned, pardon my language. They were lovers once, until he dumped her. But what's all this got to do with your disks?"

"I don't know really," I said. "I guess I'm just fishing."

At that moment Kevin-buddy returned and Davies took off.

Kevin held out the two films and looked at me as though I was naked. Why did some men do that? If my lecherous thoughts about Patrick could be read as easily I would be mortified. But some guys seemed to thrive on it.

"You a tree hugger?"

"Depends on where the tree is," I said.

"All right. A witty lady. I can give you a room for a couple of hours but I'll have to kick you out at two o'clock. I have a whole slew of kids coming in then to edit their assignments."

He showed me into a tiny viewing area and made sure he brushed up against me in the small space as he handed me the tape. I moved away from him and looked for the button to open the machine so that I could put the tape in.

"It's not edited or anything so there's lots of garbage. If you want I'll stay and help. It can be complicated, this machinery." His leer was wide enough for a ten-ton truck to drive through.

I gave him my best ice-cold glance, which probably wasn't very cold or icy because I hate hurting people. Gets me into a lot of trouble, but there it is.

"Isn't this just a standard machine with pause, play, and stop buttons?"

"Uh well, yeah, I guess it is."

"Then I can manage it myself, thanks." I turned my back on him and I heard the door shut quietly behind me. God, I hated sounding bitchy, but how else was I supposed to get rid of a guy like that without kicking him in the nuts?

chapter fifteen

The machine whizzed and whirred and then a large room, like a school gym or auditorium the size of a hockey rink, jumped into view. The camera panned the room slowly. The lighting was soft and dim, but there was no way of knowing if it was day or night as there weren't any windows in the whole of that gigantic room. The off-white ceilings were very low, giving the impression that this was a basement room. On the stuccoed ceiling some tattered white gauze streamers hung languidly over strings of fairy lights not turned on, presumably leftovers from some previous party.

There were groups of people moving about looking at what appeared to be displays at the back of the room. Someone had arranged hundreds of regulation school-type chairs in neat rows down the length of the room. There was an aisle down the middle and a lectern and seating for eight at the front table. The film picked up the muffled footsteps and the shuffling, laughing, and coughing of fifty people, but the size of the room deadened the sound. The organizers had obviously expected a much bigger crowd.

Most of the first thirty minutes was taken up by speeches from foresters and loggers giving background information and regulations. It was obvious that the timber licence had already been granted and this was purely a public relations effort to sway dissenters to their side.

The audience was unusually passive, and I was beginning to think Kevin-buddy had given me the wrong film when the meeting was suddenly opened to the floor for questioning. It looked as though no one was going to ask anything, but then someone rose to ask the first question.

I was surprised to see the camera swing over to Don Allenby in the front row clearing his throat. His thin voice squeezed around the auditorium like a lost waif, but for all that it was steady and clear, if vaguely apologetic.

"I have a question for the forester, Ray De Roach."

A tall, thin, mustachioed fellow on the stage nodded his head and said, "It's Raymond Desrochers."

"Pardon me. Mr. Desrochers. You're a biologist and a lumber company employee. You advise the lumber company on forestry issues. Surely, you can understand that the lumber industry has never shown much leadership in doing what's right. We all know it took decades to get them to even replant after they clear-cut, and then it took decades to convince them that clear-cutting was causing havoc by eroding the rivers and mountains and creating moonscapes where trees would never grow again. I mean no offence, but can you tell me why we should trust the lumber industry to do the right thing when they don't even know what the right thing is?"

There was a murmur of voices and some applause

as Don sat back in his chair and wiped his forehead with a big handkerchief, looking relieved at having gotten his question out. The camera swung over to Raymond Desrochers, who rose from his chair and walked over to the podium.

He took a long time adjusting the mike, fiddling with its height so that he didn't have to stoop over it.

"There have been mistakes made in the past. We can't ignore that. The lumber industry, like all of us, is not perfect, but we're helping them remedy the situation by improving forestry techniques."

"By logging what little there is left?" The voice was deep, low, and rumbling with menace. The camera swung over to a man I recognized as Diamond from his pictures. He was sitting in the first row.

"Some remedy," he growled.

Desrochers cleared his voice and responded in a calm, quiet voice.

"We don't go in and clear-cut any more, if that's what you're saying. We are practising sustainable development now. Razing the area is not environmentally sound. We've discovered that. We admit we were wrong. So we don't clear-cut any more. We cut selectively and we replant when we're through. We leave buffer zones around the water. We leave any trees that hawks and other endangered species might be nesting in. We leave them standing with a buffer zone around them and we don't cut down trees near bear dens and habitats like that."

When Diamond didn't respond Desrochers continued.

"Loggers are people too, they care about the wildlife the same as you do."

The film panned to the loggers, who began to whistle and clap.

"I've been really impressed with how they phone up

and tell me they've got an eagle's nest, or ask us to come out and help them with a bear den. These guys care, not just about their jobs, but about the animals too."

There was more applause from the left side, and the forester turned back to his chair as the applause died down. Into the ensuing quiet, clear and strong, Diamond said, "How can you claim to be a forester and advocate this baloney? I'm ashamed to admit you and I went through biology together before you sold out." The camera swung jerkily over to Diamond, who pushed back his chair and stood up, the scraping of metal against the floor sounding ominous in the sudden quiet of the auditorium.

"Sustainable development, bullshit," he said, spitting out the words. "You've twisted the concept to mean anything goes as long as everyone gets a chunk of the pie. Oh sure, you leave trees around the hawk nest, but those trees are vulnerable to wind. Ever heard of the 'edge effect,' or were you asleep during that lecture? I can jog your memory. It's the little problem where wind screaming in from over the clear-cut areas hits the edge of your buffer and knocks the trees down. And you make it sound as though all loggers spend their days and nights nursing abandoned fawns and baby eaglets. That's bullshit and you know it. Once in a blue moon, maybe. There's a far sight more loggers out there who swerve in their big bulldozers, not to avoid the hawk's nest or the bear's den, but to flatten them.

"And what about the trees themselves? All you see in these trees are dollar bills, but what about their value as trees and as habitat for all those animals? For God's sake, Ray, we're losing maybe two hundred and fifty acres of trees every frigging hour in this country. Our wilderness is shrinking faster than plastic in fire, and you're willing to leave a couple of trees for the hawks?

Well bravo! What a thoughtful man."

I could see Shannon lean over and try to pull Diamond back into this seat. She was whispering furiously, but Diamond shook her off and glared at Desrochers.

When the camera panned back to Desrochers his face had flushed a lively red colour and he gripped both hands around the mike, knuckles white. His voice was low and even when he spoke, but he recited his words as though they were a set speech.

"I don't want to get into another fight here, Diamond. It doesn't get us anywhere. All I can say is we are practising good forestry techniques now and the animals and trees will benefit from that. We'll keep erosion down and manage the fish and other wildlife like that. You know as much as anyone that when we cut down the trees, new growth moves in and the forest regenerates. It's healthy, and the moose and deer and lots of other plants and animals thrive on it."

Diamond leapt to his feet again.

"Why the hell do we need to manage the forest and the animals? They've managed on their own quite well for millions of years. Isn't it rather presumptuous of us to say we can do that? It's like asking us to manage our own circulatory system. It can't be done without irreparable damage. Why the hell can't you leave them alone to manage themselves?"

"As I said before, the forest has to be managed. Old trees need to be cut before they die or cause massive forest fires that destroy valuable timber and kill wildlife."

"You dirty, rotten quisling. You sold out to your own profession, Ray. You know that? Why the hell did you do it? How much are they paying you? Trees need to be cut before they die. Hallelujah. Euthanasia. Killing the trees for their own good. A really dignified death.

Don't let them suffer or cause others to suffer. Don't be such a coward, Ray. Say what you mean. You've got to cut down the old tree before it falls and rots and becomes worthless."

Ray moved closer to Diamond, anger suffusing his face. The hate between the two men was palpable, even in the film.

"You bastard. You call me a quisling after what you did to me? You got it. If the tree's going to die anyway, or choke the life out of trees around it, then why the hell shouldn't we take it? We're not talking human lives here. This isn't a debate on euthanasia. We're doing the forest a good service by renewing it and making a buck as well. What the hell's wrong with that?"

"Damn fuckin' right," came a call from the left side of the auditorium. The camera swung around and focused on a big behemoth of a logger. *Cameron*, I thought.

Cameron had leapt to his feet and was waving his arms around as he said, "I've been a logger a long time and I've walked through old growth forest, and you know what? They're just a bunch of big tall trees that cut the sun out. There's nothing growing there, nothing living, and it's been a bloody grave for a hundred years. What'll happen to it if we leave it another hundred years? You got it. The bloody trees will die and fall down and rot and that is a bloody sacrilege. It's a frigging useless forest until we cut it."

"Jesus, are you really that stupid?" The camera caught Diamond's eyes glinting in the light as he shifted his attention to the logger. Shannon tugged on his arm again, but Diamond ignored her. It was like a barroom brawl. Diamond was looking for a fight. Cameron's face turned crimson with anger.

"Who you calling stupid?" Cameron took a deep breath as though trying to control his rising anger. "We let the forest go along on its own and we waste it. You hear? Now that's stupid. It's like letting a field of corn go to seed. All that energy that went into making it wasted, if we don't harvest at the right time."

"Attaboy, Cameron. You tell the bastard."

Cameron turned and looked at his colleagues. Encouraged by their support, he turned his back on Diamond, raised his arms, and addressed them.

"We loggers like to think of the areas we log as one big happy family farm, and that's how we should run it, like a farm. Old growth is like an old cow. Farmers get rid of old cows that can't produce milk anymore. If he kept all his old cows he'd have no milk. You have to keep regenerating, and that means cutting."

"All right," someone yelled and the men and women around Cameron applauded and whistled.

"The problem is," yelled Diamond above the din, "it's like selling rubies for a song. You're selling out your grandkids' future for a lousy buck. You just want to keep your own bloody job and to hell with the real cost to the country."

"Damn right I do," yelled Cameron as he faced Diamond. "And you're telling me you're not trying to do the same? I know all about you, Doctor Jake Diamond," he said with a sneer. "We loggers aren't as dumb as every- one tries to paint us. We log the area and you lose your goddamned study site. All that work, poof, gone up in smoke, and maybe you lose tenure too, eh? Who gives a good goddamn about your fuckin' study animals when hundreds of jobs are at stake here?"

Cameron paused as applause broke out and whis- tles and stamping of feet filled the room.

Diamond clenched his fists and glared at Cameron. In a voice barely above a whisper he hissed, "Do you really think this is an issue about a couple of moose, a few lynx, and a bunch of jobs? This is about the survival of the planet, survival of the plants that nourish it, and the animals that give it diversity. This is about the survival of the natural world that has given us cures for countless diseases, fed and clothed us, and now, by our own hand, we could be losing species to extinction at the rate of several a day. Who are we to say we are not destroying, even as I speak, that very plant or animal that holds the secret which would unlock the cure for cancer? So yeah, I'm not above using animals to stop the logging. If we had here in these woods a rare species like the spotted owls of the west coast that stopped all logging instantly there, I'd stop at nothing to tell the world."

The camera panned over to a short stocky man who stood up.

"You tell him Donaldson," someone yelled at him.

"I run the Donaldson Mill, the one that's for sale, and I can't find a damn buyer because of your shenanigans. Thank God we don't have spotted owls around here, is all I can say. This area was built on logging, and we have a good number of mills in the area and hundreds upon hundreds of people are employed in the lumber industry here. That represents big dollars."

He turned and looked at the audience.

"This tract of land will keep my mill and the other mills in the area busy for five years. Without it, some of the mills will have to close, including mine. I'll have to lay off my workers and sell the mill for peanuts. I'm getting old and I was counting on the mill as my pension, so was my partner. Logging this hunk of crown land brings much-needed jobs to the area."

"And five years from now they'll all be gone," came a voice off-camera.

"I'm not talking about five years from now. I need trees to make my mill go now. If I don't get trees my job's mud. I'll never sell the mill and I'll have to go on welfare. I'm too old to start a new career," Donaldson said.

"Let me tell you something else, Diamond," yelled Cameron. "We got families to think of. You got no right coming here and telling us the land gotta be left as it is, left nice and beautiful for its own sake. Bullshit. Nice and beautiful doesn't put a meal on the table, doesn't clothe our kids. Jesus. Put yourself in our shoes, man. We don't have the luxury of philosophizing about wilderness values and future generations."

"Can't you see?" Diamond's voice was low, almost pleading. I felt sorry for him. "Five years down the line the trees will be gone, kaput, pulped, so you're only delaying the inevitable by five years, but you'll be destroying a forest of untold worth. It all comes down to jobs versus the environment. Do we blithely cut down all the trees? Or do we take a stand now and give future generations a kick at the can? I understand your fears of losing your jobs, but it's a matter of face it now and save the forest, or face it later and lose everything. Your kids won't have a thing to show for it. Trust me, the government won't leave you high and dry."

"Like hell they won't," snarled Cameron, raising his middle finger at Diamond.

Diamond's anger sputtered to life again.

"You don't give a shit about the future, about your kids' future, our kids' future. Cut and run. Make a fucking buck and to hell with everyone else. You have no long-term vision. We have to stop you. If we don't, there'll be nothing left a generation from now and every buck you've made from this devastation will be gone, with nothing to show for it but greed. I've had enough of being diplomatic, trying to see both sides. To hell with you."

"What do you mean?" snorted Cameron. "They'll have had five years of food and shelter and an employed father. You're asking me to look long-term and sacrifice for the long-term benefit of others. What the hell do you expect us to do? Quit and go on pogey so we can take nice peaceful walks in the forest we decided not to log? You can't tell me that if you were in my shoes you wouldn't do the same thing, you hypocritical bastard."

Pandemonium broke loose as loggers and environmentalists cheered on their man. Cameron suddenly lunged at Diamond and ripped the chain with the tooth pendant from around his neck. Shannon tried to hold Diamond back and Desrochers made a half-hearted attempt to rein in Cameron but it was no use. Diamond swung at Cameron and missed, but Cameron didn't. A loud sickening smack rang out and Diamond dropped like a stone. The camera panned the audience. I saw Leslie stoop and pick up Diamond's chain to give back to him. Donaldson and Desrochers were grinning from ear to ear. The loggers were cheering, fit to be tied. Cameron towered over Diamond and sneered. Diamond slowly rose on his hands and knees and stared at Cameron. It was deathly quiet.

The camera zoomed in and suddenly Jake Diamond's face took up the whole screen.

"You're a bunch of fucking ignorant bastards," said Diamond as he wiped the blood from his nose. His eyes glinted. In a soft, menacing voice he said, "You'll never log that area. You've left us no alternative but to fight dirty. I'll make sure of that if it's the last thing I do."

He turned his burning stare straight at Cameron, and I could almost feel his eyes boring into my skull from beyond the dead. It was an eerie feeling. A man once both alive and vibrant was no longer either. Abruptly Diamond turned his head away from the camera, but not before Cameron yelled back, "It might just be the last thing you do, asshole."

chapter sixteen

It took a little while to adjust to the brilliant sunshine, and I was deep in thought as I walked back to my car. It was late afternoon and I was trying to decide where to park myself until my 8:00 p.m. appointment with Don, trying to forget that I could have been having dinner with Patrick.

As I was heading toward my car a smart little sports car turned in and Leslie jumped out.

"Any luck with your disks?" she called out.

"Not yet," I said as she walked over to me.

"Is that why you're here? I must say, I didn't expect to see you again. Or are you here to lecture?" The innuendo was there, I could feel it, but the smile on her face seemed genuine.

"I wanted more information on the logging north of Dumoine. Patrick Whyte said he could get me the film of the info meeting. I came up to take a look at that."

"What a zoo that was," she said. "Don't know what good it'll do you, but it sure is entertaining, if you like controversy that is."

"I've just taken a good look at it. There were a lot of angry people in that room that night."

"Yeah," said Leslie with a half-smile. "You can say that again." She started turning away, "You going inside?"

I wasn't, of course, but I nodded, and the two of us began to walk back the way I had just come.

"I didn't notice Patrick Whyte there," I said, as nonchalantly as I could. "I thought that was odd. Was he sick?"

"Patrick? No. He just isn't interested in the logging up there. He's a gung-ho environmentalist, but he opted out of this one. Don't know why. You'll just have to ask him." Again, the little dig was there, not in the words themselves but in how she said them.

"I noticed you didn't take part in any of the discussions."

"What's that supposed to mean?" she said, turning to look at me.

"Just that you seem to be in a delicate position. You're studying moose, and logging makes great moose habitat. Maybe you stood to gain something if the area was logged."

She stopped suddenly and stared at me.

"Are you kidding?"

We reached the double doors of the building in icy silence, and Leslie hauled one open.

I hesitated, then said, "Davies tells me you and Diamond once had a relationship."

She stared at me, cold as a glacier stream, her mouth tight and narrow. Suddenly she smiled. "Boy, you are nosey, aren't you? So's Davies. Yeah, we were lovers once. And he was a royal asshole when it came to women."

There was a hardness to her voice, and something flashed into her eyes that made me feel uneasy.

"What do you mean?"

"He used women, although to be fair I don't think he knew he did, but he did. He'd gobble them up, chew them to pieces, and then spit them out."

The bitterness leaked through her smile like overflowing bathwater seeping through a ceiling.

"Is that what happened to you?"

"I don't know what you're trying to get at. I don't mean to be rude, but it's really none of your business." She scowled. "We were lovers once, okay? We fell out of love. It was no big secret. He's dead now and so what does it matter what we were to each other?"

"You got his job."

"Sure, I got his job. I should have had it years ago, but that doesn't mean I wished him dead. Anything else?"

"Actually, yes. What would Diamond have done with film he took on his trip?"

"He'd bring the roll back here to be developed, but obviously he wouldn't have had a chance on this last trip."

"Has anything showed up here?"

"I wouldn't know. You'll have to ask Patrick. Why are you so interested, anyway?"

"There was no film found among Diamond's belongings — not even any unexposed film. It just seems odd, that's all."

"Sorry, can't help."

We parted company and on impulse I stopped in at the library, found a pay phone, and put in a call to Duncan. I waited for what seemed like an age before his booming voice blasted my ear.

"What can I do for you, girl?"

I filled him in on what I'd accomplished over the two days since I had talked to him last.

"Interesting, my girl, but no evidence to warrant reopening this case." He paused and then asked, "Have you got a theory?"

"Sort of," I said. "He could easily have been taking sleeping pills without his girlfriend knowing. He was the sort of macho man who wouldn't want to admit to any weakness. But she also said he'd never take sardines into the bush because they're too smelly and attractive to bears."

"Do you believe her?"

"Yeah, I do. He knew the bush well. It would have been dumb. As for the sleeping pills, I don't know of anyone who has to take a sleeping pill in the wild. He'd been out there three weeks. He must have been in great shape, working hard all day in the sun, working up an appetite and then sleeping like a baby. No need of sleeping pills. And the weather was beautiful until late on the night he died — hot and humid and sunny. Easy to go swimming, even after the sun was down, and easy to dump any soiled clothes in the water to clean out the oil, but he didn't. She's probably right, although you could argue that he got too tired and simply fell asleep before changing. But it would be like a bloody beacon sending out an invitation to the bear for supper."

"You do see the complicated in life, don't you, Cordi? Diamond probably had someone else with him who had brought sardines and it all happened so fast that Diamond couldn't get rid of them before the bear attacked."

In one blinding flash I saw it. Why hadn't I seen it long before this?

"Or maybe there's another reason," I said excitedly.

"Maybe, just maybe, someone spiked his water and then planted the sardine oil on his pants."

"What?" Duncan's voice shook down the line like a jackhammer hitting metal.

"Put it in his water flask."

"Put what?"

"Sleeping pills."

"Hang on there, girl. You're getting carried away. Even supposing someone did, he'd be sure to taste it," protested Duncan.

My mind was racing, some of the pieces starting to fall into place. I thought back to his mess tent and the iodine tablets I'd seen.

"Not if he was using iodine tablets to purify his water. They'd mask the flavour of anything. What if the oil was spilled later, when he was sleeping?"

"My dear girl!"

"No, it's not as crazy as it seems. I was talking to Don Allenby. He was very evasive, but he said something about sardines, and then he said something like, 'Why would I bait him?' At first I thought he meant 'bait' as in 'taunt,' but I'm not so sure now. How did he know about the sardines? It wasn't public knowledge, was it?"

"No. It was never considered important enough to be reported as anything but fish oil. The public was given reassurance that the fish attracted the bear and if they're just careful in the woods, it won't happen to them."

"Don was scared, Duncan. His comment made me think someone could have deliberately used Diamond as bait. The sort of thing bear hunters do in the spring. They set out bait in the bear's known haunts and then they sit behind a blind and wait."

"You're talking murder, girl," he said, and when I didn't respond he said more forcefully, "You're talking gibberish, Cordi. Even if what you say is true, how would they ever be sure the bear would be there? You've got to admit that it's a very unpredictable murder weapon to choose."

"I don't know, Duncan. I haven't yet worked that part out."

Duncan was silent. I wanted desperately for him to agree with me, or at least to think my theory was possible.

"Don used the word *murder* before shutting up. But there's no way I can prove it even if it were true and I found out who was responsible. It makes the fumigating of my larvae and the stealing of my disks make a lot more sense, though. Whoever did it wanted Diamond out of the way but for some reason didn't want his body found where he died, most likely because it would incriminate whoever it is. That could be just about anybody, but my bet's on Don. He has the strongest motive of all: his child's welfare."

"And he knew about the sardines, a fact I never released publicly. You be careful, girl. I'd hate to lose you now that I've found me a forensic entomologist."

I pulled the receiver away from my ear and looked at it. "I beg your pardon?"

"I've decided you should become Dumoine's first forensic entomologist, girl, on a consulting basis whenever we need you. You have most of the criteria, and it wouldn't take you long to get the hang of it. We'd just need you to help pinpoint time of death and stuff. You see, there is a dearth of qualified people willing to do this work. I know I'm being a little presumptuous, and you don't have to say a thing right now. Just think about it and we can talk later."

He was being unbelievably presumptuous, but before I could say anything there was a loud clanging juddering noise over the lines and I jerked the receiver away. Through the noise I could barely hear Duncan's voice:

"Gotta go! They're drilling holes for a new fancy-dancy telephone line. Think about it." And the line went dead.

Since I was still in the building I wandered back to Diamond's lab, hoping Patrick would still be there so I could ask him some more questions. Transparent reason, but better than none. The door to the lab was open, and I hesitated before I knocked and walked in. I heard a quick breath, a rustle, and a book or something falling.

"What are you doing here?"

"I might ask the same of you," I said as Lianna moved out from behind a bookcase and stared at me. She said nothing at all, and the silence became uncomfortable. I folded first.

"I was looking for Whyte. Thought he could tell me more about Diamond's role in the logging issue. Maybe you can help me."

Lianna still hadn't blinked, still stared at me with her carefully made-up eyes, and it unnerved me.

"You were there. I saw you on the film. Sitting with the loggers. Isn't that an odd thing to do? Supporting the loggers when your husband was so against them?"

"Look, lady. I'm my own woman. Just because I was married to the guy doesn't mean I have to agree with everything he did. In fact, I actively disagreed with most of his ideas. I own a cottage up in the area. There's no road access, no hydro, but it's a beautiful spot. I'd love to get a road in there. I hate rustic living, but I love the country. Go figure. The loggers claimed they would put in a road. Besides, it annoyed Jake to see me there and that made me feel good."

"You hated him that much?"

"Hate isn't the word. I resented him. I resented all that he did to me. I resented his work. It took me away from me, and even when it didn't he'd bring his damn work home."

"Is that why you left him?"

She looked at me, tilting her head to one side, and I thought she wouldn't answer, but instead she spat out, "Yes, that and his continuous string of mistresses. He paid more attention to them and to his goddamned study animals than he ever did to me. He started bringing his bloody cats home six years ago. The first one was a little three-month-old cub. It was pretty cute and it didn't stay long, but then there were more and most of them needed to be bottle fed at all hours of the day and night. They'd mew and puke and pee and the house smelled awful all the time. I couldn't bring anybody home it was so bad. We couldn't even make love when the damn things were around. If they mewed he'd be gone in a flash."

She looked at me defensively as if wanting my support. I nodded in sympathy, not because her life had been invaded by cats but because of the string of mistresses. Even if I didn't like her I could feel sorry for the pain he had caused her and the hatred that had resulted from it.

"The last straw," she said, "were two ugly, naked cubs, so young their eyes weren't even open. He and Jeff had brought them in one night a few years ago after returning from New Brunswick to pick up some sperm for Jeff's artificial insemination project. You know about Jeff?"

I nodded and she continued.

"They only stayed a night, I made sure of that. I threw them all out the next day. I guess he went up to Jeff's, but we didn't talk to each other much after that. It was over even then, you see. I just hadn't wanted to admit it. But then that little bitch Shannon appeared and I couldn't take the humiliation anymore. I'd given him so many chances. I threw his stuff out in the yard six months ago, changed the locks on the door, and filed for divorce."

"Why did you lie about the little black book?"

She looked at me and smiled. "So you've been talking to Shannon, have you? I wondered how long before you'd find out from the bitch. You suspected right from the start that I was lying, didn't you? I know that now, but I thought my act had convinced you."

When I didn't answer she continued.

"If I'd told you I was looking for something that belonged to Diamond, as his bitter ex-wife, what would have been my chances that I would have got a straight answer from you?"

"But how did you know Diamond had written his will in it?" I said, evading the question.

"My lawyer told me Shannon was claiming there was another will. She's not very bright, you know. She told my lawyer it was in Diamond's diary. But she couldn't come up with it, so I knew she didn't have it. I hoped the police did. I figured he owed me and that the bitch didn't deserve a thing."

"Didn't you get anything in the divorce settlement?"

She laughed again, a sad, sorry little laugh.

"Oh sure, but not my fair share, never my fair share. I'm just lucky he forgot to change his will in time. I deserve to get something out of his death. I got nothing out of his life."

chapter seventeen

I had a lot of time to kill before my meeting with Don so I cruised around Dumoine looking for a park to walk around in and then I went hunting for a nice little restaurant. I settled for a little cafe that had only one waitress for eight tables — and they were all full. My nose was so plugged up that the food was tasteless, and I regretted that I hadn't gone to buy some antihistamine. I didn't get away from the restaurant until 7:45 and I was afraid I'd be late for my appointment with Don. It took me a while to find his house, and it was just past 8:00 when I finally pulled the car up in front of it. The house was a small, rundown two-storey affair squished between its neighbours and sporting a postage stamp–sized front lawn. There was no car in the skinny driveway and the garage door was tightly closed.

I parked the car on the street, collected my box of Kleenex, and walked up the front walk. The lawn was neatly cut, but there were no flowers at all. The screen door was a marmalade colour and the bilious green paint of the inner door looked like some terminal disease. There was a sheet of paper taped to the door. I opened the screen and looked at it:

> Sorry I'm not here. Come on in and make yourself at home. I'll be back at 8:30 or so. Please don't leave. Beer in the fridge. Sorry. Don.

Feeling like an intruder I cautiously opened the front door and called out, just in case he was back and had forgotten to retrieve the note. But there was no response, so I went inside and closed the front door behind me. I found myself in a tiny foyer crammed with a neat row of boots below an equally neat row of old jackets, each on its own peg, totally at odds with the outside of the house.

I moved into what appeared to be a living room, tables neatly stacked with magazines, nothing out of place, and the curtains drawn even though it was still light outside. The house was stuffy and incredibly hot, not a single window open and no air conditioning. I wondered how Don could stand it. I was sweating already and I'd been inside for only thirty seconds.

A large oil painting of a hare took prime spot above the mantelpiece that framed a bricked-in fireplace. There were two pictures on the mantel. One was a family photo of Don and his wife and their little girl, who looked to be about four years old in the picture. She had blonde hair like her mother's and dimples, but her eyes were deep brown like her father's, whose hand rested proudly on her tiny shoulder. Don was looking down at his daughter with such an expression of raw love that I was momentarily dragged into his tragedy, until I forced myself to turn and look at the other picture.

There was very little left of the four-year-old in the scarred face and vacant eyes of the girl securely strapped into the wheelchair. I looked at the picture, wondering about the depth of the pain and guilt to which Don's little girl had taken him. Had it poisoned his mind and dragged him down into desperation in his need to provide some sort of life for her? Had it driven him so far as to turn him into a cheat? Had it perhaps driven him even further than that? Had he been involved in some way with Diamond's death to prevent the fraud from becoming public — from ruining his life and destroying his ability to care for his little girl?

I continued on through the living room to the kitchen, which was immaculately clean, from the gas stove, with two brightly coloured pots sitting on the front burners, to the tiny refrigerator. No microwave, no dishwasher, no frills here, and the dishes were mismatched. There was a sort of hissing sound, coming from the basement near the stove, and the fridge's motor suddenly leapt to life and made me jump.

A door led out of the kitchen into a back room, which Don had turned into a study of sorts. Unlike the other rooms this room was messy, as if someone had been in a great hurry and been interrupted or something. I put my Kleenex box down on the desk and glanced over the papers, but there was nothing there except some unpaid bills. One was huge — a third and final notice for $20,000.00 from a private nursing home.

I put it down, feeling suddenly dizzy, and gripped the chair back, my stomach heaving. The wave of nausea passed, but my head was feeling heavy and achy. I thought about what I had eaten at the restaurant and wondered about food poisoning. At least I knew I couldn't be pregnant. It had been months since I'd left Luke. I hoped Don would come soon. If I was getting sick I wanted to get home and be sick in private. I went back to the living room, not wanting him to surprise me in his private study. A car door slammed and I jumped. Guess my nerves were on edge along with my queasy stomach.

I moved to the window in the living room and parted the curtains to see if it was Don. But it was an old man carrying some parcels up his path. Another wave of nausea slammed into me and I grabbed hold of the curtains to support myself. As I did something tumbled out from the curtain box above my head and fell to the floor.

When the nausea passed I stooped to pick it up — a small black book with a bright orange slash — Diamond's diary. So Don had the black book! How had he got hold of it? I remembered the day I had met him. So concerned that the body was Diamond's. It had been Don who had insisted Ryan and I could leave and that he would lead the police to the scene. Could he have found a chance to pocket the diary before the police searched the tent? Maybe there was something in the diary to implicate Don in the fake data?

I was sweating now and feeling very weak, so I sat down in a chair and flipped through the diary. No will, but then several pages had been torn out, and in the centre was a folded letter from Diamond.

> Don:
> Unless you can come up with a damn good explanation I have no choice but to fail Roberta at her defence next month, unless you postpone it until we've sorted this out. I have no way of knowing whether Roberta was involved in what appears to be wholesale data faking or

not. You can understand my refusal to
pass a student without knowing the
truth. I have also put the publication of
our joint paper on hold until this is all
settled to my satisfaction.

Jake

So Roberta was involved too? Diamond's death
had certainly made things easier for her and for Don.
Maybe they had conspired together in some way that
had led to Diamond's death, either premeditated or
accidental. Maybe Don had gone up to reason with
Diamond and had failed. The bear had appeared and
he'd taken advantage of that. It was obvious Don
couldn't afford to lose tenure. He was barely scraping
by as it was, and it looked from the unpaid bills as if
he would have to find another, much cheaper, place for
his daughter. I wondered what that would do to him. I
suddenly felt tremendously uneasy as another wave of
nausea gripped me.

The words on the page in front of me began to blur
and jump, and I thought for a moment that it had been
smudged when it was printed, until I shifted my gaze
and realized everything was looking blurred. My head
was pounding and I felt weak and dizzy. I felt an overwhelming urge to lie down and sleep.

I stumbled through to the front door, knocking over
the vase on the hall table on my way, my head growing
more fuzzy and woolly and my heart pounding so that I
thought someone was knocking on the front door even
as I tried to fill my lungs. Too late I remembered the
humming sound coming from near the stove. I needed
air. The door was just inches from me, and I watched in
quiet desperation as my hand reached out for it just as
my mind swirled into darkness.

"My dear Cordi. You're just lucky to be leaving this place vertically instead of horizontally."

Martha was perched on the windowsill of my hospital room, right by a huge bouquet of daisies — there being no chair big enough for her. Ryan was trying to stuff my oversized dressing gown into a tiny overnight bag.

"You were damn lucky, Cordi," agreed Ryan. "The place was thick with carbon monoxide fumes. If Roberta hadn't needed to pick up some papers from Don and dropped by when she did ..." his voice trailed off.

"You'd be fodder for my med students, dear girl." I looked toward the door, where Duncan stood framed. "The lethal effects of CO poisoning on the human body. Great topic. Aren't you going to ask the old codger in and introduce us all?" Duncan slid his eyes over Martha and Ryan and winked at me as their faces went through the usual contortions on being faced with a nose the likes of Duncan's.

Ryan gripped his hand, muttered some inanity, and looked at Duncan's left shoulder, but Martha, whose face had raced through surprise and astonishment to sheer delight, chortled with glee, "Goodness gracious, man, what a nose you have."

Duncan's smile turned into a huge grin, as he strode over and gripped her pudgy hand in his own two massive ones. "Music to my ears, my dear woman. Most people tend to look at my left shoulder and pretend my nose isn't there, while their minds are thinking about nothing else."

He turned his twinkling eyes on Ryan and raised his eyebrows.

"This nose was a gift from my dear dead parents."

He released Martha's hand, having held it for slightly longer than necessary, and strode over to the chair by my bed.

"How did you know I was here?"

"I have admitting privileges at this hospital and saw your chart lying at the nursing station this morning. Figured there couldn't be more than one Cordi O'Callaghan, so I called the cop who brought you in, before coming to visit. They told her, as you know, that the gas stove in the kitchen was left on and malfunctioned." He looked at me and grimaced.

"I think you've stirred up some muck and it's beginning to swirl around you like a bloody tornado. No proof, of course, but it's not exactly easy to leave the gas on. The police version is that Don turned on a back burner to cook some stew, received a phone call that made him rush out of the house, writing you that note, which was scribbled and almost illegible, and then forgot the gas on. Not only, that but he accidentally turned on the wrong burner and then the burner malfunctioned and you wouldn't have noticed because carbon monoxide is odourless." With my hay fever I wouldn't have noticed a frightened skunk at five feet. But I did remember now the hissing sound that must have been coming from the kitchen, and not the basement, and the pot on the front burner. "And that's how I almost died?" Duncan nodded. "His neighbours told the police that Don had had a problem with it last week and had tried to get a repairman in. But they were fully booked and he'd vented his frustrations at them.

"His neighbours? Why didn't the police talk to Don?"

"Because he hasn't shown up, and I don't think he's going to," said Martha.

Everyone swivelled to look at Martha, who was twirling one of my daisies in her right hand. I wondered if she'd sneaked a peak at Patrick's card when she fished out the daisy. Roberta must have told him right away for the flowers to arrive so quickly.

"Why not?" I asked.

"Because he's pulled a bunk, as they say in the movies, hightailed it out of here, disappeared, because he couldn't face going to jail for what he's done."

"And what do you think he's done?" asked Duncan his lips twitching in amusement.

"He faked data and then when Diamond found out he somehow manoeuvred Diamond in front of that damn bear and while he didn't throw the killing blow he still murdered the man so that he wouldn't lose his job."

"Cordi's old baiting theory, huh?"

I looked at Duncan and said, "Did you know Don has a severely handicapped daughter who lives at a very expensive nursing home and he was having trouble paying the bills?"

"There. See? What did I tell you?" said Martha. "The poor man couldn't afford to lose his job or he'd have to move his poor kid to some horrible place. A parent's love of a child is a very powerful thing, you know — strong enough to kill for."

"And now he's just abandoned her forever?" asked Duncan dryly.

Martha fluffed up her hair and said straight and cool, "He's abandoned her and himself. I say he intended to kill himself but some fool phone call or something interrupted him and whatever it was, it was important enough for him to race out of the house with the gas left on. Cordi just got unlucky and was in the wrong place at the right time. He hasn't returned, and I'm telling you he won't, because he's dead. Killed himself out of remorse for his daughter, guilt over Diamond, and shame over the faked data. At least he didn't have to know that he almost killed you by accident, too." She nodded at me.

"But, Martha, if he was going to kill himself why would he then write a note and tack it on the door for me to find?" I asked.

"He wrote the note before the phone call. He'd already decided to kill himself before you came. He meant you to find his body."

I rolled my eyes to the ceiling, and she valiantly continued on.

"He lives alone, right? Maybe he was afraid no one would find his body for days. He was a fastidious man by your account. Everything neat and tidy and whatnot. A slowly rotting corpse wouldn't be to his liking."

"Really, Martha," protested Ryan.

"No, I'm serious," said Martha. "He writes the note at seven-thirty, pins it on his door, turns on the gas, which he must have known was malfunctioning, and then the phone rings or someone comes to the door or he remembers some last thing he needs to do, like make a will, and he has to put his plans for suicide on hold. But he forgets to turn off the gas because he's in such a hurry to leave."

"That's hogwash," said Duncan.

"Okay," said Martha, her eyes flashing. "How does this sound? He arranged to meet Cordi, then wrote the note to entice her in, having already turned on the gas before leaving. He gets rid of her and his problem is solved."

"But that's attempted murder," I said.

"It is, isn't it?" Martha said with a little shudder.

chapter eighteen

"Y ou think it's this Don guy?" asked Ryan when he and I had finally made it back to my place through a rainstorm. The fresh air of the farm was reviving my spirits, and I was coddling a drink in the hammock on my porch watching the lightning light up the fields in electric white. "He's not the only one with a good motive for getting rid of Diamond. They all seem to have one."

I fiddled with my drink. "Yeah, that's what I was thinking. For a popular man he was in dicey water with lots of people. Lianna stood to gain financially, so does Shannon if the handwritten will is found. Leslie got his job and by the sounds of it had fought long and hard and bitterly for it. Is she the type of person to be vindictive? I think so. Is she strong enough to murder? I think so. Is she likely to have murdered him? I don't know. Then there's Roberta. If she's guilty of faking data she stood to lose a lot. In this job climate that

would have been suicidal. Even Davies felt that
Diamond was the reason he might be passed over for
university president. As for all the loggers, Cameron,
Ray, the miller Donaldson — with Diamond out of the
way they have their jobs. Any one of them could have
done it."

"But that doesn't explain why someone tried to kill
you. Certainly lets Roberta off, doesn't it? After all, she
saved you. Unlikely that she would, if she was trying to
kill you."

"Unless she was trying to make us think that."

"So what are you going to do now?" My phone
began ringing through the open porch door, and I
glanced at Ryan. Neither of us made a move to answer
it, and the answering machine clicked on. We listened to
a low, sandpapery disembodied voice floating out to us,
cutting the air with its menace like the lightning that
streaked before us.

"Stay the hell out of it, O'Callaghan ... or next time
we'll succeed."

The click of the machine turning off was drowned
out by a roar of thunder and the beating of my heart.

"It's time I went up there to see for myself," I said early
the next day as I pored over the faculty's directive for
course material.

"Go where? See what?" asked Martha absently from
her position on her little milk stool as she filed papers. I
couldn't see the milk stool but I knew it was there,
strapped to Martha's rotund figure, because there was no
way Martha would be squatting in mid-air.

The milking stool had been Martha's idea. She'd
come out to the farm one Thanksgiving and watched
Mac putting the tubes on the "girls," as he liked to say.

He was wearing a milking stool, a round seat on a metal peg that strapped to the waist and looked like a miniature pogo stick stuck to his rear. Martha was so excited about it she made him take it off and show her how to use it. The belt had been way too small, but with Mac's help they later fashioned a custom-fitted one for Martha. She always wore it on the days she did her filing, moving from one cabinet to another and then squatting on her chair. Now she stood up and moved over to the next filing cabinet, her temporary tail waggling behind her.

"I've set up a meeting with the forester, that Raymond guy in the film. We know Diamond was killed in a cedar forest. Maybe I can find out where from him."

"Mmm?" Martha rested her bulk on the tiny stool and began filing.

"The forester said he could show me maps of the area with tree types and stuff. "

"Oh, Lord love me, Cordi. You weren't crazy enough to tell him you suspect Diamond was murdered, were you?"

"Of course not. I just told him about my disks and also said I was writing a paper on the logging issue and that I needed maps of the vegetation. He wasn't too keen until I said the paper was going to deal with pure economics to see which side should win, so I'd be looking at the types of trees and what they would fetch on the market. I'm going up to the logging camp this morning to meet him there."

Martha slowly swivelled on her chair, a shudder rippling through her face.

"You're going with someone, right?"

"No," I said, knowing what was coming and wondering with some amusement how Martha would resolve it.

"My dear Cordi. Surely you're not going alone? After what happened the other day?" Martha's eyebrows darted sky-high in disbelief and then plummeted precipitously toward her chin in alarm.

"Not on your life, Cordi. I'm not going to have your death on my conscience. This time I'm coming too." She glowered at me, daring me to object, and when I didn't she turned back to her filing, her whole body fairly jiggling with victory.

Half an hour later I manoeuvred my car out of the parking lot and we headed up to Dumoine, stopping off quickly at the farm for a backpack, some food, binoculars, and our Series 111 Land Rover.

"I got another good suspect for this 'maybe murder' theory of yours," said Martha as I turned right onto Highway 148. "Did you know Diamond was worth a bundle? More than $1.5 million?

Startled, I turned to look at Martha. Where did a biology professor earn money like that, I wondered.

"Eyes on the road, please. I can't stand it when you do that. It was in the paper two days ago."

"Why didn't I see it? I read the paper."

"The *Libelled Times*?"

"Oh really, Martha. You read that rag?" It was Ottawa's gossip paper and the first choice of dog trainers.

Martha fluffed out her hair and pouted.

"Really, Cordi, even gossip pieces are founded in truth. And at least they don't pretend they've got all their facts right. Besides, it was in the other papers but not with quite the detail. Anyway, apparently the will was read and Lianna gets it all, including the insurance policy. Shannon comes up empty-handed. That's why it was in the paper at all. Shannon was vowing to get what was her due, saying she would find the other will if it took forever. They had pictures of the two women looking like murder — you know, the human interest stuff they like. According to sources, Lianna laughed and said forever suited her just fine."

"Where did Diamond get that kind of money?"

No biology professor I ever knew earned anywhere near that amount even over fifteen years.

"He didn't. His father was some wealthy U.S. tycoon and left his sons a small fortune. Diamond was quite prudent with his investment and it grew nicely. He was independently wealthy. Nobody but his close family knew it, apparently."

"So what you're saying is that Lianna gets $1.5 million from him, and the life insurance policy makes it another million. Rather convenient for her that he up and died."

"Too convenient by half. My bet is she was somehow involved in his death. A real Jezebel, she is. Mark my words. A painted lady like that has no good up her sleeve." Martha's face glowered darkly.

"Oh, for heaven's sake, Martha. You're starting to sound like the *Libelled Times*. On the other hand, if the other will shows up, she's out of luck and Shannon comes into a small fortune."

"Right, but Lianna didn't know about the other will until after the dastardly deed was done," said Martha, relishing her words and rolling the Ds off her tongue like a professional bowler rolling a strike.

"Remember, Cordi? You said Lianna's lawyer contacted Shannon's trying to find the black book. Of course, if my theory is right then Lianna will be trying just as hard as Shannon to find that will."

"Whoa, Martha. The black book was found. I saw it at Don's. There was no will in it."

"So it was the wrong black book."

I told her about the torn out pages, and we speculated that someone already had the will.

"What about Shannon?" asked Martha suddenly. "She did know about the will, and Diamond had promised to put it in the safety deposit box. She could have gone up there intent on killing him, thinking the will was safe in the deposit box."

We fell into silence then, as we moved into rougher country.

The back roads were all washboard and bumpy, and Martha hung on to the Land Rover like a leech. The dust swirled up through the floorboards as we neared the turn off to the biology station and the portage trail into Diamond's site.

"Who's Patrick?" Even though I had known the question was coming ever since she'd taken the phone message from Patrick about the film, I wasn't prepared for it and stammered around for an answer, like a guilty kid caught red-handed.

"Ooooh. Lord love you, Cordi. You've fallen hard." Was there nothing I could hide from this woman?

When I tried to protest she just chuckled and asked me when she could meet him. Before I could answer I felt a strange vibration judder through the Land Rover, and I instinctively jerked it over to the right-hand side. As we came around the corner I watched in fascination as the monstrous snout of a tractor-trailer carrying a full load of logs came barrelling toward us, smack in the middle of the road. There wasn't room for both of us. I pumped the brakes and jerked the wheel frantically further to the right. I could see the driver's eyeglasses glinting in the sun, his mouth set in a scowl. The tractor-trailer swerved back to its side, its body groaning and wailing. A horrendous deep, continuous squealing scratched the air like nails on a board as the man at the wheel struggled to keep the truck on the road. It careened past us, missing us by centimetres, and roared out of sight.

I could feel the sweat standing out on my forehead and I gripped the wheel harder as I tried to control the shaking. I guided the Land Rover over to the edge of the road and stopped. I took a deep breath and looked over at Martha, who was frozen in a moment of pure terror, her eyes wide and bulging, her body still, and her face drained of all but its rouge. Still gripping the wheel I sank my head on my arms and breathed deeply. Was it my imagination or had that truck taken its own sweet time about swerving, my reflexes being all that lay between us and death. God was I being paranoid!

"You stupid fuckin' idiots!" The voice was loud and menacing and unpleasantly familiar. I whipped my head off my arms and looked in my side-view mirror. Cameron was hoofing it toward the Land Rover from the direction in which the truck had disappeared.

"What the hell are you doing on this road? You could have got us all killed, you know that? The driver just managed to keep the rig on the road. He's pissing his pants right now. Jesus."

I rolled down the window. Cameron's big red beefy face approached like a storm cloud.

Martha was squirming in her seat. "*We* did? *We*?" she croaked. "It was his stupid truck going too fast in the middle of the road on a corner that nearly killed us."

I motioned Martha to be quiet and controlled my own seething anger.

"You both okay?" I asked. He stopped, bewildered by my question, his anger spluttering, but then he recovered.

"This is a logging road, lady. You shouldn't be …" He stopped suddenly and peered at me more closely. "Hey, aren't you the nosey parker who found Diamond's body? Yeah, sure, you were the one pawing around in my truck that day. You were with those damn screaming greenies. What the hell are you doing here, anyway?"

"Trying to find out who murdered Diamond." *Why the hell did I say that?* I thought. But it was too late. I couldn't take it back, even with Martha's face staring at me incredulously.

"Murdered?" Cameron's voice rose an octave, but its loudness never varied. "Who the hell's talking murder here?" He looked behind him quickly as if making sure no one was listening, his eyes darting around like worried marbles.

"Look, lady, we don't need any more trouble around here. Leave it alone. It's all in the past now. Whatever happened out there that night, it's all over. The guy's dead."

"You hunt?" I asked on impulse. He looked at me, taken aback, and a look of pure calculation flitted across his face.

"What of it?"

"Bear?"

"Yeah, so?"

"Were you the one who shot the bear they say killed Diamond?"

"Damn right." Bingo.

"How did you find it?"

"What the hell's this got to do with anything?" he said.

I said nothing, and the silence lengthened until Cameron could stand it no more.

"We baited him. Threw out some old fish where we knew he'd be — near Diamond's permanent camp there — and then waited until he came and then we nailed him. Easy as anything and they're suckers for fish."

"Is that how Diamond died? Someone baited him and threw him to the bear?"

Cameron leapt back from the truck as if he'd been bitten.

"Jesus, lady, are you nuts?"

I shrugged and took a different tack, aware that Martha was squirming beside me.

"Why didn't you wait for the wildlife guys to shoot the bear? Why do it yourself?"

Cameron licked his lips and wiped the sweat forming on his brow, looked behind him and leaned forward.

"We'd had some trouble with a bear. A real rogue bear he was. One of the guys got mauled just before Diamond got nailed."

"You?" I pointed to the scars on his arms. He kept quiet. I tried again.

"Who knew about the rogue bear?"

Cameron shuffled his feet and looked away. "We kept it pretty much to ourselves. Didn't want any trouble up here."

"Too bad you waited until the day after Diamond's body was discovered to get the bear." I paused. "Or was it?"

"What the hell are you getting at?"

"You were pretty angry at Diamond that night at the information meeting. You looked pretty damn smug after belting him one. You must have felt pretty good when his body was identified."

"Sure, I was angry. You would be too. The fool was looking to take away my livelihood and couldn't see my problems for his bloody trees. But that doesn't mean I wanted him dead. Transferred somewhere far away would have suited me just fine."

I could hear the sound of a chainsaw somewhere deep in the woods and a lone mosquito hovered around Cameron as he glared at me. I shrugged, feeling considerably less confident than I looked.

He gripped the side of the window and said, "If you're fool enough to be thinking murder, leave me out of it. There're people a lot happier than me that Diamond bought it. Go ask Raymond about his hot-pants wife. She couldn't keep out of Diamond's bed." He gave me a lop-sided leer and said, "Stay off these roads if you know what's good for you."

"Is that a threat?"

"Nah, just a friendly warning."

With that he slapped the window and, suddenly laughing, strode back down the road. Martha and I exchanged glances.

"Busy man, that Diamond," said Martha.

chapter nineteen

I shoved the Land Rover into gear and headed on down toward the turn to the biology station. A small red convertible, top down, was signalling to turn onto the main road, and I recognized Roberta at the wheel. I pulled up alongside her, rolling down my window.

"Just wanted to thank you again for rescuing me."

Roberta smiled. "Anybody would have done the same, you know."

"Any news about Don yet?"

"Nothing. Not a word. Three days and no sign of him anywhere."

"He had a lot to be depressed about, didn't he?"

Roberta jerked her head up and stared at me, the wine-dark specks in her blue eyes standing out like the reverse of snowflakes on black velvet.

"He was cooking his data, wasn't he?"

She tried to stare me down but her heart wasn't in it and she looked deflated.

"How did you know?" she finally asked quietly.

"He told me, the day I was to meet him. He said he could explain it all and not to tell anyone until he had spoken to me."

Roberta smiled a long sad smile. Finally she said, "He's a good man, Don is. It must have broken him to have to resort to cheating like that. I knew he was having trouble paying his bills for his daughter. I'd even questioned some of his data. It didn't seem to fit, but he was good at what he did. I never suspected he was cooking it until he admitted to me he was in deep shit. He only spoke to me because he knew that I might be affected just by association. He *is* my supervisor."

"So you knew that Diamond was going to tell the Dean and that your own thesis would be suspect? Rather convenient for the two of you that he died before the cat was let out of the bag." God, I felt horrible saying this to the woman who had saved my life, but I had to get to the bottom of things and I knew being nice wouldn't cut it.

Roberta stared at me, a hollow, vacant look in her eyes.

"I guess you could say that, but you don't understand. Fate was really mean to him. He felt he had to choose between his daughter and his ethics. When Diamond found out, Don came up here to his camp to try and reason with him, to get him to give him some time to redo the paper, undo the damage."

"He came up here? When?"

Roberta hesitated, looked down at her hands, and then shrugged.

"It was a bunch of days before Diamond was found dead. He left the barricade and sneaked up to talk to him. When he came back he was upset, white and trembling.

He said Diamond had agreed to wait, but he was really uptight. It seemed odd at the time, and since then I've thought about it a lot. He could have been there when Diamond died, you know." She paused as if she felt she'd said too much, and then she blurted out, "Don't you see? His daughter was far more important to him than his work. He was willing to risk anything for her. Can't you understand that?"

"I can understand it, but I can't condone it," I said, feeling like a righteous prick. "His research is based on data that has been made up and he was going to publish it. Now that Diamond's dead he's off the hook."

"If you don't go and blab it, he is. But that's why I'm so worried about his disappearance. In his state of mind he could do something really dumb."

And with that she put her car in gear and left me with an unanswered question on my tongue.

Martha was busting a gut beside me.

"Cordi, did you hear that? Don went to see Diamond around the time he died."

"That means he might have seen what happened. Or he might have found him already dead and was just too afraid the police would think he had had something to do with it to report the body."

I thought back to the first time I had met Don: nervous, jumpy, so sure it was Diamond up there in the bush. Too sure?

"What if he stumbled on the killer moving the body back?" suggested Martha.

"What if he was the killer? He could have gone up the night before, killed Diamond in the cedar forest, and for some reason couldn't move the body, so he went back for it the next night and used the barricade as an alibi."

"Except that Roberta knew he went to see him."

"Yes, but she had a lot to lose if any of it came out."

Our conversation came to an abrupt end as we rounded the corner and there in front of us stood the lumber camp, carved out of the woods in record time with bulldozers and backhoes and other equipment I didn't recognize. I drove down the makeshift street until I saw a handwritten sign on a door saying "Office." I parked and we got out of the Land Rover and looked around. The place was a hodgepodge of trailers, prefabs, and machinery. I headed toward the office but stopped when I realized Martha wasn't with me.

"Come on," I said.

Martha shook her head at me. "You go on ahead. I'm going to check out the cookhouse."

"What about my life you were so worried about?" I asked.

"Oh, you're okay here. I'm going where the gossip is." I watched as she gingerly picked her way through the muddy ruts, her bright crimson shift swaying around her like a tent as she headed off toward what appeared to be the cookhouse.

I took a deep breath to gather my nerves. I was not looking forward to the conversation ahead because I didn't know what to expect. I climbed the steps to the makeshift office, and as I held out my hand to knock on the door it was yanked open and Donaldson stood on the threshold.

"Well now, what do we have here?" he said as his eyes roller-coastered over me, taking in every curve and valley in wide-eyed pleasure until they finally ambled back to my ice-cold brown eyes.

We have a woman, in case you haven't met one before, I thought while I offered him my hand. "Cordi O'Callaghan. I'm here to see Ray."

"Right-o. Hey, Ray! We got a live one!" he yelled,

ignoring my hand and ushering me in with his arm draped over my shoulders.

Ray came to greet me, glanced reproachfully at Donaldson as I shrugged off his arm, and hastily shook my hand.

"You'll have to forgive Donaldson. He's from the old 'letch' school."

Donaldson's smile became sweetness and light.

"He's here on sufferance," said Ray, shooting an intense frown, full of meaning, at Donaldson. "Just here to see where I've decided he should start cutting first."

Donaldson cracked his smile and was about to speak when Ray waved him into silence and said, "This is the Doctor Ph.D. I told you about who found Diamond's body. Thinks her data disks were swiped because of Diamond."

Donaldson's pale blue eyes narrowed, and he and Ray exchanged glances. Donaldson stroked his chin with short stubby fingers but didn't say a thing. Ray moved over to a table by the window.

"Want some coffee?"

I shook my head and watched as Ray poured some thick black liquid into the cup and then drowned it with milk and sugar. As I started to say something, a huge bulldozer rumbled by.

"Are you cutting already?" I asked, startled.

"No, but we're finally gearing up now," said Donaldson. "The injunction was only just overturned, but we want to get a head start. Ray and I and our foreman, Cameron, and a bunch of the lads have been up here since May without a break, setting up the camp." When he saw the look of surprise on my face, he said, "Sometimes you gotta gamble in this business, and we knew we were going to win, that the injunction would be overturned." He shrugged. "We didn't want to lose precious time, and besides, we needed someone up here to guard all the equipment from the loonies at the barricade."

"She doesn't need to know our entire history, Donaldson," snapped Ray. He turned to me. "I've pulled out some topographic and vegetation maps of the company's logging areas for you, as you asked on the phone. The company logs right across the country." He pointed to the crown land areas where the company held timber licences throughout the east. They were extensive.

"As you can see, the loss of this logging tract" — he pointed to the area where we were — "would make only a dent in their balance sheet, but the two mills in this area stand to lose their shirts."

"Yeah, mine in particular," snorted Donaldson. "Just look at the map. Most of the area's been logged around here." He pointed to his mill, situated perfectly for the area now about to be logged, but otherwise surrounded mostly by logged forest. "If the logging had been stopped my mill would have been worth practically nothing, and I would have had to declare bankruptcy. We'd taken all the wood we could from the area except this and were hauling logs from a hundred miles away. It was not cost-effective. As it stands we have a buyer, thanks to Diamond's death, and the court's reversal of the injunction I can now retire, let the young guys make some bucks with it."

"You have a partner," I said, stating it as a fact.

"Yeah," said Donaldson slowly, the word oozing out like molasses, as if reluctant to leave his lips. "Why do you ask?" he said cocking his head on one side like a bird and squinting at me.

"Just curious. You said 'we.' I just wondered who 'we' is."

He un-cocked his head and said, "I have a silent partner." He laughed. "A very silent partner."

"You mean Whyte?" asked Ray. Donaldson dragged his eyes away from me and squinted at Ray.

"Yeah, Whyte. One hell of a lumberman was my partner. He started the mill, remember, brought me on board and treated me like a brother. He'd have throttled Diamond with his bare hands. When he died in a car crash I found he had left me fifty-one percent, and the rest went to his wife, on condition she not sell until their son turned thirty. Strings from the grave. The old bugger. He liked control, did Whyte. She was furious. Went back to using her maiden name, Santander, she was that mad."

I felt a sinking feeling in the pit of my stomach.

"What happened to her?" I asked, risking the raking of those eyes for the end of the story I thought I already knew and wished I didn't.

"Quite sad, really. She and the kid had no money to live on. But she had spunk, I must say. Went out and got a job and put her kid through university and then her mind gave out on her, kinda shrank into nothingness. We tried to declare dividends, but the last five years have been hard and things were just too tight. The kid's been supporting her, but I think it's been rough."

"What happened?" I asked.

"Business had been bad for a number of years — there just wasn't the lumber — and we couldn't declare any dividends. About two years ago she came out to persuade me to sell, but by that time there was already controversy about the logging. Diamond had got on his high horse, you see, and the worth of the mill plummeted because of the uncertainty. I had to tell her that her shares were not worth much with the controversy and all, and that we could command a much better price if she waited. I told her it would die down — I really believed it would at the time."

Ray laughed, "Nobody really knew what was going to happen. Diamond was so volatile, always coming up with some new trick. Anyway, with him gone the protest kind of died."

"And now the old lady's son has contacted me," added Donaldson, "and we have a firm offer that we've accepted."

My thoughts went back to Mrs. Santander in her strange clothes, and the tiny sparse house where she lived with Patrick. I remembered his quiet dignity and his protectiveness. Of all Diamond's colleagues, only Patrick had had no motive for wanting Diamond dead. Now he did. And it made me want to cry.

"I guess lots of people have reason to be happy he's dead." I said quietly.

When no one said anything I looked up, suddenly aware of the silence in the room. Both men had stopped talking and were staring at me, their faces blank, smiles tight and withering. I could hear the crickets chirruping outside and the wind rustled through the trees, and I felt defeated. Trucks were moving around the complex getting ready to build a bridge across the river to the new stand of timber. I wanted to be somewhere else.

"What kind of suggestion is that?" Donaldson's voice was sharp, defensive, angry. I could read nothing in the blankness of his face or in the now granite coldness of his eyes. I wasn't sure which I liked less, the frozen eyes or the soft, lecherous eyes of moments before. I suppressed a shiver, suddenly very glad I couldn't read all that was in his mind.

"Just that a lot of people who knew him now have a life, a job, money, when before they were …"

Ray and Donaldson suddenly laughed in unison, naked, raw, humourless laughter that raked the air. It was unnerving, and I cleared my throat to give me something to do other than to stare at them.

"You may be right, but I for one didn't stand to lose my job, so other than the fact that I didn't like the man, I had no reason to wish the poor guy six feet under. But his death did make life a lot easier for a whole bunch of people, no doubt about that. Donaldson here, among others, as you now know, has a damn good reason for being glad the bastard's dead."

"You didn't like him?"

"What can I say? He rubbed me the wrong way. Constantly. He dominated all the hearings so that we couldn't get any consensus or any work done. It was infuriating. He presented brief after bloody brief, faxed, phoned, and emailed us to hell. I dreaded turning on my computer every morning. He loved the limelight, did Diamond, and he loved a good fight, verbal and physical. We were lab partners in animal behaviour at university before I became smart and switched to forestry. I think he finally drove me to it — just to get away from him. You see we were both Ds so I usually drew him for my lab partner. But enough of Diamond." He shook his head in mock wonder and pointed to the map on the table.

"I think this is what you are after. They're perfect for your paper, but I can't think how it can help you with your disks ..." He paused, waiting for me to say something.

All I could think of was, "Where are we on this?

As Ray made room for me beside him, Donaldson raised an imaginary hat and left us to it. It was a large-scale map of the area with all the vegetation marked on it, just like the map at the zoology building that I had pored over, but this indicated what areas were going to be logged. Ray spread out the map, pushing away the coffee mugs and a half eaten bag of chips. He jabbed his squat round finger at the map. "We're here. This whole area is slated for logging." He spread his hand over hundreds of miles of bush.

"What kind of timber is it?"

"Mostly white and red pine."

"Any cedar?"

Ray looked up with interest, or was it something else? "Some, but it's not a large percentage of the logging tract.'

"Where is it?"

He glanced at me curiously, and then looked back at the map. He pointed with his finger. "The cedar is pretty much concentrated here across the river at the base of the escarpment. It goes inland quite a distance, maybe ten miles. It's low and swampy in there — a natural valley. Starts about a mile above the rapids near where Diamond had his camp, but on the opposite side of the river. It's quite extensive along the escarpment. There's a big cliff area over there and the land is really wet because of the many natural springs in the area."

"Can you see the cedars from the lake?"

"Yeah, sure. If you want to, then just take the path past the cookhouse down through the woods to the water's edge. There's always a bunch of boats there if you want to paddle across." He glanced at the clock. "Bit late now, though, if you want to get back home by dark." He rolled up the maps and put them away as I moved toward the door. I had my hand on the knob, hating myself for what I was about to do, but I had to find out.

"What about your wife?"

Ray stopped dead and our eyes locked in an ugly embrace.

In measured words he said, "What about my wife?"

"I just heard she and Diamond had a thing going. Must have been kind of hard on you." God, that was hard to say. I had nothing against this guy and here I was bringing up what must be a painful memory, but I needed the information. I could brood about it later.

I watched as his face crumpled and his hands lost their grip on the maps as he struggled to control his emotions. "That was a long time ago." He turned his back on me and I quietly let myself out, feeling like a pariah.

chapter twenty

It was a hot, humid day and the dust from the new road was clogging every one of my pores. I kicked the dust with my feet and headed off toward the cookhouse and the path to the lake. As I approached one of the mobile trailers I heard a noise and stopped.

"Psst." It came again. "Psst." I turned toward the sound and there, perched on an overturned bucket between an outhouse and what I took to be the cookhouse, was Martha. Her back was to me, her head twisted around like an owl to keep me in view, and her thick, solid ankles were wobbling in time with the protesting wobbles of the aluminum bucket. I watched in fascination, wondering if the bucket would continue to hold her weight or would decide to crumple and, if so, what Martha would do.

"Good god, Martha, what the hell are you doing?"

"Shhhhh." Martha's low, insistent command slithered

toward me and caught me just as I was about to laugh.

Martha motioned quickly with one hand for me to join her and judging by the protesting groans of the bucket would have lost her balance except for a rather remarkable balancing act.

I stepped into the alley between the two makeshift buildings and looked up at Martha as I struggled to adjust to the gloom. She was leaning against a fence that crossed the alley, her head just topping it so that she could see what was on the other side.

"There's something fishy going on around here," she said in her best Perry Mason voice. I rolled my eyes skyward.

"No really, Cordi. The cook told me all about it."

"About what?"

"The fish," said Martha in a dark, ominous voice as she strained to look over the fence.

"For heaven's sake, Martha, get down before you kill yourself," I said in a whisper.

"I can't."

"What do you mean you can't?"

"I can't get down. I'm caught on something."

I moved around behind Martha and saw that her shift was caught on a wicked-looking spike. I squeezed my arm in between Martha and the fence and untangled her. She dropped to the ground with relief, took out a large pink handkerchief, wiped her forehead, and slapped a mosquito on her arm.

"Really, Cordi, I don't know how you can stand to be out here with all these bugs." She looked at me and sighed, as if all her lifeblood had just been sucked out by that one lone mosquito.

"Check out the freezer on the other side of that fence."

I looked at her in puzzlement and hesitated, wondering what she was getting at. "Well, go on. I can't do it.

You'll get your answer when you see what's inside it, mark my words." I could almost see each of her words being ticked off with a little checkmark in Martha's head.

I repositioned the bucket and leapt up, gripping the top of the wooden fence and scrambling over to the other side. The freezer was snuggled up against the fence and another fence with a gate in it, well hidden or presumably well protected from any animals. I opened the lid and looked down thoughtfully at the contents, pushing aside the top layer and rummaging down in the lower levels to be sure I hadn't missed what Martha was advertising with her wildly dancing eyes.

By the time I had climbed back over the fence, Martha had rearranged her shift and fixed up her appearance by applying some more lipstick and brushing her hair.

"Well?" she said triumphantly.

"Well what? Your lipstick's on crooked," I said.

Martha pinched her mouth with her thumb and forefinger to wipe away the lipstick. "Gone?"

"Still some in the lower right corner." Martha scrubbed some more and raised her eyebrows at me. I nodded.

"The stuff in the freezer. Did you see it?"

"So the loggers like corn. What of it?"

"Corn?" Martha said her mouth opening in a grimace and her eyebrows struggling to meet her widow's peak.

"Frozen corn," I said, and Martha's features crashed down in bewilderment as I took her by the arm and led her out of the alley.

"No fish?"

"No fish. Now why don't you tell me what the hell is going on here. What's all this about fish anyway?"

I made for the path Ray had pointed out to me, dragging her along with me.

"Where are we going?"

"I want to see the lake."

Martha dawdled and picked her way around rocks and branches most people would have stepped over. She doggedly pursued her latest theory.

"The cook really liked my dress, so when I told her I'd made it she asked me to send her the pattern." Martha looked sidelong at me. "She's a little bigger than I am, and it's not always easy to find things to fit. Anyway I agreed and she took me into the kitchen for a bite to eat. She was cooking up a mess of fresh fish for the men and it smelled so good I asked her where it came from.

"'Just down at the lake here. They bring 'em in by the barrelful,' she said to me, and I swear she winked, but I wasn't sure. But that's when I got suspicious. They were having trout, Cordi, and I'm pretty sure it's out of season."

I stopped in my tracks and looked open-mouthed at Martha.

"How would you know if it's out of season, Martha? You hate the outdoors and anything to do with it."

"Ah, but Cordi, I love fish, fresh fish gently sautéed with a bit of lemon and garlic." She closed her eyes and licked her lips. "Anyway, even if it is in season I'm sure they must have been way over their limit. Besides, the cook said they had a whole freezer out back that they kept stocked full of the stuff. Then I swear she winked at me again."

"Did she say anything about bears?"

"Yeah, that was really curious. She said Cameron came into camp a while back all clawed along his arms. He'd been across the lake and said a bear had mauled him after he'd spilled a can of tuna fish on himself. Then that zoologist turned up dead and Cameron and his buddies told the wildlife guys that they'd shot the beast. The cook didn't think they had, though."

"Why not?"

"Because they always give her the pelts or the fish to clean. She gets paid extra under the table. But there was no pelt, she said. I suppose if she knew they were poaching fish she'd just keep quiet so that the extra money would keep coming in. She stopped talking after that because I think she knew she'd told me too much."

"Did anyone else know about this rogue bear?"

"All the loggers, she thinks, but she wasn't sure if they had told any of the biologists. They weren't really on speaking terms, after all, but she figures it was only the decent thing to do. Although they all hated Diamond so much they may have practised selective amnesia with him. Served him right that he got killed by it anyway, was what she said. But she wasn't supposed to talk about it. The loggers didn't want the wildlife officers up here. One can see why if they were pilfering trout out of season."

Martha paused and then in excitement said, "Maybe that's the motive for moving the body. Maybe Diamond knew about the poaching and so they killed him. They moved him because they were afraid it would be discovered, either when the cops came out for a peek or when the wildlife guys came up to shoot the bear. They moved the body and then shot the bear to make doubly sure their secret would stay a secret. And maybe they tried to kill us just now to keep it all under wraps."

"They'd go to all that trouble for a bunch of fish?"

"Maybe it's something else besides fish. I've suggested it before. Maybe they have a still in the woods, or they've been making hash, or they've kidnapped some wealthy Arab prince. Maybe they've set up a trade in bear gall-bladders. There's a lucrative market for those. I don't know what it might be, but a dead body turning up near any nefarious doings would definitely cramp your style. You'd have to move it. Or maybe they baited him, just as you said. You heard Cameron earlier. He hunts bear, knows how it's done — even spilled fish oil on himself and lived through the result. They save their logging jobs and their still, or their poaching, or whatever. Double motive."

I was mulling over Martha's latest theories when we finally broke out into a small clearing. The land sloped down to a pebbled beach and the lake stretched out before us. I took out my binoculars and scoured the shore on the far side.

"I got the gossip on Raymond and his wife," Martha said.

I continued looking through the binoculars scanning the far shore. I thought I could make out a few cedars near the cliffs of the escarpment, but it wasn't easy from this distance to see any detail. What was frustrating was that it wasn't a small pocket of cedars but as Ray had said a fairly extensive forest. I had had vague hopes of finding a cedar forest of a couple of acres in size and being able to comb it and find out where and why Diamond died. It didn't look good, and I knew I'd been incredibly naive in hoping otherwise.

"And?"

"Happened more than ten years ago, and apparently Ray has never forgiven Diamond."

I lowered the glasses and eyeballed Martha.

"So Cameron was right?"

"Looks like it. Apparently she and Ray were an item and already married when he and Diamond were at university. Ray introduced them at a party and lost his wife a month later. Ray was beside himself with jealousy and threatened to kill them both. Can't blame the poor guy, can you? Gives him a motive for murder though: jealous husband gone berserk. Held it in all these years, the bitterness growing like some cancer until it strangles his reason. Lots of those around.

"So he went up to kill Diamond and saw the bear, and made use of the bear to do it for him. The perfect murder, if the bear cooperates. It'd be awfully dicey though. Maybe it happened on the spur of the moment. Diamond's sitting there watching his killer eat sardines when suddenly his killer sees the bear heading toward them. The killer throws the oil at Diamond and takes off, coming back when Diamond is dead to move the body. Or maybe they drugged him and dumped sardine juice on him in the area where the other guy got mauled."

I swung the binoculars along the far shoreline and then scanned the area of the cliff face. Martha continued jabbering away, but I wasn't listening anymore. My mind was racing a hundred miles an hour as I stared at a huge cliff soaring skyward. I adjusted the binoculars, focusing in on it, and there, on the full face of the cliff, glinting in the sun, was a livid jagged slash of rust red streaking diagonally down its face, like a huge red welt.

chapter twenty-one

On the way home Martha rummaged around in her bag and took out a CD and inserted it into my CD player. I was expecting something musical like the Rolling Stones or even Elton John but what came blasting out was the play-by-play of a hockey game. I stared at Martha open-mouthed and then said, "What in heaven's name are we listening to a hockey game for? Or hadn't you noticed it's summer."

"But, Cordi, this is the Montreal Canadiens. Just because it's summer doesn't mean we fans go to sleep." She wasn't kidding. Martha was not exactly reticent about where she stood when it came to the Habs. All the way home we listened to the Montreal Canadiens getting thrashed by the Florida Panthers, while I chewed over in my mind the significance of what I had learned so far. I wasn't sure what I'd found but I was on the verge of something, I just knew it. Something in the back of my mind was screaming to get out — it just couldn't find a route.

I was so lost in thought that when Martha suddenly bounced up and down on the edge of her seat and screamed, "Go Habs!" I nearly lost control of the Land Rover. When I finally wrestled the beast back onto the road I marvelled that Martha had been so engrossed in an old game that she hadn't even noticed the Land Rover and the side of the road making intimate eyes at each other. I listened to the game, my mind now frayed from too much thought to want to do anything else. It sounded bad for the Habs. I glanced over at Martha, wondering why she'd want to listen to a losing game.

"I brought the wrong CD," she whispered as the Habs went down in a shootout.

Martha was deathly quiet and the announcers from the U.S. channel were having a field day. "The Panthers have won it!" they yelled. "The Florida Panthers kick butt. The stealthy cats came out soft-footed and strong." The game swirled into my mind, infecting my thoughts, and suddenly I knew what Diamond had been doing up in those woods in the weeks before he died.

The sun was dripping off the escarpment like gold as it moved toward dusk when I finally wheeled the Land Rover into the farmyard. The smell of freshly cut hay was heavy in the air and the indolent mooing of the cows out in the paddock indicated that it was getting close to milking time. I could see Mac in the paddock and waved at him as I saw Martha into her little Volkswagen and watched as she bounced down the road toward the highway. Ryan's motorbike was parked outside his office, and I raced upstairs two at a time to his loft. He was reviewing some photos by the skylight as I came in and wound my arms around him from behind. He stopped as he saw my face splitting in a grin from ear to ear.

"What's up?"

I turned on the computer before even sitting down, barely holding in my excitement, and said, "I'll show you in a minute, I hope."

Ryan came and peered curiously over my shoulder as I inserted Shannon's disk and then opened the files for each of the six cats Diamond had been monitoring that spring. I moved the cursor, looking for their vital statistics. There were no vital stats for the sixth cat, but I knew Diamond must have recorded them somewhere. I looked up at Ryan, who was now standing beside me wondering what was up. I pointed to the files for the other five cats.

"Look at this, Ryan. For each cat Diamond has recorded their weight, length, and other physical characteristics, how often they had travelled, and how far."

"So? Isn't that standard information anyone would gather?"

"Exactly," I said excitedly. "No biologist worth his salt would track an animal and then not weigh and measure it. He's done that for five of the cats."

"What are you getting at, Cordi?"

"The sixth cat has no physical characteristics recorded." I clicked the window and pointed to the computer screen. "He's recorded movement and activity and general location in western Quebec, but no physical characteristics at all."

"It must have been accidentally deleted."

"Does this word processing program have hidden text capability?" I said, trying to contain my growing excitement.

Ryan looked at me curiously and nodded. "Yeah, sure it does. Move over and I'll see if I can bring anything up."

Ryan keyed in some commands and suddenly the text of Diamond's sixth cat doubled in size. I grabbed the mouse from him and scrolled to the beginning of the document, and there it was. Height. Weight. Length. My heart was beating like a bloody racehorse at the photo finish.

"Take a look at the weight, Ryan."

"Fifty kilograms. What of it?"

"That's a hell of a size for an adult Canada lynx."

Ryan looked at me, and then clicked on all the other file windows. Not one of Diamond's adult lynx weighed more than ten kilograms. Not surprising, since female lynx average about 8.6 kilograms.

I looked at Ryan, blowing out my cheeks in excitement. I pointed at the computer screen. "This cat's at least five times the weight of an adult lynx. There's only one cat in Canada that big."

I let the words hang in the air for effect. This was my moment of triumph and I wanted to savour it. Ryan looked at me expectantly.

"It was a cougar, Ryan. Diamond was monitoring a pregnant cougar!"

Ryan stood looking at me, uncomprehending, my dramatic little revelation having had no effect on him.

"So what? Even if he was studying a cougar I don't see what that has to do with Diamond's death. He was a cat man. He studied cats. What's the problem?"

"Cougars haven't been found in Western Quebec for generations."

Ryan let out a long, low whistle and said, "You're joking. Are you sure?" Ryan's shift from boredom to excitement was palpable, and I spoke quickly.

"Of course I'm sure. Lots of people have claimed to have seen them over the years but there's been no believable evidence. Most biologists think they are extinct, gone, vanished, forever dead here in Quebec, but they are officially listed as endangered in eastern Canada because there have been so many unconfirmed sightings over the years. Recently someone found a small population in New Brunswick. If Diamond really had found a cougar, it would be dynamite. Logging would stop on the instant. The spotted owls in the old growth on the west coast forced the loggers to stop out there not too long ago."

Ryan heaved out of his chair. "I'm famished. Let's celebrate with something from your fridge." Ryan was going to eat me out of house and home before Rose and the kids returned from her parents' cottage. Still, it was nice to have him around to myself every night to talk things over. I knew I'd miss his nightly company when Rose got back. Oh sure, I'd get my fill by visiting them as I always had, but it wasn't the same. I wouldn't have his undivided attention. I thought of Patrick then, as Ryan and I linked arms and walked across the farmyard and down the road to my house.

The sun was spilling its guts all over my porch when we got there. I threw some steaks on the barbecue and Ryan made a salad. The crickets serenaded us as we continued our conversation on the porch.

"How the hell did you make the connection?" he asked.

"The baseball game, a necklace, and that crumpled scrap of paper I found by Diamond's pack." I told Ryan what I thought I'd read on the paper. "Anyway, Shannon had a necklace with a tooth embedded in silver. She told me it was a cougar tooth and that Diamond had found it in Florida. I didn't make the connection then, but when I listened to the uproar as the Panthers won the game I realized that what was written on that smudged scrap of paper wasn't 'antlers' at all. It could just as easily be 'panthers,' another name for cougars. I suddenly figured the cat with no statistics might have no stats for a reason."

"You're talking about a career-making discovery here, and he sits on it? Why didn't he break the news earlier instead of radio-collaring the beast and following it around for a few months?"

"He wanted solid, irrefutable proof I guess. Not just a photo of a cougar but a photo of a cougar with cubs! What a coup! He'd never lack for grant money again."

I was on a roll. Theories leaping all over the place.

"It had to be ironclad," I said. "He must have sat on it to keep sightseers out until he had it all well documented. Maybe he was afraid of someone coming in and blasting the beasts out of the world if he announced his findings too soon."

I stopped suddenly and looked at Ryan

"What? I hate it when you look like that."

"The film we found out on the portage. Suppose ..."

"It was pictures of the cougar?" said Ryan, catching my excitement and running with it.

"You got it! You know what this means, don't you? It means that just about everyone has a double motive. Everybody except perhaps Lianna and Shannon stood to gain in a big way if they were sole party to Diamond's secret."

"How so?"

"Supposing Roberta and Don were working together and discovered Diamond's cougars. It would make their careers. If they steal Diamond's discovery for themselves they'd hit it big, and instead of losing their jobs and going down in disgrace, they'd cement their reputations."

Ryan got into the act.

"Then there's Leslie, right? She kills three birds with one stone by inheriting Diamond's job, getting revenge on an old lover, and taking over his discovery. She did tell you she was working on something new."

We were really getting into our stride here.

"Even Davies could have done it. He's so crazy about the reputation of his university and this would bring kudos and likely cement his appointment as university president."

"Wait a minute, Cordi. We're getting carried away here. If any of these guys killed Diamond for his discovery then why hasn't anyone announced it yet?"

"Because maybe they haven't been able to find out where the cougars are. Maybe all they have are Diamond's photos and they've been spending time trying to find the cougars. That might explain the break-in at Shannon's, maybe the lost pages in the diary. Maybe it wasn't a will. Maybe whoever it was was looking for something that would indicate where these cougars are."

"On the other hand," said Ryan, "if the killer is Cameron or Donaldson or any of the loggers, as soon as they find the cougar they'll shoot it and bury it into oblivion to keep the logging going."

I looked at Ryan in horror.

"God, I hope not," I said, but I knew it was as plausible as any of the other theories we had been kicking around. "The miller's crowing because the worth of his mill has climbed back up since Diamond died and he's accepted a firm offer to buy. Having an endangered species suddenly pop up hanging around your logging area is a death sentence for logging. For all we know they may already have found and killed the cougar." What a depressing thought. I quickly changed gears.

"Martha has a completely different theory," I said. "She's convinced that Cameron and his cronies are poaching fish or something and that Diamond found out. Cameron knew there was a rogue bear in the area. He could have baited Diamond no problem. He gets rid of Diamond and saves his poaching business and his logging job."

"Possible," said Ryan. "It also explains why the body was moved. Suppose Diamond died in their poaching area and they didn't want the wildlife people coming around to kill the bear and find evidence of poaching."

"Yeah, that's what Martha thought. But the cougars also give a good reason for why the body was moved, assuming he died somewhere near the female's den."

"What about Shannon?" asked Ryan.

"This wouldn't alter her motive. I don't think she'd gain anything from a cougar discovery. She's still a suspect because of what she stands to inherit if that will is ever found. If it ever existed."

"And Patrick? What about Patrick?" asked Ryan, and I felt my heart jump. I had been trying to ignore any thoughts I had about Patrick because they all seemed to point in a direction I didn't want to go.

"I wouldn't want to be in Patrick's shoes if he's the killer," I said reluctantly. "He has a double motive that splits him right down the middle." I told Ryan all about Patrick and his mother's ownership of the mill.

"Patrick presumably gets his mother's shares if she is judged incompetent?"

"You got it. So he obviously had to decide which stood to bring a bigger bonus for him: the sale of the mill so he and his mum would have money to live on right away or the announcement that he had found cougars in the area, which would immediately decrease the value of the mill to practically zip. From what Ray said he's chosen the latter. Or has he?" Did he know about the cougars? Was he trying to have his cake and eat it too?

"So basically we can't eliminate anybody."

"Yes and no," I said. "According to the book Roberta showed me, if I remember correctly, most of them were in the bush. Leslie and Don were at their study sites on those dates — Roberta was with Don. Leslie was alone. Patrick had gone out to collect samples from east of the river and returned some days after Diamond's death. Lianna said she was at her cottage, which is up in that area somewhere. Shannon was cooking meals at the barricade while Diamond was gone."

"What about the loggers?"

"Apparently Ray and Donaldson and Cameron and a skeletal crew were up there to build the camp and protect the equipment from the barricaders, or so they told me."

"Jesus, the woods were jumping with people. No wonder we can't find any remote wilderness anymore."

I lapsed into silence and watched a moth fluttering frantically at the lighted window.

"How's work going, Cordi?" It was another question I was dreading, but I also knew that Ryan wasn't asking just to make conversation. He really wanted to know. But I didn't want to talk about it, so we sat there deep in thought watching the sunset. There was a long wisp of a cloud just above the trees, and the sun had lit it up in tints of deep red and purple. It looked like a nasty scar slashing its way across the horizon, reminding me of the red welt on the rock. Upon remembering, I jumped up so suddenly that Ryan spilled his drink.

"Good god, Cordi. What is the matter with you?"

"I was thinking about that crumpled piece of paper. The words 'red welt ock' were on there with some numbers and 'NV,' but it could have been 'NW'."

Ryan looked up. "Compass reading?"

"I hope so," I said, trying to remember what the numbers had been as I pictured the little scrap of paper. "310!" I said triumphantly.

"It won't do you much good unless you know where he was standing when he took the reading."

"I think I know that," I said, and I told him about the cliff I had seen with the huge red welt streaking down it.

"I think he's blazed a trail from 'red welt rock.' Maybe it will lead to his cougar or to some other clue that will help me find out who took my disks."

"Sounds like wishful thinking to me, Cordi."

"Yeah, but I think he was following the cougar when he died. I know it holds the key to all this." I could feel my resolve starting to waver.

"And what if you're wrong?"

I didn't want to think about that.

chapter twenty-two

I woke the next morning long before dawn and had a running battle with myself as to whether it was worth it to go up and take a look at the red welt or not. I kept coming up with good reasons to postpone it — I was getting more and more down on myself. I knew if I got up I would start to feel a little better, and if I didn't I could always go back to bed again since it was Saturday. I lay in bed awhile longer, but my thoughts just got darker. I got up to go to the bathroom and things did brighten up. I decided to go. I stuffed a backpack with some extra clothes, food, compass, and pepper spray, and grabbed my day pack, sleeping bag, and a small tent just in case. Then I manhandled my canoe onto the Land Rover and lashed her down.

I caught the sunrise as I swung the Land Rover out of the farmyard and headed north to the logging camp. The Ottawa River picked up the rose red glow and blue of the sky. The area had received a lot of rain in the last few days and I had to throw the Land Rover into four-wheel drive to make it past one quagmire just outside the logging camp. There was a funny little rattle coming from some dark and oily place. I'd have to take some time to track it down; it was getting worse.

I almost didn't see her because I was so preoccupied with the niggling little rattle, which was pretty incredible, seeing as how she was standing in the middle of the road waving her arms like windshield wipers, Land Rover–style. I coasted up beside her and rolled down my window. At first glance I didn't recognize Roberta. Her designer jeans and silk blouse were covered in mud, and her hair was raked up inside some sort of cap, but her high-pitched voice gave her away as she explained what was wrong. Not that she needed to tell me. The skid marks were visible on the road and I could see her car was nose down in a small swamp, with someone still at the wheel.

"Is anybody hurt?"

Roberta looked back over her shoulder at the car.

"Oh, no it's okay. That's Shannon, Diamond's girlfriend. She's been steering and I've been trying to push the damn thing out of the ditch.' She indicated the mud and dirt on her clothes and smiled sheepishly. "I think I just made it worse. Can you help?"

I loved moments like these. There isn't anything that a Land Rover can't haul out of a tight place. I backed the Rover up and waved at Shannon, who indicated she'd stay in the car to steer it. Roberta helped me secure the chains. As we were wrestling with them I took the opportunity to ask her what she was doing up here so early in the morning.

"You know biologists. Up with the birds," she said cheerfully.

I looked over at Shannon, and Roberta followed my gaze. She laughed, a short nervous laugh.

"I tried to persuade her not to come, but she wanted to see Diamond's camp. Davies has offered it to me as my field base for a Ph.D. if I want it, and he and Patrick are up there right now packing equipment. She showed up at his lab yesterday and found out that I was coming up. Begged for a ride."

I glanced at Shannon. I could see her pale, haggard face looking back at us.

"What could I say? I couldn't refuse her — she's been through so much. And a couple of days spent up here might do her good."

"Did she ever find the will?" Talk about being blatant. Roberta looked at me with well-deserved distaste.

"No, as a matter of fact she hasn't, and if you think that's why she's come up here then you don't know the difference between a grieving lover and a greedy widow."

We let that hang between us like a bad taste as we finished securing the chains. I got behind the wheel of the Land Rover. Roberta's car popped out of the swamp like a cork, just as I knew it would. Such a satisfying feeling of power. Roberta came over to thank me, and I asked her if she'd heard any news about Don.

She started as if she'd been bitten and looked at me guardedly.

"No. No word of him at all. It's not like him, you know?"

I didn't know so I didn't say anything, just nodded and threw the Land Rover into gear.

Five minutes later I pulled into the main yard of the lumber camp. The early morning sun carved deep, long dark shadows across the huge hulking machinery. I drove down to the old road that led down to the lake.

I got out of the Land Rover, stretched and walked around to the front and began untying the canoe.

"Well, well, well. If it isn't Doctor Ph.D." The voice came flying through the air like a homing pigeon. "What brings you here again so early in the morning?"

I stood up and peered over the hood to see Donaldson striding toward me, followed at some distance by an anxious-looking Ray and Lianna. Donaldson's leer put the sun to shame, and I nimbly steered clear of his handshake by keeping my hands busy with the rope.

"Just following up a hunch," I said. I looked at Lianna, and my face must have asked the question for me because she said, "They're putting in a road for me up to my cottage. Ray here is showing me just where it will go."

I nodded and looked at Donaldson.

"Have you sold your mill yet?"

Donaldson's smile stole across his face like a kitten stealing cream. "Just signed the papers yesterday. Came up to sort everything out with Ray here."

Ray and Donaldson exchanged glances, and then Ray said, "You're welcome to one of the canoes down there. Save you untying your own, but better take your paddle. I don't think there're any decent ones down in the boat shed. Leslie's down there, she can help you."

"Leslie? What's she doing around here?" I looked up, startled.

"I think she's carting out some of the field equipment that she brought out of the bush late yesterday."

I must have looked confused, because he continued.

"Her study site's just up past the next portage. She always takes her equipment out here, has for years. Saves her two portages. We couldn't exactly tell her she couldn't do it anymore when we moved in. We've improved the road for her. It was a real cattle track before we came."

They asked me if I wanted some coffee. I politely refused and watched as they ambled off in the direction of the cookhouse.

Ray turned back then and called out, "Cameron and some of the loggers are out on the lake checking out some stuff for me. If you see him, would you ask him to get the hell back here? We need the outboard motor pronto."

I nodded and absently swatted at some mosquitoes hovering around my ears. I hauled out my pack and paddle and headed down the woods road to the lake to see if the canoe Ray had offered was okay to use. The air was fresh and clear with a mounting wind, but somewhere off to my left I could hear the buzzing of a chainsaw that neatly eviscerated what would have been the deep, calming quiet of a wilderness morning.

I came out onto the pebbled beach and saw Cameron and two other loggers helping Leslie hoist the last of some big boxes into the back of a rusty old pickup truck. The outboard was pulled up on the beach behind them. I walked over, and after saying "Hi" I told Cameron what Ray had said, and he and his friends dropped what they were doing and headed up to the cookhouse. Ray may not have seemed like a leader, but apparently his requests were not treated lightly.

When they had gone I turned to Leslie and said, "I thought you and the loggers were at loggerheads, so to speak."

Leslie gazed at me, a quizzical expression transforming her face.

"Cam and the others, they're good hardworking men. Who am I to criticize them for wanting to make a living? I sympathize with their plight; I may not agree with their line of work, but I sympathize and they know that. They help me out a bit." She paused. "What brings you up here so early?"

"Just following up a hunch. Ray offered me a canoe to go over to the other side here and snoop around a bit. Does it matter which one?"

Leslie looked surprised. "You going over there? Now? To the campsite? The one the loggers use sometimes?"

"You mean the big cliff?" I asked.

She nodded, looked pensive, and scratched her chin. "This is terrific. Would you mind giving me a lift? I promised Davies I'd pick up Diamond's spare canoe at the end of the portage across from here. I was going to get someone to paddle me over tomorrow from Diamond's permanent site near the biology station, but this would suit better, since you're going over there anyway. You can solo this one back again. That way I can paddle over and help them at Diamond's camp, and then they can drive me up to get my own gear when we're through."

I looked at the choppy waves and felt the wind strengthening. It would make the paddle over a lot easier with a second paddler, even if it meant I'd have to make small talk with her. I waited while Leslie scrounged around in her truck and got out a small pack, a fishing rod, a paddle, and a lifejacket. Without hesitation, she headed for the stern. I shrugged, changed direction, and headed for the bow. *What the hell*, I thought. It was more work to stern in this weather anyway. As we lifted the canoe down to the water I asked her why Diamond had a spare canoe at the portage.

"Sometimes he had a spare canoe at either end of the portage so he could move through some of his study area without having to portage a canoe," said Leslie. "He could have taken out here and saved himself a lot of trouble, but he refused to do that. He liked to fish at the base of the rapids there, too. It's a great spot and close enough to his camp for him to fish for breakfast. Now that he's gone, nobody uses the canoes and Davies wants them back. He and Patrick and Roberta are out near the bio station sorting through Diamond's gear and divvying it up. Gives me the creeps."

"Has there been any word yet about Don?" I asked as I threw my pack in, grabbed the gunnels with both hands, and crab-walked up to the bow.

She didn't answer, and I looked back over my shoulder at her. She was staring out across the lake, her eyes unfocused, far away in some other part of her mind.

"Is he a good friend of yours?" I asked gently.

She started, and I watched as her eyes came back into focus, thoughts dissolving as others coalesced, like milk swirling in coffee.

"Don?" She smiled. "He was, I guess."

"Was?"

Leslie grunted as she clambered into the canoe and pushed off.

"He's a harmless sort of guy but clingy. He was really nice to me when I first arrived on campus, introducing me and all that stuff — a real friend. But then he started trying to horn in on my research program, steal my students. I guess he thought it would be easier to do with a woman than a man, but he chose the wrong woman. We haven't been close for a long time."

"Since his wife died?"

Leslie turned the canoe with an expert J-stroke, aimed it toward the narrows leading to the lake, and said, "Who told you about that?"

"Roberta. She said he was devastated, that his work really got quite shoddy after that, and there were rumours of data falsification."

"I wouldn't know about any of that, but if he was faking data, God help him."

"Any theories on where he might have gone?"

"No idea. The police have been prowling around

campus all week getting the lowdown on how depressed Don was. They think he might have just run away from it all. Maybe he couldn't take the responsibility anymore, so he just kind of disappeared. Poor Don."

I remembered how the police had grilled me about Don and his kid. How I'd tried to find out if my disks had been found at his house, and what a load of questions I'd gotten over that. But in the end they hadn't been interested in my disks and said there was no evidence that Diamond's death had been anything but accidental. They did ask me to call them if anything changed though.

"Do you agree with them about Don being depressed?" I asked.

"Yes and no. There's no question that he had a lot of problems and pressures. I don't even know half of them, but even if the rumours of data falsification are wrong, he had his poor daughter and Dean Davies on his back. He was very depressed when I last talked to him. I'm worried. What more can I say?"

"You mean suicide?"

"It's a possibility in his frame of mind, but somehow I can't imagine him abandoning his daughter like that. But I guess everyone can reach breaking point, and Don had more reasons than most. It's amazing he's lasted as long as he has. Some people get no luck."

We moved through the narrows of the bay and turned into the wind and talking was made next to impossible. We paddled in silence, the wind lapping at the waves against the boat as we beat into it. I was thankful that I had company. Paddling solo would have been a grind.

The sun was still quite low but the clouds were scudding across the sky like scared rabbits. The wind was warm and the water splashing against my hands was tepid as I carved my paddle through it. The air smelled the way it felt — warm and free. The wind snuffled my hair and the gentle slap of waves against the canoe almost made time stand still. The cliff reared up out of the water like some prehistoric beast, and I wondered how many natives had paddled this self-same lake hundreds of years ago to paint their stories on the face of that imposing cliff.

I shivered as time suddenly pummelled me with its aloofness, its cold, inexorable, relentless need to move on, inexplicably changing some things but leaving others virtually untouched after centuries. At moments like this, I thought, time telescopes upon itself and the past becomes one with the present. It was as close to immortality as I'd ever come, and I felt an almost physical wave of sadness sweep through me as I saw the past millennia, tantalizingly close yet inaccessible, stretched out behind me.

I squinted into the sun, looking ahead at the shoreline, shoving the sadness away to some hidden corner of my mind. I didn't want to be sad, but it was hard shaking it off. Not that it was ever easy.

The cliff thrust a good sixty feet up out of the water, its weather-beaten face jagged and rough from the wind and rains that had blasted and stained it for many millennia. Slashing down its face like a knife wound was the deep rust red rocky vein that I had seen from the logging camp the day before. Even though the sun had not climbed high enough to wash the face with light, it stood out like an angry red scar against the nondescript grey granite of the rest of the massive rock. Here and there, small cedars had grappled for their meagre place in the sun, growing stunted and twisted in places that seemed impossible for even a single root to take hold.

The canoe leapt and danced through the waves like a ballerina as Leslie skillfully steered it in toward shore. I could feel the pull of the current and the roar of the rapids around the corner to our right. Leslie turned the canoe when we were some ten feet from shore and then we hugged the shoreline. The canoe picked up speed, and Leslie yelled at me to get ready to jump out at the beginning of the portage, which I remembered was alarmingly close to the beginning of the rapids.

I could see the deep black of the water pale as the water became shallow and rocks and sand came looming up. There was a small pebbly beach and smooth rocks that sloped up into the trees, but there wasn't much between it and the start of the rapids. It wouldn't do to dump here. As the canoe ground against the sand, I leapt out and pulled it out of the strong current. While Leslie clambered out and got her gear, I secured the boat to a small tree and turned to look around.

There were cedars here, all right. Massive mothers of another time, they soared overhead in a logger's dreams, growing in the wet moist shadow of the cliff, giant younger cousins to those on the exposed cliff face. I turned and saw Leslie watching me. She had donned her small backpack, picked up her paddle and lifejacket, and stood as though waiting to say something, but before she could make up her mind we heard the roar of a motorboat as it came around the cliff behind us, heading up to the head of the lake. Leslie galloped up to the top of the rock to get a better view of the boat. I followed at a more sedate pace. She shook her head as the first of the waves from the boat crashed against the shore.

"I wish they wouldn't allow motors up here — they wash out the loons' nests, but the loggers swear they need them to check out the land on this side of the lake." She suddenly turned and looked at me.

"What are you interested in over here, anyway?" It was asked casually, as if she didn't really care, but the intensity of her eyes made me wonder.

"Just a hunch that maybe Diamond was here," I said. *He has to have been*, I thought, looking at the cedars. I didn't want to think about the fact that it might be just a wild goose chase or something my imagination had magnified into something it wasn't.

Leslie chortled, which didn't help my confidence.

"Of course he was. He came here sometimes, just as we all have. If you don't want to shoot the rapids, it's the only portage. It's a nice ride in an empty canoe, but fully loaded it can be difficult. But as far as I know, he seldom used it when passing through to his study site or to fish — that's at the other end."

She smiled and patted her rod. "Maybe I'll paddle over in the morning and catch me some fish for breakfast. It's a great fishing hole, but this end of the portage was too popular with the loggers for Diamond to want to use it often, and there's nowhere at the other end to pitch a tent. It's a rock garden down there."

She stared at me as if I had egg on my face, then shrugged and said, "I hope you find what you're looking for."

chapter twenty-three

I rubbed my face and watched Leslie disappear into the woods in the direction of the portage. I turned to survey the area around me. It was a beautiful campsite with lots of open rocky areas and smooth flat granite sloping down to the river and the lake. The amount of garbage strewn about — from tins to beer bottles to the carcasses of fish — was alarming. Easy pickings for a bear. Instinctively I felt the pocket of my pack to make sure my bear scare was still there and then hauled the pack onto my back.

The smell of cedar was strong. I climbed up the rock and walked in among the cedars. The ground was bare beneath the towering trees with evidence that it had been used and misused many times as a campsite. I counted three different fireplaces, and there were rings of rock and flattened brown cedar boughs in two places where people had pitched their tents. Someone had left a laundry line strung up between two trees and a ratty old blue sock hung limply from it. I absently kicked a couple of charred tin cans lying by one of the fire pits and the noise startled a crow. I saw with some annoyance that the loggers had posted a brand new "no trespassing" sign.

The cedars blocked out much of the sun here and it was cool and dark, but where the sun filtered down through the trees the sunbeams danced near the base of the cliff as it angled inland and struck something in the near shadows that gleamed. I looked up and saw that the moss, which had covered one side of the massive rock that had whelped from the cliff behind it, had been stripped off fairly recently, almost as though someone had slipped and fallen from the top of the fifteen-foot rock.

A twig snapped nearby, and I looked up quickly, but there was nothing except the gentle wind causing the tree's shadows to blow the sunbeams all over the forest floor. What I did see were several long, deep scratches streaking down the trunk of a cedar where the bark had been ripped away and the new wood laid bare, glistening and vulnerable. The bear that had made them had made them recently.

With mounting alarm I turned and scanned the trees and found one other with claw marks. Although I had hoped to find signs of bear I hadn't counted on the signs being recent. After all, the bear had been killed more than a month ago by the loggers, and on the other side of the river. Hadn't it? These markings were new. The place was crawling with bear sign, but that wasn't all. Poking out from under a rocky overhang I saw what looked like a piece of leather. When I stooped and picked it up I saw that it was a small collar, sliced in half, but with the buckle still fastened tightly. I turned it over in my hand. There was a tag dangling from the buckle, and when I wiped the dirt and muck from it, the name jumped out at me: Paulie.

I felt the goosebumps rise on the back of my neck, and when a twig snapped I whirled around. No one was there. The woods were quiet, but what tales could they tell? Was this where it had happened? Where Diamond had died? Had Paulie witnessed it, and then tried to make her way back to civilization? Or had she followed her master's body back to the other campsite, hitching a ride in the murderer's canoe?

I looked back through the woods and thoughtfully eyed the claw marks on the trees. If this was where Diamond had died then the bear sign might belong to the rogue bear. A disturbing thought, but the loggers could have lied about killing the bear near Diamond's camp or killing it at all. I looked out along the shoreline and figured it'd be a good place to fish. Would they go to all that trouble to guard their illegal fishing for a few measly fish? But there had been no bear to show the wildlife guys, who had taken the loggers at their word, so maybe they hadn't gone to much trouble after all. You'd think they'd want to kill the bear for their own safety. Unless, of course, they wanted it to scare everyone away.

I stared out over the water, wondering if Diamond had seen any of this view in those last agonizing minutes of his life. I shivered as the wind caressed me. It didn't seem right somehow, that a life should have ended alone, here in this beautiful, timeless place, that a man should have died and no trace of his passing remained but the broken collar of a cat. I tried to picture it through Diamond's eyes. What had he been doing? What was so important that he had died for it? Had he really discovered some cougars in an area that hadn't seen them in years or was I just being too fanciful? Yet it all fit my theory: the bear sign, the cedars, the paper with "red welt" and the compass coordinate on it, and now poor Paulie's collar. I pictured the three-legged cat as she had run back to me and rubbed against my leg on the portage trail. Not for the first time I wondered what had become of her.

I shook myself out of the gloomy mood I was falling into. I studied the cliff and realized there was no way up here without ropes. I'd have to skirt it. I pulled out my small daypack and stuffed it with an emergency blanket, some food, a map, compass, matches, flashlight, and pepper spray, reluctantly foregoing my collection pack. I threw a rope over a branch of one of the cedars and hauled up my pack to keep the bears from tearing it to shreds. I hoisted my daypack onto my back and headed up into the cedars. I skirted the base of the cliff as it ran inland and after ten minutes found a way up.

It was a long narrow cleft in the cliff that angled gently up through the rock. The going got worse as the crack narrowed like a funnel until my shoulders touched both sides and the trail ended abruptly. I looked up and saw blue sky twenty feet above my head. Before I could give myself even a second to think about my fear of heights, I braced my back against one wall, my feet against the other, and began the slow shimmy up. My legs were aching from the effort by the time my head emerged into the dazzling sunshine. I hauled myself out and looked out over the lake as I took a swig of water from my canteen. I hoped I could find a better way down than the route up.

I walked along the edge of the cliff face trying to get my bearings. The sun was almost directly overhead and beat down relentlessly. The sheer drop of the cliff made my stomach queasy and my knees weak, but what I was looking for was unmistakable.

The thin jagged red welt in the face of the cliff cut up through the top and ran back behind me toward the woods. I sat down astride the welt with my back to the lake and took out my compass. Diamond's compass reading, if he had taken it here from astride the red welt, pointed off to the left. Northwest. I could feel the excitement building in me as I followed the compass reading across the top of the sun-baked cliff, the wind blowing through the trees and a veery singing its water-fall song somewhere off to my right.

When the rock of the cliff gave way to the forest, I stopped and scanned the trees, searching for a blaze, willing it to be there. There were no easy bright orange markers, but then I hadn't really expected Diamond to be so obvious. In the silence I could hear a motorboat in the distance.

I started walking a transect back and forth, looking at every damn tree within a hundred and fifty feet of the rock, and in a path twenty feet on either side of the welt. It took me fifteen minutes before I found the first blaze, a hundred feet from the open cliff and practically invisible to anyone not looking for it, because it was low down, well below eye level. I took a compass reading from the first blaze and almost didn't see the second, Diamond had placed it so far ahead. A very cautious man, but once I reached the second blaze, the rest were easy to follow, coming every twenty feet, which was a good thing because there was no trail and the going was rough. I checked to make sure he'd blazed both sides of the trail before chasing his blazes into the bush. It didn't look as though anyone had used this trail except Diamond the day he had blazed it. Curious. Surely he would have used it often.

I followed the blazes for several hours, taking compass readings every so often. I began to worry about getting back before dark. Twice I thought I heard an animal in the woods, and once I saw the back end of a moose as it ambled away from me, its huge bulk somehow making no noise as it moved quickly through the forest. It was nearly 2:30 p.m. by the time the blazes ended abruptly at the edge of a huge rocky outcrop studded with cliffs and boulders that stretched ahead of me for perhaps a hundred yards or more before descending again into the trees. It was a high point of land overlooking a vast wild forest, uncut for as far as the eye could see and dotted with lakes and rivers too numerous to name. No wonder the loggers were drooling over this country.

I looked about me and wondered what to do next when I caught sight of a piece of burlap waving gently in the sickly hot breeze. I stopped and studied it from a safe distance. It was some kind of shelter or blind built between two boulders with the burlap acting as a roof and back wall. What the front looked like, or how big it was, I couldn't tell from where I stood. I could feel the excitement building inside me.

I waited and watched the blind, but after ten minutes, when there was no movement, I cautiously approached, moving quietly and carefully until I reached the flap. Gingerly I pulled it back and peered inside.

I wasn't sure what I expected to see, but it wasn't the fully furnished affair that I found myself staring at. It was still crude, but as blinds go, it was like Buckingham Palace. Diamond certainly had been a man who liked his creature comforts. At the far end was another burlap wall with the telltale peeping flaps of a blind littered throughout it. There was a hunk of foam rubber leaning against the rock, almost obliterated by a mountain of pillows and several blankets. It was positioned right under one of the peepholes. Beside the makeshift sofa was a small crude bookshelf made from slabs of rock holding a dozen whodunits and some papers. There was even a square of carpet on the rough rock floor. I made my way over to the peephole nearest the sofa. It was a square patch of burlap attached only at the top and loose on three sides. I lifted it up and found myself staring out over a small ledge and then down what looked to be a sheer drop of thirty feet onto a jumble of rocks and caves that wended their way down the cliff into the forest floor below.

The blind was actually a natural crevice between the rocks of a much larger cliff. Diamond had simply run two overlapping pieces of burlap across both ends on a wooden pole and then roofed it with more burlap. There was a pair of new miniature binoculars with Diamond's initials scratched onto the left-hand tube; the hand that did it had jerked on the D so that it looked like a P. I picked up the binoculars and put the cord around my neck out of habit, cautiously pulled back the flaps, and looked out. I looked down through the jumble of rocks, but if Diamond had indeed been watching cougars, they weren't there at the moment. There was nothing to see. Disappointed, I quietly let the flap fall back and turned my attention to the blind itself.

I picked up a *Macleans* magazine that lay on the crude wooden desk to the left of the chair, looked at the date, and sucked in my breath. It was a very recent issue, so recent that I had only just received mine in the mail the day before. I looked at the subscriber, and a chill went through me: Don Allenby. I looked about in alarm and saw a black and red checked coat flung into the corner near the chair, and a small leather satchel hidden in the darkness. I picked up the satchel and opened it. It was full of papers, old magazines, a change purse, and a wallet. I flicked open the wallet and Don Allenby's face stared up at me. I felt a swift flicker of fear.

I stood there like some brainless idiot holding the wallet with his licence in my hands as a million thoughts careered through my head. Don Allenby was out there somewhere. I could hear my heart beat in the calm of the blind, and the sudden grating of rock against rock sounded like an explosion in the silence. I dropped low and moved quietly toward the lookout flap. The sound had come from somewhere below me. Was he out there waiting for me? If Don was out there somewhere I was a sitting duck and we both knew it.

Through the binoculars I could make out movement in the shadows of one of the rocks, and I held my breath and watched. Suddenly a small spotted golden animal tumbled into view, followed by two more furballs rolling and tumbling and biting each other as they frolicked, their ringed tails flicking in the sun. I let out my breath slowly and, despite my fear, savoured the sight below me. So I had been right. Diamond had found a family of cougars. He had pulled off the unthinkable — finding an endangered species on the eve of a chainsaw gang moving in to clear-cut. What a coup — not only for this piece of forest, but for Diamond as a researcher. And the find was all the more impressive because the home ranges of these creatures were so large. I held my breath as the long, lithe, golden body of the mother glided into view, her cubs gambolling around her as she blithely ignored them and curled up in the crevice. I sat spellbound, watching them tumble and chase each other, rolling over their mother and playing with her tail. The den must be very close, I thought.

Two of the cubs were locked in each other's arms and were rolling over and over and the third was still playing with the mother's tail: as she flicked it away he'd leap and pounce. The mother was wearing a radio collar with a plastic tag on it, and I focused the binoculars and tried to read what it said, but she was uncooperative until she suddenly looked straight at me and I made out the letters S-i-a-n. The name rang a distant bell, but before I could summon up the memory, I noticed the complete immobility of the cougars. The family froze, like a family caught in a portrait, all turning to look up straight at me. And then they vanished without a sound.

I had a sudden blinding, unnerving, and overwhelming urge to get the hell out of there. I was halfway to the entrance to the blind when I heard a sharp scraping sound overhead, followed by a rain of pebbles onto the roof of the blind. An ominous rumble grew in intensity even as I dived for shelter toward the cougar side of the blind, not knowing if I had chosen correctly or if I was diving right into the line of the rocks crashing down on the blind. The binoculars swinging from around my neck rapped me hard in the chest. There was a sharp bullet-like sound as a boulder ripped open the roof, and I could feel, more than see, the avalanche coming down. I launched myself at the burlap wall, praying the ledge beyond it was big enough to take me.

I felt the burlap tighten and resist me, and for one dreadful moment I thought it would shoot me back into the line of the boulders, but suddenly it gave way and I was catapulted out onto the ledge. The momentum of my launch caused me to roll right over the edge, the strap of the binoculars catching on a rock and snapping as I scrambled to cling to something solid, clawing with my hands, scrabbling to retain a grip as my fingers slipped and I could feel myself falling.

chapter twenty-four

It was deathly quiet. I lay in the pile of rubble five feet below the ledge, clinging to a stalwart little cedar that had broken my fall. I looked down below me and saw that it wasn't the sheer drop I had thought but a steep series of boulders and rocks that rolled down to the forest floor. My left leg was screaming bloody murder and I moved gingerly, afraid of any broken bones. My baby finger was mashed to a pulp, but there was no pain and I felt a moment of unreality, looking at it as if it belonged to someone else.

The moment was shattered when I heard Don scrambling somewhere up above me. I struggled to my feet, scanning the cliff, but I could see nothing. Footsteps sounded above and to my left, coming closer, causing a cascade of pebbles to fall. In the noise it made I moved quickly, angling away and down to keep out of sight. One of the loose rocks struck me on my baby finger and I viciously bit off the scream welling up inside me. I stopped when the noise stopped and waited, crouched behind a large boulder. I was just ten feet from the woods, and the silence went on and on. Suddenly the footsteps sounded again, much closer, and as I held my breath I heard rocks being moved. Bent double I bolted for the woods, not daring to look behind me, and when I reached them I kept on running.

When I came to the first blaze I sat down in the hollow of an old cedar and tried to stifle the nausea that threatened to overwhelm me. My mashed finger was bleeding and I wrestled with my shirt, ripping off a hunk and applying a dressing. I struggled to my feet and kept moving, following the blazes back, but it was hard work. I stopped often to listen to the woods, but I heard nothing. Maybe he had decided to ambush me further along the trail, a trail that he presumably knew a lot better than I did. I froze at the thought and then, in total panic, I crawled under a rock outcrop, too afraid to go on. I must have lain there for fifteen minutes before I heard a twig snap somewhere off in the woods and I froze again, waiting, listening, like a wild animal trapped by fear.

Something was moving toward me, cautiously, quietly; the telltale snap of a twig here, a twig there, was unmistakable. I held my breath, shrank back into the rock crevice, and waited.

I could hear the footsteps coming closer, the shallow breathing, but from where I lay I could see nothing at all. My mind was pitched to the screaming point, the terror boring holes into me like worms into apples. I was afraid I couldn't stand it, that my fear would explode out of me, like some horrific sneeze of the mind, that I'd stand up and in desperation call out, "Yoo-hoo. I'm here." Time passed. I struggled with my fear. The footsteps slowly receded and I lay in the crevice and watched for hours as the sun move inexorably across the sky, while I tried to regain my sanity.

Where was he? What was going through his mind? I tried to imagine what he would do, tried to build up my confidence. He was not a big man, and I didn't think he'd ever counted on having to kill someone with his own hands. He'd baited Diamond, after all, and let the bear do the rest. He'd not had the guts to do it himself. Indecisive too. A coward as well. He'd tried to kill me with gas fumes and had thrown a rock in our canoe to destroy the film. I had a chance against a coward.

I began to feel a bit more confident, my fear subsiding to a dull roar. My mind cleared. I knew I couldn't follow the blazes back out. He'd be there somewhere waiting for me — waiting for me to manoeuvre myself near a cliff, and make it look like an accident. My throat was parched as dry as paper, but I'd lost my pack somewhere along the way. The palms of my hands were wet and I was breathing far too fast. I tried to calm myself down and think about what I had to do — tried to stop the panic from welling up again. I took out the compass from my pocket and decided to take a new line that I hoped would bring me out somewhere below the campsite. What I'd do when I got there would have to come to me as inspiration.

The sun had long since set when I finally made my move. It was rough going, and very slow, as I tried to avoid any dry branches. I felt like a thundering jumbo jet trying to be quiet. Every time I stepped on a dry twig I'd freeze, afraid even to swipe the mosquitoes from my face, straining my eyes searching the darkness of the woods for the telltale shape of a man lurking in the shadows. I stopped and rested often as the night wore on.

I'd been walking for what seemed like hours when I stumbled on a root and came down hard on something soft, yielding, and wet. I pushed my upper body off whatever it was with my arms, looked down on what had cushioned my fall, and gagged. In the dim light of dawn, the unseeing face, contorted in death, gazed up at the last of the stars. I rolled violently to one side and did some heavy breathing. Don's face was badly mashed and bruised and his lower body was at an angle God never intended. I looked behind me and saw the dark looming shape of a cliff, perhaps twenty feet high. *He must have fallen in the dark while stalking me*, I thought.

I felt the relief flood over me like a tidal wave and then as quickly ebb away, leaving in its place a void of emotion before the next flood of feelings filled me with a sense of dread. Even in this light I could see that he'd been dead for more than a few hours. My blood ran as cold as the blood in Don's veins when I realized what Don's death meant.

It was someone else out there stalking me, and all the rules were different now. I felt the strength of my initial fear cascading back. At least with Don as an opponent, I had had a fighting chance. Now I didn't know who my stalker was, how strong or how well-armed, decisive or driven. I had no information at all, other than that whoever it was wanted me dead, just as surely as they had wanted Don dead.

Donaldson, Ray, Cameron, or even Lianna could easily have followed me. They all knew where I was going and had access to a motorboat. Roberta and Shannon had gone to join Patrick and Davies at the biology station, close enough for them to have paddled over here. Even Leslie could have doubled back and followed me. If any one of them knew about the cougars, there was a lot at stake for each of them.

I hadn't realized just how much I'd clung to the unformed thought that if I had come face to face with

Don I could have talked him out of killing me. But the others? I had no such confidence where any of the others were concerned.

I had to get out of here. I travelled slowly, stopping every few minutes to listen, waiting for whoever it was to leap out and nail me, bracing for it, whittling my fear into a sharp point. I came to a grinding halt as the woods suddenly ended at a huge rock outcrop. I glanced behind me and thought about heading back into the woods, but caught my breath when I saw a dark silhouette sliding through the trees toward me, moving silently and surely. Had I been seen? I threw myself down in panic onto the cold, hard rock and belly-inched my way forward, hoping to find a crevice. Instead all I found was air. I cautiously raised my head and, to my horror, found that I was at the edge of the cliff, and thirty feet below me lay the black waters of the lake. There was a small cedar growing out of a crevice, and below it I could see a small ledge. I grabbed hold of the cedar, swung my legs over the edge, and tried not to think about the drop. I let myself down to my full length, hanging there, my legs scrabbling for the ledge and not finding it. As I hung there, I started silently reciting *The Cremation of Sam McGee* to steady my nerves. I concentrated on pretending I was only two inches off the ground. No problem. I could hang here forever. Suddenly a stone rasped and tumbled down past me and I heard it scattering on the rocks below. Not two inches. I was too afraid to look up even if I could have. If someone was up there I could only hold my breath and pray they hadn't seen me.

And suddenly someone was there. I could hear them breathing and then the pain seared through my fingers as something slammed into them. I let go and at the same time instinctively bunched my legs against the cliff face as I spun around and pushed off. All that went through my mind were thoughts of all those countless people who have died because they dived into water without checking for rocks first. *I don't want to die*, I thought as the lake rushed up at me in the dim light. I plunged into the coldness of the water, bracing for the hit, but nothing happened, just the peaceful silence of the depths. I kicked up to the surface, angling in toward shore so that when I surfaced the rocks and cliff face would hide me from above. I clung to a rock for a long time until I heard footsteps slowly move away. I pulled myself out, and as the sun came up I scrambled over the rocks and into the woods, heading toward the campsite. I knew I was close to the canoe. All I had to do was get to it. At least that's how I comforted myself as I struggled through the woods.

I could hear the rapids now, slowly getting louder, and I saw a clearing ahead. I approached cautiously, moving from tree to tree until I could get a view of the open area. It appeared that I was approaching the campsite from downriver. The beginning of the portage was quite close. I hadn't yet formulated a plan as I crept closer. Suddenly I caught a movement out of the corner of my eye. I shrank back against a tree and watched as a man, who had been stooping over something, stood up and looked around. I stifled a gasp. Patrick was standing over my pack, which now lay on the ground, the rope attaching it to the tree still dangling above it. In his hand he was holding a tin and looking about him furtively.

Suddenly he dropped the tin on top of my pack and turned to stare right through me. I froze. I was downwind and the smell of fish was strong. I could see enough of the tin to tell me it was sardines and it was open. Patrick's hand went for his pocket. I bolted, racing between the trees heading for the water. I heard a loud bang even as Patrick yelled something I couldn't hear.

I felt the bear a split second before it attacked. The blow, silent and sudden, sent me sprawling forward. I felt a sharp row of painful jabs sear through my arm, and I smelled the hot breath of the bear on my face, the stink overpowering in its intensity. The weight of its body pressed me to the ground. I went limp trying to remember if I was supposed to play dead or fight like the devil. With some bear species you fight them, with others you play dead. As he began to nibble my arm I knew I could no more play dead than a bear could play a violin — the pain was too excruciating. I let out a murderous bellow fuelled by adrenaline, fear, and pain, and at the same time I wrenched my arm, flung myself sideways, and rolled away. The bear growled and came at me as I scrambled to my feet and whirled around. Then, standing at my full height with my arms raised, I bellowed again. But the bear kept coming, bowling me over. I went limp again, not because I wanted to but because I had no strength left and I was terrified. My arms were pinned under the bear's weight, my nose jammed into the smell of the cedar twigs, my ears blocked by its weight — all I could think was, *What a horrible way to die*. Suddenly the bear let go.

I lay immobile in the dirt, and from where I was I could see the water and the canoe and the reason the bear had left me. Patrick was yelling and bolting for the water, repeatedly looking over his shoulder to see where the bear was. The murder weapon turning on the murderer, I thought, and wanted to scream at my rotten choice of men. The bear caught up with him at the water's edge and swatted him in the head with his paw. The blow catapulted Patrick into the current of the river, and I watched him trying to keep his head above the water as the current caught him. The bear followed him along the shoreline, and I lost sight of them both.

I exploded from the ground, my head ringing, my vision blurred, but there was no pain, only a momentary fear of blacking out that surged through me but then was gone, and I was running, staggering under the fear that the bear would return. I resisted the urge to run into the woods and made for the canoe. I pushed it into the water, and then realized it was still tied to the tree. I scrambled up and struggled with the knot. I kept looking up toward the woods as I frantically tried to undo the knot. Finally it gave at the exact moment that the woods erupted with an enormous bellow and the bear came bursting out as if in slow motion, its massive forearms flung out at each stride, muscles rippling, the huge jaw open. The roar of the hunter hunting its prey boomed through the woods.

Frantically I pushed the canoe off with my right foot, but as I did I slipped and fell headlong into the canoe and lost momentum. The canoe rocked dangerously to the left, the gunwale almost slipping beneath the water as the bear charged down toward me. I frantically groped for the paddle and pushed myself up onto my knees. I could feel the current begin to pull me even as the bear gathered itself at the water's edge, its legs bunching into a coiled spring, and then it leapt at the canoe, one long, graceful jump at full stretch.

It missed the canoe by inches, and the waves it sent out caught the canoe broadside, throwing me off balance. I felt the canoe begin to go over. For one frantic moment, it sat suspended on the edge of tipping as I tried to regain my balance. I slapped the water with the open face of my paddle, and the canoe fell dizzyingly back to a level field. As I did so the bear reared out of the shallow water right next to me. I brought the blade of the paddle high over my head and brought it down on the bear's open jaws. The shaft of the paddle broke and the bear lunged at me, grabbing the broken end of the paddle and jerking his head back.

The strength of the movement was terrifying and instinctively, I released the paddle and grabbed the gunwales to try and steady the canoe. The bear sensed the danger before I did, but it was too late. I could hear the roar of the rapids, feel the pull of the water against the canoe. And suddenly the bear and I were one, the power of the bear reduced to basics as the power of nature took over. I had to move to the stern to get the second paddle if I was to have any chance of running the rapids in the canoe.

Leslie had said there was an easy route through them along the outside curve of the river, the route that was always taken in a lightly loaded canoe. It was a fast, straight run with no obstacles, and I remembered that Ryan and I had been able to run them almost fully loaded. However the western shore, the side now drawing me down, was a roiling, boiling mass of foam and standing waves, boulders, and small shelves. I shuddered at what must have happened to Patrick and marvelled at how I could still feel something for him.

I scrambled forward, holding both sides of the gunwale, grabbed the paddle, and hunkered down inside the canoe. I jammed the paddle into the water with a powerful forward stroke against the strengthening current. I had to hold my own against the current long enough to get me over to the other side. With my back to the rapids, I angled the canoe upriver, pointing toward the eastern shore, and paddled like a madwoman. If I got far enough across I could steer my bow around and safely head down the clear channel.

The rapids were roaring in my ears, the sound inexplicably dividing in my head into all its parts: apart from the homogenous noise of constant wind through the trees I could now hear, as in a symphony, the gurgles of water moving around the rocks that I could sense creeping up behind me; the sucking, squelching sound of whirlpools near a keeper where the swirling of the water has been known to spin and swallow a canoe; the crashes and splashes of the standing waves set up by water rushing over boulders many feet beneath the surface; the pounding of the waves against a rock island; and the quiet gliding of water flowing over rocks far beneath the surface. Like the instruments in a symphony, they all played their own tune, joining in to present a crescendo of raging, roaring water that overwhelmed the quality of its separate components.

I could feel the pull of the water on my paddle at every stroke as the river gathered speed. The small riffles on the water suddenly vanished, and I knew I would never make it to the other side. I was going down stern first into the rapids, held in the powerful grip of something I couldn't beat.

Instinctively I turned around in the canoe to face downriver, grabbed the paddle firmly, and studied the river, my fear swirling around me like the water before me. I was being drawn toward the wide open V of water funnelling between two gigantic boulders. As I approached, all the riffles and white of the splashes further up were suddenly pulled taut as the water was hauled down an incline of the earth's surface and then stretched through the rocks and boulders.

I hit the V dead on, my canoe gathering speed so that I had to back paddle to slow it down. Ahead lay a boiling jumble of froth and foam, impossible to read because the angle was so flat. Briefly, I stood up for a better view, but all I could see was a field of unforgiving boulders. I concentrated on what was directly ahead of me: on the right a jagged, evil-looking rock and to the left a nearly completely submerged boulder with water dancing on its gleaming pate. I went right, squeezing between the jagged rock and another boulder, and danced down through some standing waves, struggling to keep from broadsiding any of them. I'd never soloed in rapids before, and I was way out of my depth.

I could see an ominous stretch of smooth water ahead, and the telltale cut-off shoreline at the waterline indicating a shelf. There was no way out: the current was going too fast and the shelf was too wide. I couldn't get around it. I had to go over it.

The canoe shot forward, and the horrendous scrape and shudder of the keel as it went over the shelf jarred me and almost flung me out of the canoe. I held fast, and the canoe dived into the churning waters. The bow went under, and I went with it.

The churning, roiling waters grabbed me and I gasped as the cold water soaked me through. As I came up for air I looked around wildly for the canoe. It was now a lethal weapon that could wedge me against a rock or knock me out. I saw it tumbling ahead of me like a matchstick. I pitched and turned and was taken by the current.

Desperately I tried to ride it on my back, legs up and out of the way of any boulders that might snag them and spell death for me. I didn't want my leg getting jammed between two rocks while my body was thrown forward by the current, forcing my head down under the water just as it had with the sweeper. I bounced and rolled and grazed some boulders and felt a dull pain in my left leg. I caught glimpses of the bear surging through the foam ahead of me, tossed like a toy, and the thought of ending up in an eddy with it made my mouth go dry. Suddenly I was pulled under by some unseen force lurking beneath the river.

I felt it pull my legs first like an enormous vacuum. I took in a huge lungful of air as it sucked me down, and then the whirlpool's powerful spiral of water took the rest of me, pulling me down with no intention of spitting me out again. There was no fighting the power of this keeper, and I knew it. If I tried I'd exhaust myself further. I had only about a minute at the most before my air ran out. I had to fight the instinct to swim up and instead go with it, letting it take me, waiting for the chance to swim out from under it. I felt a moment of panic as my body tried to move up, against my mind's wishes, but my mind won.

I fought my way down through the spiral, down, forever down, until I could feel my lungs screeching for air. When I hit the bottom I swam along for as far as I could before I knew I had to let my body take me up, whether or not I had swum far enough to escape the clutches of that deadly spiral. I burst out of the water spouting foam and gulping air in great wracking heaves as I struggled to stay afloat. I was out of the worst of the current. It took me gently now and swirled me through into an eddy behind a large boulder. With what strength I had left I hugged the boulder and lay there, retching and coughing uncontrollably.

The bear was less than fifty yards from me, but on the other side of the river with fast water between us. It was hauling itself out of the water right next to where my battered canoe lay wrapped around a boulder, a gaping hole spouting water like a sieve. There was no point in even trying to get over there. Even if I did, the canoe was useless, and with the bear now on that side I wasn't feeling very brave. I hugged the rock and lay still, gathering my strength.

The bear staggered up onto the shore and stood swaying on the river's edge, peering back at the rapids as if looking for me. It started moving drunkenly toward the woods, and then stopped. It shook the water from its hair. Starting with its head the shake travelled like a wave down its body to its rump and tiny tail, shaking the water free. I watched it amble off unsteadily into the woods, and then I released my hold on the rock and was swept down into the quiet pools at the very bottom of the rapids.

I clambered onto the rocks and eyed the shoreline dubiously. The forest came right down almost to the water's edge. It would be one hell of a bushwhack back, even with the portage. My legs ached from the bashing against the rocks, and my arms and hands and back were throbbing from where the bear had raked me in its efforts to turn me over, but there wasn't a lot of blood and I seemed to be okay.

I was still thinking about the sickening sound the claws had made when something made me look up. About twenty yards upriver I saw Patrick, lying motionless at the water's edge where he had dragged himself half out of the water. I watched him closely for five minutes, but there was no movement. I picked up a good-sized rock, hefted it in my hand, and cautiously approached him, bracing myself for him to spring to life with a blood-curdling yell and strangle me with his hands. When I was five feet from him he moved and I jumped back in alarm, but it was only the current pummelling him.

I approached him warily, gripping the rock so tightly my knuckles showed white. Gingerly I turned him over with my free hand. He was out cold, his handsome face ashen, highlighting an angry slash across his temple. I quickly felt for a pulse. Slow and steady. I thought about leaving him there in the eddy, wanting to let my fear of him get the better of me, but then I thought of my disks, and what I had foolishly thought he once meant to me, and realized I couldn't. So I pulled him out of the water and took off my belt to tie his hands; my nerves, tighter than a spring, jumped at every perceived movement, expecting those bedroom eyes to flash open with murderous intent. I fought my imagination as hard as my fingers fought to tie a knot around his hands before he could wake up and turn nasty.

chapter twenty-five

I needn't have worried. The blow to Patrick's head had been a dilly — it was incredible that he'd stayed conscious long enough to haul himself out of the water. Even after I'd mopped up the blood and badly bound the wound with chunks of my shirt, he was still out cold, and I was simply cold. My teeth were chattering, partly from relief that I was alive, partly from the physical cold that the sun couldn't seem to dissipate as it rose higher in the sky, and partly for the emptiness I felt when I looked at Patrick.

I looked at my own wounds and figured they could wait, except for the baby finger. I bound it up again, and when I finished I figured it was about seven o'clock in the morning and I wondered what the hell I was going to do. I was on the wrong side of the river to hike out for help unless I left Patrick where I'd hauled him out and swam across to the other side. I took one look at the swirling water at the base of the rapids and the far shore a hundred yards away and I knew I did not have the energy to do it. I was wondering if I could float one of the old logs piled like matchsticks at the base of the rapids, and paddle across astride that, when I heard someone yell.

I thought at first that I was delirious, but the yell came again. I turned and saw a canoe approaching down my side of the little lake from the direction of the biology station. The canoe was backlit, and I couldn't make out who it was, just that they were wildly waving their paddle, which flashed silver in the sun. Nothing had ever looked as nice as that canoe. As it got nearer, I saw that it was Leslie kneeling amidships, strong-arming the canoe toward me, a fishing rod wobbling up and down as it trailed behind the canoe. I felt an enormous wave of relief that nothing had changed Leslie's mind about coming here to fish for breakfast.

Leslie nosed the canoe in as close to where I was as she could get, and then leapt out and hauled the canoe out over the rocks. She came running over, leaping from boulder to boulder.

She was out of breath when she reached me, but the concern in her eyes was evident.

"Jesus, what happened to you?" she asked, as she fumbled in her backpack and pulled out a tiny first aid kit. I couldn't imagine what she saw as she looked down at me. It was likely not a pretty sight, and I couldn't imagine her little first aid kit doing much good. She was about to set to work fixing me up when she caught sight of Patrick's body slumped behind the boulder where I had pulled him to safety. The colour drained from her face as she took in the horrid gash on his face, the claw marks, the blood, and his bound hands. I thought he must have looked worse than I did, or maybe it was the bound hands that bothered her, but she took a while regaining her equilibrium.

She slowly returned her gaze to me and said, "What the hell happened here? You both look as though you've been through a meat grinder. Is he alive?"

I nodded, and told her about Patrick's attempts to stalk and kill me as she cleaned me up far better than I had been able to do. I told her about finding the blind and the cougars, and tripping over Don's dead body. Leslie turned pale at the mention of Don's name, and some garbled sound came from her lips, her distress building with every new word I uttered. When I'd finished my story, Leslie was dumbstruck. In the end, all she could manage to say was, "Poor Don, no one deserved what he got."

She turned her attentions to Patrick after handing me a windbreaker.

Gratefully, I put it on. I was shivering so hard it was difficult to pull it over my head. I watched her cleaning the gash on Patrick's head and thought sadly of what might have been. He was still out cold, and I hoped he stayed that way until after we'd turned him over to the police. I didn't think I could bear to look into those beautiful murderous eyes. How could I have been so wrong?

Leslie came back and asked me if I thought I could help drag Patrick to the canoe. I didn't want to touch him. I felt so betrayed by my own feelings. It took all my strength, physically and emotionally, to help Leslie carry Patrick, and we dumped him unceremoniously into the canoe, his hands still bound. Leslie stowed the fishing line, took the stern, and handed me a paddle. We pushed off, rounded the point, and headed across the lake to Diamond's old camp, with me paddling like a toddler.

Leslie steered the canoe to the beginning of the second set of rapids, and not to the gravel beach of the campsite where I assumed she would head. "It'll be easier to get Patrick out if we go alongside the rock ledge of the portage," she yelled.

"Why don't we just land at the beach and I'll go for help?" I waved in the direction of Diamond's campsite, where Roberta had said she would be with Davies and Shannon.

"Nobody there. They all went back to the biology station last night. Left me to clean up." I nodded and turned to look at the beginning of the portage, where Ryan and I had almost died. I could see the cliff where the rock had come plummeting down, and I watched as the water began to swirl and gather strength around us. I could hear a veery calling in the woods near the campsite, and the sun touched my face like an old friend. I should have felt relieved, but instead I felt jumpy and on edge. I quickly looked back at Patrick, who was lying amidships. I half expected to see his eyes boring into my back, but he was still unconscious.

Leslie steered us expertly in and along the shelf by turning the canoe at the last minute and coming up into the current and the small eddy. I was seizing up, and it was awkward to get out while holding the knotted bowline. I nearly fell between the canoe and the shelf as we got our signals mixed and Leslie, without warning, got out at the same time. She stumbled, and the bag she was holding in one hand fell and something metal clattered toward me. We both reached for it at the same time, but I got to it first and Leslie backed away. I glanced at her and then looked back at the object in my hand. Time stood still. I was holding a pair of miniature binoculars. Even as I turned them over in my hand, I knew what I would see. A shaky D that looked like a P. I raised my head and our eyes locked.

The sudden jolting fear in my stomach crashed through my body like a physical vibration. Leslie must have picked them up while she was searching for my body in the rubble. I remembered the tug of the strap on my neck and the snapping sound as it had broken. I slowly put my hand up and rubbed the sore spot on my neck. I couldn't peel my eyes away from Leslie's. It was like the sick fascination of a spectator at a car crash — I could only stare at her and wonder what was going through her head.

Leslie broke the spell by backing away from me and reaching for her pocket. I suddenly found myself looking at the dark, round hole of the gun that suddenly materialized in her hand.

"Took you long enough," came the snide, cutting voice. I saw a cruel smile of triumph spread across her face. "Untie Patrick's hands."

She inclined her head in Patrick's direction. When I didn't move, not out of bravery but out of pure and simple shock, she said calmly, "Don't you understand? It's got to look like an accident. If he goes down those rapids with his hands tied, everyone'll know it wasn't an accident, won't they? And that could raise very inconvenient questions." She smiled sweetly, and I felt as though a vacuum cleaner had suddenly sucked my mouth dry.

"Don't you see? You both got caught in the current. I saw you heading downriver trying to reach shore. The canoe swamped and you were thrown out. I tried to throw you a rope, I really did, but it was no good. I couldn't save either of you."

She smiled again, almost sadly, waved the gun, and gestured toward Patrick. My mind was cluttered with too many thoughts and snippets of information for me to take in anything except for the fact that I was in deep shit, and Patrick wasn't a murderer! In the midst of fear there was joy. I moved toward him with mind-numbing slowness.

I knelt by the side of the canoe, leaned over, and started fumbling with his hands. He was semi-conscious and moaning and his eyes were open, but they were clouded with pain and disorientation from the blow to his head. I felt any hope vanish as I realized I would not be able to count on help from him. But then I realized the corollary to that. It was up to me to help not only myself but Patrick as well, and the thought suddenly gave me courage and dispelled the helpless feeling that had threatened to shut me down. I groped with the knot, stalling for time, eying the distance between Leslie and myself, wondering if I could get to her before she pulled the trigger. But if she wanted our deaths to look like an accident, would she really pull the trigger? I couldn't read her well enough to take the chance. Or perhaps I was just too scared and was hoping for a miracle.

"Is that what happened to Jake? An accident?" I said, frantically trying to keep her talking.

She laughed. "The bear got Diamond. You know that."

I shook my head, still crouching by the canoe. "I don't think so. I think you killed him and made it look like an accident. You seem to like that scenario."

She gave a derisive snort but said nothing, just stared at me, waiting, watching, like a cat watches its prey.

"You found out about the cougars and couldn't stand the thought of your old lover and rival getting the kudos."

She snorted again. "The bastard didn't deserve it," she growled.

"So you drugged his water, and when he was asleep you deliberately baited him and left him for the bear to finish him off."

"You make it sound so cold-blooded," she said. "It wasn't really like that, you know." She paused, and then shrugged. "You see, Jake told me about the cougars the morning before he died when we bumped into each other at the portage. He didn't tell me out of friendship, but because he wanted to see my reaction. He meant to break the news the next day," she said bitterly. "He laughed at me, told me even if I lived to be a hundred I would never be as good a researcher as he was. Damn it. It was a fluke he found those cougars, not skill, and he knew it. But he laughed at me. He laughed at me. I hated him. I hated what he'd done to me. He had taken my love and my job. I hadn't thought he could do anything else to me, but I was wrong."

"So, you came back."

"Yeah. I came back. I made sure he wasn't there. He'd gone back up to his cougars. Of course, I didn't know that at the time, but he'd left with a full pack, so I knew he'd be gone for the day and would have to sleep at the loggers' campsite overnight. Macho as he was, he didn't much like canoeing after dusk. I drugged his water, and I waited until he came back. I watched him drink the water and finally, when he was asleep, I snuck into the campsite."

She was looking at a point above my left shoulder, her eyes unfocused. I stood up, the cramps in my legs screaming for mercy. She waved the gun at me, narrowing her eyes, and I saw the hatred, hard and cold.

"I thought if I hit him on the head hard enough to keep him from waking, and then dragged him to the water and dumped him in, it wouldn't be like actually killing him. He'd drown — everyone would think it was an accident and no one would come snooping around. There'd be no chance of anyone stumbling on the cougars, and I could break the news after I'd gotten his photos developed to prove it and located the bloody beasts." She laughed derisively and continued. "I pocketed his full film canisters, but they all turned out to be unexposed film. The only good film was the one I took from his camera. But then I lost it." She put her left hand in her pants pocket and wiggled her fingers through a hole. "And then you almost kyboshed it all by finding the bloody film and I had to sacrifice it."

Not to mention almost sacrificing us, I thought, as I remembered the flash of purple up on the cliff.

"You thought it was the larvae," she said, "but I didn't know about the larvae until I read it in the papers."

"So you fumigated my lab and stole my disks."

She nodded. "I couldn't take the chance. And it was so easy. Your colleague, Jim Hilson, is a good friend of mine. We understand each other. He gave me a key to the building."

Hilson! I felt a spasm of anger burning through my fear like sun through fog. She looked through me and an odd look of revulsion rippled through her face like a wave on a beach, mirroring mine. She shook herself and refocused on me.

"I couldn't do it. I couldn't hit him with the rock. Isn't that funny?" She laughed, the hollowness of it sounding like an echo without its source.

"He was lying there sound asleep with Paulie curled up beside him, and I just couldn't do it," she said, separating out the last five words as if they were contaminants. "I was disgusted with myself and I went back to my canoe to lick my wounds, and that's when I saw the bear downwind of Diamond."

She moved the gun to her left hand and said, "It was heading my way and everything else happened so quickly that my mind had nothing to do with it. It was as if I were on autopilot — my body did it all. I retrieved my pack and I took his flare gun and then opened one of the cans of sardines I'd brought along for lunch the next day if I didn't bag a fish. I dumped it on his shirt. I moved well away from him and the bear and waited in the shadows. Paulie nearly ruined things by waking up and staggering toward me, meowing, but I knocked her out with the rock. The bear took its own sweet time and I thought it wasn't going to get to Diamond, especially when the bastard woke up and spotted me. He was pretty groggy, though, and the bear got him before he could get to me."

"What made you so sure the bear would attack him?" I asked.

Leslie smiled. "I didn't know for sure, but I had nothing to lose once I'd discovered I couldn't do it myself. Cameron had told me there was a rogue bear over here and that they had tried to get it a bunch of times but with no luck. He had a close call with the beast while he was eating fish when the bear came out of nowhere. So I thought the percentages were in my favour. I had nothing to lose."

When I didn't say anything she kept on going.

"Of course, I couldn't be sure and I had no plans if it failed, but it didn't, did it? But then I realized I had a big problem. I didn't want anyone snooping around the area before I could find the cougars. I had to move the body, so they'd search for the bear somewhere else. I knew Cam and his buddies would never tell the police about the rogue bear because they routinely poached fish in this area. They didn't want anyone snooping around either."

"But what about the trace of tranquilizer they found in his bloodstream?"

Leslie narrowed her eyes.

"You don't miss much, do you?" Suddenly she smiled again and turned the question back on me, becoming professor to my student. It was an unnerving feeling. "What do you think happened?"

"The bear hung around the body too long. You tried to dart the bear so that you could move Diamond and his things quickly back to his permanent campsite, but you missed the bear and got Diamond instead."

"I'm not as cold-hearted as you think," said Leslie angrily. "I hate to see anything suffer, and the bear was awfully slow with Diamond. He was in too much pain. I couldn't stand it, so I climbed a nearby cliff and got out the tranquilizer gun. It seemed to take forever to get it loaded. I shot him with it to ease his pain. He was already dying. The tranquilizer wouldn't have killed him. I was just trying to ease his pain. It was daylight by then. I darted the bear afterwards with enough to keep it out of action for a while. I hid Diamond's body, gathered up his stuff, and waited until nightfall to shoot the rapids and bring him back to his permanent campsite. I couldn't risk moving him during the day. It would have worked too, if it weren't for you and your bloody meddling."

"And the food at the campsite?"

She smiled. "Yeah, that was a stroke of genius I thought, putting the Mars bar in the tent and leaving empty sardine tins lying about. I thought you'd cottoned on to me when I accidentally told you the cops had said they'd found a Mars bar in the tent."

I suddenly remembered back to the conversation, to the niggling feeling I had had that she had said something important.

"The cops never said it was a Mars bar," I said in a flash of tardy insight.

"Too bad you didn't see it before, eh?" She waved the gun in my face and said, "They never clued into the lack of any bear sign, and when the loggers claimed to have killed the rogue bear it was case closed. I did take a bit of a risk there, but it worked."

"And Don?" I asked, taking a wild stab and hoping I'd connect somewhere.

Leslie stared at me, her mouth slack, and then she sighed.

"Don. Yes, dear, kind, nerdy Don."

"He found out what you'd done to Diamond," I said.

"My guess is that he came to Diamond's camp late one night to persuade Diamond to forget about the problem of the fake data and saw me lugging Diamond's body out of the canoe. You could smell the sardines a mile away, and Don was no dummy. The crazy bastard tried to blackmail me, but after he talked to you he panicked and called me, said he'd have to go to the cops. I couldn't let him do that."

"So you went to his house," I said. She nodded.

"I offered him half the kudos and told him I'd show him the cougars and we could make it to the biology station if we left right away. But he didn't want to leave with me. He was all worried about you, for God's sake, but then I said I'd scrawl a note and leave it on the door while he got his stuff. I knew I couldn't handle both of you so that note and the malfunctioning stove were strokes of genius."

"You took a risk. He might have read it," I said.

Leslie laughed. "With his eyesight and my handwriting? Anyway, after that he came like a lamb to the slaughter. Pity I never knew about the fake data," she said wistfully. "I could have blackmailed him back and he wouldn't have had to die. But I had no choice, and when we left, I turned on the faulty back burner he'd been complaining about all week, as if any of us wanted to hear about it. He kept saying he was going to die of carbon monoxide poisoning but then didn't do anything about it. Exasperating man. Anyway, I took advantage of it. I left the burner on as a shot-in-the-dark surprise for you. You were getting much too inquisitive. But it didn't work so I had to make that anonymous phone call." She sighed again. "When I found you'd collected some insects from Diamond's body I nearly panicked. Didn't take much, though, to trash your lab and take your disks. I couldn't risk the possibility that the larvae might identify where he died."

"Except that the larvae I collected turned out to be ordinary blowflies endemic to both areas," I said, hoping to take her off guard. "They're found everywhere, and it wouldn't have meant a thing to me. It was the cedar twigs in the wounds and the fact that you had fumigated my larvae that twigged me to possible foul play."

She barely blinked her eyes as she took in what I said.

"Where are my disks?" I asked, hoping I could at least learn that, if the price for all this was going to be my death.

She waved the gun at me and smiled.

"Better get in the canoe now."

"I don't think so," I said, glad that my voice sounded a hell of a lot braver than I felt.

"What do you mean you don't think so?" she shouted angrily. "Are you blind? I have a gun." She waved it to make sure I could see it.

I forced my mouth into a smile while the rest of me screamed inside at the risk I was taking. I listened in fascination and heard myself say, "You won't use that gun on me." I prayed that I was right.

Leslie advanced menacingly.

My mouth was as dry as sawdust, and every muscle in my body screamed at me to run and never stop. But I held my ground, and Leslie came closer still.

"I'll use it, you know," she said between clenched teeth. "Now get in the goddamned canoe."

"It won't be like the other times," I said, praying my gamble was right. "The bear got Diamond, a cliff killed Don, gas and a bunch of boulders nearly got me. But this time you're holding the murder weapon in your hand and you'll have to look me in the eyes when you kill me."

I saw her arm falter, and the gun begin to dip down as a puzzled look spread over her face. I felt a sense of elation and tensed my muscles as I judged the distance between us, but then the gun came up and she started to laugh. She raised it and pointed it right between my eyes.

"You think you can trick me?" she shouted. "What do you take me for anyway? I've killed twice, and it's true what they say: it gets easier every time. I may not have killed Diamond directly but I pushed Don over that cliff. And I stepped on your fingers. It's not much of a leap from that to pulling this trigger."

I was unnerved by the sudden coldness and resolution in her voice, and the sudden steadiness of her gun arm as she pointed the thing at me.

"Besides" she said in a flat monotone, "I don't have to kill you, do I? Just shoot you in the leg and then the arm. I have six bullets and I'm prepared to use them all until you get into the bloody canoe."

I almost gagged then, as I realized I had seriously underestimated her.

"It won't look like an accident, though, will it?" I said, desperately clutching at straws if they could delay my death for even a minute.

Leslie looked at me and nodded.

"You're really thinking, aren't you? You're too bloody calm by half. But think of it this way. You have more to lose than I do. If you get in the canoe you have a chance, a tiny one I admit, of surviving a trip over the falls. You have no chance at all with this gun."

I stared into her unblinking eyes, as transfixing as a snake's, and my body went cold. The fear was building up to a crescendo — I didn't think I could hold it in much longer, and suddenly I knew that that was my key. Use my fear. But choose the moment.

I let my eyes shift from Leslie's to a point just beyond her left shoulder, willing myself to imagine the arrival of help. I felt my face begin to loosen the way it does when relief floods it, and I brought my eyes back to focus on her face without ever having turned my head. She was looking at me, first with curiosity and then with growing alarm. We held each other's eyes until once more I let mine flit over her shoulder, head as still as death, and then quickly looked back at her. It was too much for her, and as she turned to see what I had seen I jumped her and let all my pent-up fear out in one shuddering, horrifying scream.

I grabbed her gun arm and tried to wrench it out of her hand. I gasped in alarm as it stretched like pulled taffy while we both struggled for possession. Leslie suddenly let go, and I staggered back as the gun snapped back to shape with a resounding thud. Startled, I hesitated, staring at the useless rubber replica in my hand, and Leslie lunged. I jerked left, but not far enough, and Leslie caught at my arm as her momentum shot her forward toward the swirling water of the river beyond. She spun me around, and I lost my balance and crashed down on the rock, slipping, my legs hitting the cold water as I scrabbled to find a purchase for my hands. A second later I heard the splash as Leslie hit the water. I felt her hands clamp down on my legs like a vise, and I started to slide back as Leslie pulled me in.

I grappled for a hold on the slippery rocks, feeling our combined weight and the strength of the current dragging us in. I could feel my mashed-up fingers slipping over the surface, my face scraping against the cold, hard rock as I tried to stop the slide into the water. And then my fingers caught hold of a crack, and I held on as

Leslie tried desperately to climb up my legs and out of the current. I could feel her hands inching their way up slowly and surely as her body rasped against mine. I still had a tenuous grip on the rock and tried to wedge my fingers down to hang on. I couldn't kick out without a good grip, or we'd both go. Frantically, I felt for a better handhold, my fingers groping over the rock. And there it was, a crack big enough to take my whole hand and wedge it securely.

I gripped hard then, and kicked out viciously with my legs. Leslie was like a leech, and I couldn't dislodge her. I waited, and the second I felt her grip loosen as she crawled further up my leg I gave a massive kick, arched my back, and felt Leslie's other hand loosen and slide down my legs, scrabbling madly, until suddenly she was gone.

It took everything I had left to haul myself out of the water and onto the rocks. I lay there gasping for breath and looked at the river. There was no sign of Leslie downriver in the white foaming mess, and I shuddered. I looked back at the canoe held back from the rapids only by the bowline still tied to a tree, its stern line under water and caught by the current. It was being buffeted by the fast moving water, and with Patrick's dead weight in it, it was in danger of swamping. Patrick!

I could hear him groaning even above the roar of the rapids. I needed to get hold of the stern line and pull the canoe into shore. I gripped the side of the canoe and hauled it in as I inched my way down to the stern. Finally, I grabbed the line and started to pull it in, but it wouldn't come. I cursed when I realized it was caught in the rocks. I braced myself, leaned back, and pulled with all the strength I had left … then reeled back in shock.

Leslie's head lunged up through the surface of the water gasping and spluttering, her hands in a death grip on the line, her wild, crazed eyes boring into me. My body reacted before my mind could think, and I dropped the rope burning my hands and staggered back onto the rocks. I watched, mesmerized, as Leslie struggled to keep her head above water and slowly began pulling herself forward again, her head forced under again and again by the power of the water. I couldn't take my eyes off the wild, hair-streaked face, and with sick fascination watched as she moved nearer. I was gripped by the inertia of fear and revulsion, transfixed by Leslie's image as surely as a mouse is transfixed by the snake moving in for the kill.

Inch by laborious inch, she pulled herself closer to safety, her bulging eyes boring straight ahead, staring at something, never wavering, with such a raw intensity that I glanced back and gasped. Patrick was draped over the stern seat, blood from his bandaged wound seeping through and trickling down his face. Slowly, painfully, he unclipped the stern line from its ring and let it go.

Epilogue

Nearly a week had passed since Patrick and I had almost died on the river, and I was on my porch lazing in the hammock, nervously thinking about my dinner party just two hours away. Everything was ready except my mind, which wouldn't stop telling me in great detail everything that might go wrong. And I didn't want anything to go wrong. I'd invited Ryan, Martha, Duncan ... and Patrick. Especially Patrick. The man I had pegged as a murderer; the man who had come to the campsite in search of me after hearing from Roberta that I was alone up there; the man who had discovered my pack covered in oil and had looked up to see the bear coming out of the woods behind me; the man who had tried to save me by firing a flare gun and then, when that failed, who had tried to lead the bear away from me, and nearly died for the effort.

As I'd watched him unclip the line from its ring and let it slide over the stern and into the fast water, before slumping back exhausted into the canoe, I had felt betrayed by my own thoughts and angry and ashamed that I could have so misjudged him. I had moved then, as fast as my battered body would allow, to get help, and Patrick and I had been airlifted by float plane out to a hospital in Dumoine. I thought back to the day in the hospital when I'd visited him as he recovered from a severe head injury. Now, tonight, would be his first visit to my home, and I was a bundle of nerves jangling in the late afternoon breeze.

"I think I know who you are, Cordi O'Callaghan."

The sudden softness of his voice drowned out the crickets with its sheer intensity of meaning. He must have walked in from the barn because I hadn't heard a car, and my heart lurched to stalling point. As I struggled to sit up in the hammock, Patrick came up the porch stairs two at a time. He sat beside me then, his body pressing hard against my own, his hand reaching for mine. The livid scar on his forehead where the bear had caught him was healing, and I wanted to touch it, but I didn't. I thought the heat inside me might burn him.

"You're two hours early," I said instead, trying to hide my nerves. He said nothing, just looked at me with that melting smile of his. He stroked my hand and his fingers moved lightly over my arm, found their way under my blouse, like butterflies, barely touching my skin, and yet I was screaming at their touch.

"Look at the cows out there," I croaked. "See how the sun makes them look red?"

"I don't want to look at the cows," he said, his eyes caressing mine. His voice was so soft it was like a blanket enveloping me. My body knew what it wanted, but my stupid mind just wouldn't let me go.

"I think Mac's going to be late milking the cows. They shouldn't still be there at this hour," I said, feeling like an idiot — wanting to be otherwise.

"Shut up and kiss me, Cordi O'Callaghan."

He pulled me to him then. I felt his lips hard against mine in an explosion of pent-up emotion that consumed both body and soul. I could still hear the cows mooing in the field and the crickets chirruping, but the sun froze in its tracks within the medley of our wildly beating hearts. We sank into each other and I allowed myself to finally believe what I had seen in his eyes.

We lay in the hammock, afterwards, peacefully waiting for the rest of my guests to arrive and listening to the sounds of night falling. No need for words. We'd just spoken them with our souls.

"Well, well, well, what have we here?"

From deep inside Patrick's arms, I looked up to see Duncan smiling down on us. I realized we must have fallen asleep, and, embarrassed, I struggled out of Patrick's embrace and the hammock's cocoon to greet Duncan, Martha, and Ryan. Martha raised her eyebrows in a knowing way, and Ryan eyeballed me and Patrick the way only a brother can. I introduced them to Patrick, who, totally unfazed, graciously rose to greet them as if he'd known them all his life.

I left them to it and went to get drinks. When I returned they had all found seats, and as I handed out the drinks Duncan said, "What did I tell you my dear girl? You'll make a marvelous forensic consultant, having single-handedly solved a murder no one knew about!"

Duncan's large form was sprawled on one of my porch chairs nicely snugged up beside Martha's. Patrick was sitting on the railing and Ryan was in the hammock sipping wine and watching the sun bathing the escarpment a deep golden yellow.

Ryan smiled and said, "So, you've decided, Cordi?"

I looked at Duncan, and then at Ryan and Martha, who winked at me. It certainly looked as though they had all decided long before I had. I went and sat on the rail beside Patrick.

"Yes," I said. "I guess I have. I figure it won't be too onerous, but we'll see." I still had misgivings. "And it'll be interesting."

"Not to mention that it's a great hook for your taxonomy course," added Martha with a laugh. She turned to Duncan, who raised his eyebrows in alarm. "Do you realize we had to put ten students on a waiting list in case any of the forty registered students dropped out? They all wanted to be part of a team solving a murder — the course description sounded like a detective novel. Of course the publicity in the paper about the murder, and the halting of the logging, and the cougars, and Cordi's role in it undoubtedly helped, but the outline is great stuff. You should read it, Duncan. Full of blood and gore and mystery."

Duncan looked a little nonplussed, and I shot a nasty look at Martha, who in turn raised her eyebrows and pointedly said nothing. All these raised eyebrows were making me dizzy.

"We're not talking human murders here," I hastily reassured Duncan, who had taken out his handkerchief and was now wiping his brow. I could just imagine him envisioning forty undergrads storming his lab for evidence or set loose on the streets asking questions. It was an alarming thought, even to me, and I quickly set things straight.

"I'm setting up my taxonomic assignments — or at least some of them — as homicides. We're talking about road kills — you know, dead coons and porcupines, even dead pigs and birds — that sort of thing." The relieved look on Duncan's face was comical.

"You mean someone's out there murdering pigs?"

"No, of course not. We're just going to set it up as though these road kills have been murdered. Each group will be assigned a 'murder' and Martha and I will manipulate the corpses so that the students will be told where to find the murder victim. They will then have to collect and raise the larvae to adulthood and identify them. We also want them to determine if the body has been moved from where they find it and how long it's been dead. So they'll be collecting flora as well as any biological entity that might help them solve the murder."

"Some of them actually are murdered, you know," piped up Martha. Her face turned dark and ominous as she continued in a low conspiratorial tone. "I've seen drivers purposely swerve to hit a turtle or a coon. It's revolting."

We all politely thought about the murdered animals for some seconds, and then I broke the silence and addressed Duncan.

"You won't have to worry, Duncan. The students will not be running all over campus. I've got permission to use some abandoned land outside the city. The students will treat it like a murder mystery. That's all. And it's just one part of the course. Once I get them into the course, I can teach them the basics of taxonomy and hopefully hook some of them for life."

Duncan broke out his best smile.

"I have to hand it to you, girl. It's a brilliant idea but, please, please, I don't want any of those undergrads osmosing over into real murder territory if and when I have to call you in on a case. I'm not sure I could handle the hordes."

I laughed and said, "I *know* I couldn't. Not all at once, anyway."

Before Duncan could respond Martha poked him playfully in the ribs and said, "Don't you dare call on her for at least three months. Now that she's got her disks back, she's received conditional approval of her grant based on seeing final research results of her work to date in three months, and revisions for her article for *Animal Behaviour* will be handed in as soon as she can do them, so she'll be very busy."

She winked at me and I laughed, remembering how ecstatic I had been when the cops, after Leslie's body had been fished out of the river, had searched her apartment and found my disks as well as photographs of the cougars. I guessed I would never know why Leslie hadn't thrown the disks away — perhaps the same sort of reluctance that had made her choose to carry a rubber imitation gun. Or the hope that something on the disks would help her own career. Whatever it was, I was grateful.

"Not to mention the fact that she's now got Hilson's animal behaviour course to teach, too," said Martha as she rubbed her hands in glee. "And you should have seen Jim Hilson's face when Cordi broke the news about Leslie and torpedoed his career. Of course, the university did the actual firing because of his role in the fumigation of Cordi's lab. But Cordi got to break it to him big time!"

Uncharacteristically Martha stopped talking and I realized they were all looking at me.

"What can I say?" I said. "I won. He lost." Keep it short and sweet. But I couldn't do anything from preventing it from running through my head.

It was indelibly imprinted on my brain. Jim Hilson had waltzed into my lab, given my rear a pat, and said, "It's farewell time."

I pushed him away, but he kept crowding me so I pushed as hard as I could and he grabbed my arm with lightning speed. I twisted away from him and said, "I'm sure you don't want harassment added to your charge of accessory to theft and murder." He dropped my arm as if I'd bitten it. "Do you?"

"What the hell are you talking about?" he asked. His eyes were glinting like daggers at me and I backed up.

"You gave Leslie Anderson the keys to this building," I said.

He looked at me uncertainly, and I could clearly see his lack of courage surfacing like a methane bubble from a swamp.

"So what?' he said. 'She's a friend. She asked me for a favour."

"She's a dead friend who just happened to kill two people and steal all my disks," I said.

He stared at me in stone cold silence. He was struggling to hide his sudden fear, darting his eyes around looking for an escape route, but he couldn't find one.

"You gave her the key, and she fumigated my insects and stole my research," I said.

"That makes you an accessory after the fact," I added.

He just stood there, at a loss for words, and in I went, straight for the jugular. "It's official. The Dean has fired you and the cops are probably up in your lab right now." He looked at me, his head at an angle like an owl, his face sagging into itself like a leaky balloon. We said nothing and as the silence lengthened I wondered what was going through his head. Finally he cleared his throat and said, "How did you know?"

"Know what?"

"Know about everything, Leslie and me, everything."

"You really want to know?"

He nodded, and for the first time in my life I'd felt sorry for Jim Hilson — but not that sorry.

"You just have to know the right people," I said, and then I blew him a kiss and left him standing there, stewing in his own words.

I was brought back from my reverie by Martha.

"What will happen to Don's daughter?" she asked out of the blue, breaking the spell. No one said anything, just let the crickets take over our silence, because nobody knew.

"And what about the will? Did Shannon ever find it?"

I looked at Martha, wishing she'd just be quiet. I hated not being able to answer questions. "The police never found out who ripped out the pages from the black book," I said. "Maybe there never was a will. Maybe Shannon lied. We'll never know."

I could see the moon starting to rise over the escarpment and felt content for the first time in weeks. It was a good feeling. "Who's going to take over the cougars?" This time Duncan broke the silence.

"Patrick is," I said and actually squeezed his hand.

He squeezed back a lot harder and said, "I'll set up surveillance up there, and I'm working on a paper based on some of Diamond's notes and some of my own stuff as well." I thought about how Patrick had sold his share of the mill just before the discovery of the cougars broke out. The company that bought the mill had been livid, but it had been sold in good faith. I felt kind of rotten about it, even though the cougars would make Patrick's career and halt the logging.

"Of course Diamond will get the credit for the discovery," continued Patrick, "but he's given me a giant career boost. I have a research grant to study Sian — that's the name Diamond gave her, apparently — and her cubs, and try to locate others in the area.

We know there has to be at least one male in the neighbourhood — Sian's mate — and hopefully more. It's wild country and they're secretive cats, so it's not such a long shot to hope that a viable population may exist up there."

His words rang like a gong through my head, moving from room to room in my mind, sounding an alarm like a town crier. Something to do with Sian. What the hell was it? It had bothered me at the blind but the uneasy suspicion now forming in my mind had been scared away first by the boulder, then by all the revelations Leslie had told me, and later by the police.

When Duncan and Martha finally left, I had to nudge my protective brother out of the house. Before Patrick could immobilize me by taking me in his arms, I grabbed his hand and said, "I have to check something in the barn."

"Said the spider to the fly?" quipped Patrick as he allowed himself to be led to Ryan's office.

I flicked on Ryan's computer and the screen came to life. I sat down in front of it, waiting impatiently for all the things to mount before I located Diamond's folder, and opened "lynx" with the password Leah22.

"What is it, Cordi?" asked Patrick as he draped his arms over my shoulders. I had to make a conscious effort to forget he was there as I keyed in a word search for Sian in the documents in the folders. And suddenly, there it was staring out at me: Dana, Simba, Sian, and Myth, the four cats Diamond had bred in captivity.

The prickle at the back of my neck grew as I began to tease around the implications of what this meant. Of course he could have given two cats the same name, but I knew, even as the thought flitted through my mind and I searched through his files, that it wasn't true. No scientist worth his salt would risk mixing up two study subjects by giving them the same name. Sian and the sixth cat that Diamond had radio-collared were one and the same. And that could mean only one thing.

"Jesus," I whispered, leaning back, staring up at Patrick. "Diamond's cougar was artificially inseminated."

"What?" said Patrick, taking his arms away and reaching for the mouse. Together we looked at the locked folder labelled "wild card," sure it held the key to everything. I started keying in Sian followed by numbers from 11 to 99. Nothing. Patrick suggested a number of passwords too, but nothing worked. We were close to giving up in exasperation when suddenly I remembered Shannon's sign and Paulie's pathetic little collar in my hand, the name glinting in the early morning sun. Paulie, not Polly.

It opened at Paulie22, and there it was in black and white. Detailed information about Sian's life. I sat back and stared at Patrick, who had sat down rather abruptly on the sofa. The whole thing had been an elaborate hoax right from the start.

"You've got to be kidding," said Patrick, but it was all there.

"According to this," I said, "Sian was one of the cubs that Jeff brought back from New Brunswick, along with her brother. It says here that Jeff had been looking for a breeding kestrel, and while making the deal some hunters came and told him about some half-dead cubs they'd found. When he realized what they were, he questioned the hunters trying to get more information, knowing that New Brunswick cougars were rare too, but they wouldn't talk. Jeff smuggled them out, flew them back to Quebec, and called Diamond, who convinced him to sit on it for a while."

"What did they do with the cubs?"

I scrolled through the document, scanning the entries.

"It appears that Jeff installed the cats in two separate compounds once they were old enough to be on their own. Diamond wanted them as wild as possible. Jeff was in the process of breeding some fox for reintroduction to the wild, and Diamond persuaded him to take on the cougars."

"So they worked on it together?"

"Seems that way. They must have hatched the plan to release a pregnant female cougar in order to stop the logging. When the female got pregnant, they radio-collared her, released her near term, and then followed her until she found a den and holed up. Jeff flew Diamond in now and again and he spent the last three weeks there before blazing a trail out when he was ready to tell the world. He had to make sure she would stay, and the cubs would be all right, before he could let the world know."

"No wild cougars," said Patrick. "That means that three people died for nothing."

I went over to him then and snuggled beside him on the sofa, wondering what he was thinking, feeling my own dark thoughts swirling inside me, just out of reach.

Maybe, just maybe, with him by my side I would finally beat my autumn darkness forever. Or was it really that simple? Was anything really that simple?

"Ironic, isn't it?" he finally said. "Leslie and Don thought they had stumbled on the discovery of their lives, and so Diamond was killed for something that wasn't real. They all died for something that wasn't real. At least Diamond got what he wanted though. The logging's been stopped."

"But for how long?" I asked. "As soon as word gets out that it was all a hoax, the chainsaws will be back in force."

"Who else knows about it, except you and me?" he asked quietly, the meaning behind his question slinking into the darkness of my night and leaving me wondering what I would do.